# FOR RENT

## The Apartment Manager Series

## ERIN HUSS

*velvet morning*
press

Published by Velvet Morning Press

ISBN-13: 978-0692694756
ISBN-10: 0692694757

Cover design by Ellen Meyer and Vicki Lesage
Author photo by Ashley Stock

Got a vacancy on your bookshelf?
Check out the hilarious

# Apartment Manager Series

*I hereby dedicate this book to the following:*

*My husband*
*My kids*
*SpongeBob*
*See's Candy*
*My neighbor's rooster*

*All without whom I wouldn't have had the support, motivation, babysitter, sugar-high, and early morning start needed to finish this book.*

# Foreword

We are all varying degrees of crazy. You know it. I know it. If aliens are in fact spying on us like every bum on Sunset Boulevard says they are, then they know it too. When in public, you hide the crazy in order to conform to what society deems "appropriate" behavior. Some are better at this than others. When you get home, within the confines of walls and away from watchful eyes, you can let your crazy run free without worry of judgment, public persecution or jail time. Home is where you can dance naked. Where you can safely satisfy your strange fetishes. Where you can role-play or engage in conversation with yourself, out loud, about *Star Wars* or *Harry Potter* or *The Real Housewives of Orange County*, and no one will judge you for it.

It doesn't matter if your home is rented or owned. If your home is an apartment in Compton, a mansion in Beverly Hills or a cardboard box under a freeway overpass—home is where your secrets are held. It's where you can let your freak flag fly high and proud.

This is what makes my job... interesting.

I am privy to all of it—the freak flags and the secrets. From the innocent ones to the fatal. Whether I want to be or not.

It's not a job for the thin-skinned, the weak-stomached or the easily angered.

It is a job for me: the apartment manager.

# Chapter 1

*Seeking an on-site Apartment Property Manager for a charming 40-unit community. Applicant must have excellent organizational skills and a calming demeanor.*

"Calm down!"

Honk.

"You're not the only one in a hurry."

Hooonk.

"Go around!"

The silver BMW roared past me. I turned to deliver a mad glare, but Captain Douche was too busy looking at his phone to notice.

"Pay attention to the road!" I yelled to his rear bumper. "Honestly, no one can drive in this city." I flipped down my visor. The zit in the middle of my freckled forehead pulsed in the tiny mirror. "You really couldn't have waited until tomorrow?" I asked the zit.

I reached over and grabbed my makeup bag, smothered the monstrosity in concealer, added a touch of gloss to my lips, and mascara'd my lashes into tiny tarantula legs. I had to look my best today. One more week of unemployment and I'd be left with no other option than to become a phone sex operator by night who flips burgers by day. I had applications in for both jobs in case this interview led to yet another dead end.

Hooonk!

"Take it easy." I flipped the visor back and continued maneuvering my dented Civic through the crowded streets of Los Angeles. I grabbed the past-due phone bill out of my bag and double-checked the directions scribbled on the back.

*Right on City Court.*

I looked up as the street sign for City Court drifted by my window.

"Crap." I made a hasty U-turn, which inspired another cacophony of horns. A man wearing a dirty Spiderman costume weighed in on my poor driving habits by flipping me a double-fisted bird. Even if I didn't come *that* close to him or his overflowing grocery cart.

My hand automatically went up as a feeble apology before I made the sharp turn.

And there I saw it. An imposing ten-story building. A cobblestoned walkway led up to a pair of whimsical wrought-iron doors. Brilliant red and yellow flowers were strategically dispersed throughout the lavish landscaping. A sign, welcoming those who were clearly richer than me, hung above a glistening koi pond near the entrance. It was beautiful.

I parked under the sign pointing to the leasing office, shoved the phone bill into my bag, and crawled over the center console and passenger seat to exit the car. The driver's side door had been stuck shut since an expensive meeting with a runaway Dumpster a few months ago. It was annoying and awkward, especially on the days when I managed to squeeze my butt into a pair of skinny jeans. My little Civic still managed to get me from point A to point B (usually), and that was all I could afford to care about.

As I stepped onto the sidewalk, I flattened the front of my dress with my hands and brushed off the tiny crumbs clinging to my thighs. I had on an Anthropologie dress worth more than my car—the one designated for interviews and first dates only because it minimized my butt, elongated my waist, was dry clean only, and the navy color matched my eyes. Sadly, it hadn't been getting much action in the last—*oh let me see*—four years.

Rolling my shoulders back, I took a deep, calming breath. The irony that I was about to interview for a job as an apartment manager when I was nearing eviction from my own apartment was not lost on me. It had been six months since I was laid off. Finding a job when the qualifications portion of your résumé ran three deep wasn't easy. Neither was being a single mother. The phone call for this interview couldn't have come at a better time. Decent salary, apartment, utilities, medical benefits and bonuses—it was the perfect opportunity to get Lilly and me back on our feet. I only hoped my lack of apartment management experience would be overshadowed by my obvious desperation.

Setting my focus on the whimsical doors, I charged toward—*oomph!*

There was a step.

A big step.

A step I didn't see until my hands and knees were plastered atop the scorching cement, and I was staring at it.

"Are you OK?" A pencil thin tube top-donning brunette stood over me, sucking on a Tootsie Pop. Each boob popping out from her chest was bigger than my head.

"I think so." I peeled myself off the ground and brushed away the chalky debris coating my knees. "That step came out of nowhere."

The brunette flipped her long ponytail over her shoulder. "Yeah, it happens a lot. Like, that's why they put up the sign." She pointed her sucker to the caution sign with a person about to plunge to the ground like I had just done. "But it doesn't seem to help. I totally see people trip here, like, all the time."

"Do you live here?"

"Nope, my Boo lives next door."

"Next door? There's another apartment complex on this street?" Panicked, I checked my watch. The interview was scheduled to start in five minutes. Story of my life—I was never late. I was always *almost* late, enough to be a frazzled, sweaty mess when I did arrive.

She pointed her sucker toward a row of tall shrubs. "Yeah, it's over there."

"Crap... Thank you!" I yelled over my shoulder as I ran to

the foliage fence blocking the neighboring apartment building. This one was smaller. Two-story with gated parking to the left. Pots filled with succulents lined the chipped brick walkway that led to a pair of sad-looking brown doors. No welcome sign. No koi pond, but a mud puddle near the entrance had a cloud of tiny insects hovering above it.

I dug out the instructions from my bag: *10, 405, Exit SM, Sepulveda, right on City Court. Apartment building on the right. Ask for Joyce.* That was it. That was all I wrote. No apartment name. No address. That would make too much sense.

I ran back to the first apartment complex. Standing between the two buildings, I shaded my eyes with my hand, trying to decide which one might house Joyce. The first building was much nicer. So I turned and ran toward the second one, because running toward mediocrity felt more natural.

When I reached the doors, I rested my hand on the rusty knob. *You've got this,* I told myself. *You are a strong, confident woman with better-than-average abilities and a kid to feed.* I took another deep breath, pushed open the door and entered... 1988?

I blinked as my eyes adjusted to the pink-and-blue-striped wallpaper. A glass coffee table was surrounded by an overstuffed peach leather couch and two floral-printed armchairs. Below my Payless heels was teal carpet, followed by yellow linoleum with a repeating brown octagon pattern across it. The track lighting gave the room a yellowish, hazy tint, and a ceiling fan clinked with each turn of its golden blades, pushing the stale, nicotine-laced air around the ugly room.

To my right was an enclosed office with a waist-high counter (also teal) overlooking the lobby. A frail old woman with scarlet hair sat behind a desk, her hands clasped and brown eyes on me.

"Hi. Are you Joyce?" I asked, hoping she'd say no and direct me to the spa-like resort next door.

"I am," she answered in a barely audible rasp. Despite the hundred-degree outside temperature, she wore a sweater, which hung loosely around her bony frame. Just looking at the cashmere caused my sweat glands to produce in double time.

"I'm Cambria Clyne. I have an interview with Patrick for the apartment management position. His secretary told me to meet him here at noon."

"Hmm, *you* really want *this* job?"

*What's that supposed to mean?* "Yes, I do," I answered slowly.

She regarded me for several awkward seconds before speaking. "OK then. Up to you." She stood on shaky legs and shuffled up to the counter. The two-foot journey looked painful. "Nice to meet you, Cambria. I'm the current manager." I took her proffered hand. Her palm was cold, but her eyes had a hint of warmth to them. "Patrick should be here in a bit. Would you like me to show you around while you wait?"

"That would be great, thank you." I smiled.

Joyce motioned for me to walk around the counter to the door that separated the lobby from the enclosed office. I followed her through the cramped space, squeezing past a row of tarnished filing cabinets and an L-shaped oak desk. She opened the door behind the desk and—BAM!

The nicotine air punched me in the lungs, knocking me back against the doorjamb. It was as if I walked directly into a cigarette. I placed my hand over my chest, mentally apologizing to all my vital organs.

Joyce stood in the middle of a square kitchen. The blue tiled counters were piled high with boxes and rolls of bubble wrap.

"Once we're gone, this would be your apartment," she said, fanning her arm out like Vanna White. "If you get the job."

I nodded in appreciation and took a gulp of air through clenched teeth, hoping they'd work as a filter. The lack of oxygen caused my head to beat in time with my heart, but I wasn't about to let a little cancerous air stop me. I *desperately* needed the income.

The kitchen looked out to a spacious living room with Smurf blue carpet and two long windows overlooking a courtyard. Asleep in the middle of the room was an old man with a beer in one hand, remote in the other, and *The People's Court* playing on the television opposite him and his purple recliner. Not just any old purple either—a two-toned mauve and lavender corduroy chair with a coordinating couch and love seat. Clearly, someone was colorblind.

I followed Joyce down a short hallway and into a bedroom.

"This is perfect for an office or guest room," she said, sliding the mirrored closet door open to reveal a space larger than my current bathroom.

"I actually have a daughter, and she'd love this room." Truth is, I would too. I'd been sharing a room with Lilly since the day she was born. The *Frozen* bed sheets weren't doing me any favors in the love department.

"Are you married?" Joyce rasped.

I shook my head.

She thought for a moment. "Interesting… How old is your daughter?"

"She's three going on sixteen," I answered with an exaggerated roll of my eyes.

Joyce let out a laugh that quickly turned into a procession of dry, hacking coughs. She placed her veiny hand on the wall for support as her coughs morphed into more of a gurgling sound. My joke wasn't *that* funny. Nor was it original, and certainly not worth dying over.

I placed my hand on her back, feeling the ridges of her spine under the cashmere. "Can I get you something?"

She took a slow, gravelly breath, then brushed off my concern with a wave of her hand. "I'm fine. Don't fuss. Let's move on." She let out one more cough before pushing past me.

I trailed behind, worried Joyce may not make it through the tour.

We next entered a room slightly bigger than the first with an attached walk-in closet and bathroom. Despite the smoke and the blue carpet and the yellow popcorn ceilings, I was in love. To have that amount of space, in a neighborhood I could never afford otherwise, was unfathomable. A little paint and oxygen would turn it into the perfect home for us.

"Joyce, I love it." Then, because my mother had taught me the way to any person's heart was through compliments, I eyed a massive oak armoire and added, "This is beautiful, by the way."

"You like it?" she asked, not masking her surprise. "I'll be sure to give it to you when I move."

I feigned excitement. "Really? Wow. You're so kind." I smiled, eyeing the monstrosity I now apparently owned.

I followed Joyce down the hall, past another full bathroom and into the living room. The old man was still lifeless in the chair. "How long have you been working here?" I asked, looking around and mentally arranging my own furniture.

She pulled a pack of cigarettes from her back pocket along with a lighter. "Almost… let's see… it's been about twenty-five years. This retirement is well overdue." With a shaky hand she positioned a cigarette between her pale lips and lit it.

*I may vomit.*

"OK… there are forty units," she continued, emitting a fresh batch of smoke. "You can take a look around, just don't go in the third courtyard—ever. Never, ever go there. Trust me." She handed me three pieces of paper with her cigarette hand. "Then come back and fill these out." Ash broke off the end of her cancer stick and rolled down the front of the application.

I opened my mouth, about to ask why the third courtyard was off limits, but she opened the front door before I could get the words out. My need for air overcame my manners, and I performed an Olympian-style hurdle out the door, seeking refuge for my burning lungs.

*I will never take oxygen for granted again.*

After several deep, appreciative breaths, I shot an apologetic grin in her direction. My exit could be deemed rude, yet an arch of Joyce's penciled-in brow and stifled smile told me she took no offense.

"There's a picnic table by the pool you can use to fill out the application." She used her cigarette-free hand to point the way. "Bring it all back once you're finished, and remember, no third courtyard." The stern shake of her bent forefinger drove the point home.

*Note to self: After job offer, get more third courtyard specifics.*

I walked along the cement pathway, exploring the open first courtyard. There wasn't much in the way of color. Brown doors. Brown fascia. Tan walls. Brown staircase leading up to the brown second story. Greenish-brown grass. Greenish-brown shrubbery. Yet, it was clean. Not a single piece of trash or graffiti. No barred windows. No couches in the walkway. It wasn't the koi-pond apartments next door, but it was better than the armpit I was about to be kicked out of.

I strolled through a short ivy-laced breezeway and found the picnic table next to the pool. Taking a seat, I began filling out the application. It wasn't too difficult, and I nailed the first page—name, birthday, social security number, current employer and previous employer. Unfortunately, a questionnaire was attached.

*Please explain how you would handle the following situations:*
*1) The tenant in Apartment 5 and the tenant in Apartment 6 don't get along. The two call you daily to complain about the other, and both refuse to move.*
*2) You notice the tenants in Apartment 6 have a constant flow of visitors. The visitors tend to arrive and leave within minutes.*
*3) The tenant in Apartment 19 plays his drums during the day. The neighbors complain constantly and have threatened to move.*

I had no idea how to correctly answer any of these questions. Sure, I could use common sense, and I had enough common sense to know there were legal forms and procedures to follow before one can start passing out eviction notices like candy. I just didn't know what those were.

Self-doubt slithered through my mind like the soul-crushing serpent it was. I should have stayed in college. Everyone warned me when I took the year off to find myself that I wouldn't return. They were right. All I learned during my quest for self-discovery was that VH1 played an entire season of *America's Next Top Model* in a single day. My one-year hiatus quickly turned into seven. I had already moved out to L.A. from my hometown of Fresno and gotten myself knocked up by the time I realized the value of a degree. I found a job as a barista and worked my way up to manager. I was doing OK until the owner decided to sell the property to some real-estate developer and use the money to retire.

I gnawed on the end of the pen, staring down at the ashy questionnaire when out of nowhere a pair of work gloves plopped down in front of me. I jumped, dropping my pen, and gazed up at the stranger sliding onto the bench across from me.

# Chapter 2

*Strong problem-solving skills are a must.*

I froze, unsure of why this random, albeit very attractive, man had shown up. The Universe was not typically this generous.

My eyes ventured down his tan shirt, past the wisps of blond hair peeking out from behind the button-up collar, to the word *Maintenance* embroidered in blue above his shirt pocket. This, coupled with the paint specks scattered across his dark blond hair, plus the gloves on the table, gave me reason to believe he worked there.

Obviously, espionage should have been my chosen career path.

"Do you need help?" the stranger asked, flashing a perfectly straight white-toothed grin.

"Um..." *Breathe, Cambria.* "Sure," I answered in a voice three octaves higher than my own. I found his scruffy jawline and unkempt hair wildly attractive. A tiny scar under his left nostril made him look edgy in an "I fell down when I was a kid" kind of way. I cleared my throat, realizing I was staring. "Hi, I'm Cambria," I said, more even-toned. I then shot my hand out like an idiot.

He slipped his hand into my mine. His strong, callused grip caused my insides to dance and flip and flutter and beg for more. It was the most physical contact I'd had with a man in years. I plastered a nonchalant smile across my face.

"I'm Chase," he said, prying his hand out of mine. He removed a notepad from his shirt pocket. "What unit are you in?"

"Huh?"

"What unit are you in?" he repeated, this time slower.

"I don't live here. I'm interviewing for the apartment management job." I held up the application in case he didn't believe me.

He scrunched his cute face and looked around. "Joyce said there was someone sitting at the picnic table who needed my help."

*Note to self: Send Joyce a thank you note.*

He looked around the empty courtyard until his stunning green eyes met mine, then ventured downward. I pretended not to notice him checking me out, but felt myself blushing anyway. "Not sure if you knew this," he said. "But you have a little something…" He pointed to my chest.

I looked down to see an unidentified stain on my chest.

"Ah, bleep…" I said under my breath. *How had I missed that when leaving the house?*

Chase planted his forearms on the table, leaning forward. "Did you just say *bleep*?"

"Oops, yeah, I probably did." I blushed again. "I try not to cuss in front of my daughter, and now it's sort of become a stupid habit." I pulled a package of tissues from my bag and began dabbing the spot.

Now I had a large stain dotted with white tissue residue. Great.

Chase laughed. "Wait, you replace profanity with *bleep*?"

"Um… *yes*." I pulled the elastic band out of my hair, releasing my Einstein-inspired dark mane. I tamed Einstein down to a side ponytail and slouched my shoulders. Trying to cover the spot. "Better?"

His face said *hell no,* but he said, "Sure." And I liked him even more for it.

He slipped the notepad back into his pocket. "What did you need help with?"

I could think of a hundred-and-two ways he could help me. None of which would be appropriate to ask for having only known him for about a minute. I glanced at the questionnaire. "Well, I'm curious, how might you handle a tenant who was getting a lot of foot traffic? I'm assuming it's drug-related."

He made a V with his brows. "Why?"

"There are questions like this on the application. I haven't been an apartment manager before, and I want to get them right."

Chase made an O with his full, kissable lips. "I'm not sure. I've never been a manager." He ran a hand through his hair. I resisted the urge to reach over and do the same. "Maybe record all the information in the apartment file?"

I snapped my fingers and pointed at him. "That's a good idea. Then I would call the police once I've gathered enough evidence. Like, who are the visitors? How long do they stay… " I began writing my answer. "I think the police code for that is, like, 10-50 or something."

Chase shrugged.

"I watch a lot of crime shows," I explained. "I need to get this right because I *really* need this job."

"I'm not sure how much help I can be. But I'll try." He rested his chin on his palm and watched me scrawl down my answer.

"Can't you give someone a three-day notice if they are being loud, or do you have to give them a certain number of warnings before you give the notice?" I asked.

Chase shrugged again. "They told you about Kevin, right? That'd be more concerning than foot traffic."

"Who?"

"He's the owner's son who lives here. He can be a real *bleep*."

My light bulb flipped on. "Does he happen to live in the third courtyard?"

He nodded and then returned his chin to his palm.

"I take it he and Joyce don't get along?"

"You could say that."

I looked past the pool and out to the third courtyard. All I could see from where I sat was Chase's left bicep deliciously bulging under his sleeve and another courtyard for Lilly to play in.

I waved off his concern. "I'm sure I can handle it." I'd met every shade of douchebag since moving to L.A.—what was one more? It would take more than that to stop me from taking the job, if I were offered it. I still had to get through an interview, and if there was one lesson I'd learned during my employment drought, it was that I was a terrible interviewee. I'd been practicing though. Watching dozens of YouTube videos on what to say, and more importantly, what *not* to say. I prayed I'd be able to come across as poised, skilled and normal.

I hurried through the questionnaire without further input from Chase, who was summoned away by a bathroom emergency. His presence served only as a physical motivator anyway—and what a physical motivator he was.

When I swung open the lobby door, Joyce was seated in the floral armchair. She looked to have aged during the time I'd been gone.

"Here she is," Joyce announced, sounding as if she had swallowed sandpaper. "This is Patrick." She motioned toward a tall man with a cul-de-sac of brown hair sitting on the couch.

Patrick half stood and held out his hand. I shook it, hoping he didn't notice my sweaty palms. A casual wipe on his pants afterward told me he had. Great.

"Have a seat." He plopped back down and began rummaging through his briefcase.

"Here, take mine," Joyce offered, sliding off the chair. "I'm going to get some packing done."

"Thank you." I slipped into the floral atrocity, feeling like a child waiting in the principal's office. Nerves crawled through my stomach and down to my intestines, butterflying around in my gut. Authoritative figures had this effect on me. It didn't matter how many deep breaths I took or positive thoughts I had, my nerves still managed to get the best of me.

Joyce leaned down. "Good luck. I'm pulling for you," she wheezed into my ear before shuffling back to her apartment.

"You have the application?" Patrick asked. He struck me

as a no-nonsense type of guy with his stern face and permanent stress lines around his eyes. He wore khakis, a checkered white and blue shirt, a silver band on his left ring finger, and stark white Nike running shoes. His attire reminded me of Forrest Gump.

I handed him the application and watched as he sat back, crossed his Nike over his knee and read through it. At one point he squinted and looked closer with a scrunch of his forehead. Perhaps moving the drummer in Apartment 19 next to the arguing neighbors in Apartments 6 and 5 wasn't the right answer. I thought the two could bond over their shared hatred of their new neighbor, and then I'd give the drummer a three-day notice to find a new hobby. Seemed like a creative win-win to me.

Patrick tossed the application on the coffee table and grabbed a yellow notepad. "First, you pronounce your name Came-bree-ah not Cam-bree-ah, right?" he asked with a click of his pen.

"Yes. The correct pronunciation of my name is Came-bree-ah." And then, for no apparent reason, I added, "I'm named after the city I was conceived in. Just two teenagers on a little road trip and bada-bing-bada-boom, here I am."

*Whyyy?*

Obviously, my nerves had taken my mouth hostage.

Patrick made a noise I believed to be a stifled laugh or a burp. I wasn't sure. I bit my lip, afraid I would ask. He made note of my stupidity on his notepad and then continued to ask sharp questions regarding my previous employment and how I might handle situations that seemed unlikely to ever occur. I stammered through, fidgeting with my thumbs, trying to use the whole "think *before* you speak" notion I'd been practicing. When we finished, he placed the notepad on the coffee table and rubbed his temples with his forefingers.

"I will say this," Patrick began. "I was impressed with how you answered the questions on the application. You seem like a 'think outside of the box' kind of person. That's a good quality for this job. I like that you've had some management experience. I spoke to your references yesterday, and they all sang your praises." I used my grandma as a reference. "I need to tell you this," he continued, "the owner's son lives on the property."

"Oh, I know about Kevin," I hastily interrupted, too desperate to recover from the whole "bada-bing" incident to remember my manners.

Patrick's eyes grew in diameter. "You know about Kevin?"

"Yes, Chase told me about him, and it's not a problem." His gaping expression told me I might have redeemed myself from the unfortunate incident. "I have experience dealing with difficult people. Even the most rational of individuals turn crazy when you don't get their coffee right." I laughed.

He didn't.

My heart skipped two beats. He's one of those people who take their coffee very seriously, I realized. He struck me as a large Americano with an extra shot of espresso type of guy. I'd been screamed at by many Americano drinkers. Crap.

"That's good to know. I still have a few people to interview today and will be making my final decision tomorrow. Thanks for coming in."

"My pleasu-roo."

*Stop talking, Cambria.*

# Chapter 3

*Applicant must be dependable, punctual and able to multitask without becoming easily frazzled.*

I rolled Lilly out of my arms and onto the bed. She flopped over without stirring. The sequins from her Cinderella dress caught the reflection of the light streaming in through the blind slats on the window, causing rainbow specks to dance across the far wall. The display was a little too cheery for my current mood.

I twisted the blinds shut and snuck out. The heat-swollen floorboards squeaked with each careful step. Transferring a sleeping toddler without waking her required ninja-like abilities, a skillset my clumsy self did not come by naturally. I was determined, though, knowing that being productive during Lilly's hours of operation was near impossible. I urgently needed the extra time to stress and sulk and stuff carbs into my mouth.

It had been one week. SEVEN DAYS since my interview. A park-like courtyard, free rent, two bedrooms, safe neighborhood and a sexy co-worker: The job was tailor-made for my needs. Then I had to open my mouth and share my conception story of all things.

*Bada-bing-bada-boom?*

The memory was mortifying. I shook my head as I crept

down the hallway, eyeing the dirty laundry tower in the corner of the bathroom. I was wearing a red lace thong I'd found buried in the bottom of my drawer. A memento of a time when a thin piece of fabric shoved up my crack seemed sexy and didn't cause chafing. Now it meant I was out of clean underwear.

With a sigh of defeat, I grabbed my laptop from the hall closet and headed to the living room. As uncomfortable as my wedgie was, it was more doable than laundry. I dragged the cord behind me as I weaved through the sea of toys scattered across the scratchy, vomit-colored carpet. If my mother were here, she'd fall into her routine speech on how I was way too young and far too pretty, with way too much potential, to still be squished into a flea-infested apartment with bars on the windows, homeless women fighting over my trash, a toilet that only occasionally flushed, a neighbor who was frequently visited by his parole officer, and upstairs neighbors who sounded like they tap danced twenty-four hours a day.

She would then take the two-step journey from the living room to the shoebox-sized kitchen, point to the collection of empty ice cream containers lining the counter, and do her signature eye roll. She had this ability to get her entire iris shoved so high up into her lids only the whites of her eyes showed. It was unnerving. I didn't know she had blue eyes until I was out of adolescence.

My mother worked as a secretary at a meat packing company in Fresno, the same job she's had since I can remember. When I was younger, I would sit in the swivel chair next to her desk after school and watch her answer phones and take down orders. She had a wraparound headset that looked like a microphone. When she'd go to the bathroom, I would slip on the headset and pretend I was Britney Spears.

With her own Einstein pouf (although blond), petite frame, naturally pink cheeks, and perfectly turned up nose, my mom was the most beautiful woman in the world. At least she was to me—until I turned thirteen. Things went south when I was adjusting to the hormonal surge of adolescence and my mom perfected the art of micromanaging. Then she wasn't so beautiful, her job sucked, and she was basically trying to ruin my life.

My dad, unlike my mom, was more of a laid-back parent. He was a plumber by day and the boys' varsity basketball coach by night. He had a full head of thick, dark hair, same color as mine, blue eyes, same color as mine, and he was young. (Both of my parents were young—they'd had me the summer after their senior year of high school. *Bada-bing-bada-boom.*)

All the teachers at my high school thought my dad was cute, which was gross (especially when he ended up marrying one of them after my parents got divorced). While my parents were married, money was always an issue. At night, I would hear them arguing over bills and rent and car payments... I'd lie in my daybed, promising myself one day I'd get a really good job, like a veterinarian or an astronaut, and make so much money they'd never have to worry (or fight) again. But before that day could come, my dad packed his suitcase and moved into a motel across town. I was ten. I spent the next eight years bouncing between their homes, staying with whichever parent wasn't pissing me off on that particular day, until I was off to college. After a year, I took my break, moved to Los Angeles, and then came Lilly.

When I told my mom I was pregnant, she rolled her eyes so far back into her head I thought she was having a seizure. Her reaction had less to do with the fact that I was unmarried, barely made over minimum wage, and couldn't keep a houseplant alive (although I'm sure it didn't help), and more to do with my determination to raise my baby in Los Angeles. I'd impulsively moved to L.A. a year earlier with my best friend, Amy. My mother, bless her controlling heart, was upset she wouldn't be able to effectively manage the situation from afar.

However, I had a secret, and the four-hour drive cushion made it easier to keep. I didn't like to think of it as a lie, but more of an omission of one detail that would break my father's heart, please that woman he insisted on marrying, and kill my mother.

Cause of death: mortification.

It happened when Amy and I were bar crawling our way down Third Street. Amy had landed the role of Smiling Girl

#4 in a toothpaste commercial, and that had to be celebrated—and celebrate we did. We ran into an attractive-enough group of law students who insisted on buying us drinks. The free-flowing alcohol proved a challenge to my system, but I was never one to back down from adversity, and I didn't want to be rude. Both adequate grounds for stupidity.

We laughed. We sipped. We flirted. We gulped. We danced. We glugged. Based on the YouTube video, I serenaded everyone with what was supposed to be *I Feel Like a Woman*, but sounded more like a Jabba the Hutt impersonation.

After a few (or ten) drinks, one of our almost-attorney fellas caught my attention. Tom Dreyer. Tall, very tall, tousled dark hair, glossed-over hazel eyes, and a side-smirk that had me seeing hearts and flowers and fireworks to the point where I questioned if I were solely under the influence of alcohol. I'd never been a one-night-stand kinda gal. But, hey, there was a first (and last) time for everything.

I walk-of-shamed my red lace-thonged butt out his door the next morning with a hangover that lasted nine months. When I told Tom, he got all lawyer-y on me and demanded a paternity test. Which of course came back positive. I'd been too busy battling morning sickness to have the opportunity to hook up with anyone else. Then he swore. He cried. He cursed. He sobbed. He attached the F-word to a variety of different nouns. Then, he accepted it.

Now, here's where my secret comes in. It was one thing to have a child out of wedlock. It was an entirely different thing to get yourself knocked up while in the midst of a drunken stupor by a guy you'd known all of two minutes. Which is precisely what I did.

When I told my parents, I may have insinuated Tom and I were in a loving, committed relationship. Even though we weren't. Not that I didn't try. Several times. Tom never reciprocated. He did me one worse. He put me in the friend zone. The FRIEND ZONE. It's the Alcatraz of zones—escapable only by death. I was devastated. In the midst of my heartbreak, I may have insinuated we broke up. I may have also implied the reason was Tom had finally come out of the closet. My parents had met him twice and never questioned me on it. It got my grandparents off my case about not getting married first, and, honestly, I didn't want my parents to hate Tom for rejecting me and then proceeding to stomp on my heart as he slept his way through Los Angeles and Orange County. There was also some Ventura County and San Diego in there. Bottom line: Almost all of Southern California's single ladies had seen Tom naked at some point.

My parents loved the idea of Lilly being raised by a straight mother and gay father, and before I knew it, my mother started marching in parades, and my father started donating to LGBT charities. The lie took on a life of its own, and, three years later, my life would be a whole lot easier if Tom would do me a favor and be gay for real. Lying is exhausting.

The saddest part of that story, aside from the fact my fake relationship with Tom was the last relationship I'd had, was that Smiling Girl #4 was edited out of the commercial. Poor Amy. Those veneers were expensive.

I opened my pink laptop. A reflection of my puffy eyes and freckled face stared back at me from the dark computer screen. I'd never considered myself a beauty like Amy. I was attractive enough. My deep blue eyes were a nice contrast to my nearly black Einstein mane.

"God gave you those striking eyes to take the attention away from your hair," Grandma Ruthie used to say. She was right. I definitely had something to work with. However, glaring back at me was a pale twenty-eight-year-old with a massive zit on her nose to match the one on her forehead. It was anything but cute. If I were to have sprung for the seventeen-inch model, the screen would've been able to fit Einstein in as well.

I wiggled my finger on the mouse pad to erase the image and clicked over to my email.

Thirteen new messages. Most from clothing stores taunting me with fall sales. Two were from my dad—one informing me of his success with a particular sexual enhancement drug. Gross. Another apologizing that he had been hacked again. Nothing from Patrick, and no replies from the batch of résumés I'd sent out.

I felt queasy, miserable and lost. Melting into the couch, I hugged the brown fake leather while yielding to another sickening wave of anxiety. *Why is adulting so hard?*

The front door flung open and crashed against the wall. The entire apartment shook as if a 4.2 had just rolled through. I jumped off the couch, ready to attack my insolent intruder. You wake my kid, I kill you.

Tom stood in the doorjamb wide-eyed and stock-still. I dropped my arms. "Lilly is asleep. What is wrong with you?" I mouthed.

"Sorry. Pie is lure door docked," he mouthed back.

"What?" I whispered.

He traversed the threshold in one long step, stopping inches from where I stood, and bent his six-foot-five frame in half, his face close. I hadn't brushed my teeth all day. Served him right. "Why is your door unlocked?" he whispered.

"Shhh." I showered him with my Funyuns breath and waited for the high-pitched shriek of a toddler abruptly woken. The only noise came from Mr. and Mrs. Nguyen, my sweet next-door neighbors who were both hard of hearing. Through the paper-thin walls, I was privy to every conversation they shouted and every show they blasted. They were watching *Jurassic Park* with Vietnamese voice-over.

Screeching dinosaurs. No screaming Lilly. Disaster averted. I swiveled my attention back to Tom. "Why don't you knock?"

"Sorry." He held up a white bag and flashed his matching bleached smile. "I brought donuts."

"Forgiven." I snatched the bag out of his hand and padded back to my spot on the couch. I curled around the bag, inhaling the sweet, greasy scent. Deep-fried dough makes everything better.

Tom dumped himself down on the couch and used Lilly's Barbie castle as a footrest, throwing his hands behind his head and stretching his long body out. "How long has Lil been asleep?"

"It's Lil-eee." I pushed his feet off the toy with my leg and shoved a piece of a sprinkled glaze into my mouth.

"You're in a good mood."

"I'm in the midst of a meltdown," I professed, in between bites.

"No news on the job?"

I shook my head.

"I'm sure something will work out," he said casually. Stress was not in his vocabulary. No matter the situation, he assumed everything would "work out in the end" without worrying one step of the way. It was a completely foreign concept to me.

"I'm sure it will," I humored, wiping the glaze off my face with the back of my hand. "What's with the donuts anyway?"

"I was in the area and thought you and Lilly might like some." He peeked into the near empty bag. "Or just you."

"Aw, that's *sweeeeet*."

He laughed. "I'm sorta seeing a girl who works there, and she hooked me up."

*Damn you, Alcatraz friend zone.*

"I've got something else to cheer you up." He reached into his back pocket and pulled out a coupon for a free burrito from a restaurant I'd never heard of. "I helped the guy who owns this place, and he gave me a couple of these. Looks good." Tom's clients showed their appreciation for his law abilities with free car washes, oil changes, haircuts and landscaping (which was of no use to him. He has a two-bedroom apartment in Mar Vista. He took a houseplant instead, which he killed. We're better parents than gardeners, I swear.) Cash would be a nicer form of gratitude, except Tom was a criminal defense attorney at a small firm with low-income clientele. He also had this thing about only representing innocent people, which, in my opinion, was just lazy lawyering. He should challenge himself and take on rich criminals, perhaps a money-laundering CEO who'd throw money at Tom to keep himself out of jail. Of course, Tom wanted no part of that. He had a moral agenda to uphold, and it paid peanuts. Or in this case, burritos.

All that schooling, and all that student debt, and in the end, he was as poor as me (before the no job situation). If only I'd gotten knocked up by a lawyer with a desire to make money, then maybe my child support check would cover the electric bill.

I shoved another donut into my mouth, letting the sweet maple glaze dissolve on my tongue before swallowing. The chunk of dough hit my stomach like a brick. I may have overdone it. I placed the bag down just as my sweatpants began to vibrate. I grabbed my phone from between my underwear and the elastic waistband of my sweats. An unrecognizable number flashed across the screen. My stomach flipped. I raced to the bathroom and shut the door. "Hello," I answered with a smile.

"You have a chance to lower your debt," a recording announced.

Smile gone.

I hit "end" and shoved the phone into my pocket. It began to vibrate again. I knew it was the same recording. During my employment drought, I had entered every online sweepstakes I could find and didn't win anything except nightly solicitors wanting to lower my debt or refinance my nonexistent mortgage.

I placed the phone back up to my ear. In my most annoyed voice I said, "Hellooo?"

"Hello?" a man's deep voice replied.

I pulled the phone away from my ear and looked down at the screen. A 424 area code. My heart regurgitated into my throat. "Hello?"

"This is Patrick from Elder Property Management."

Palm, meet forehead. "Hello, Patrick! How are you doing this night?" *Crap. Crap. Crap.*

"I'm doing fine. I'm calling because I would like to offer you the apartment manager job."

...

"Hello?"

...

"Cambria? You there?"

...

"Cambria? Hello?"

"Um, yes. Sorry. Yes, I'm here. That's… wonderful!"

"I'd like you to start Monday. That'll give you five days

with Joyce before she moves. We should be able to get her apartment turned over by Sunday. I realize that doesn't give you much time to move. Due to the short notice, I'll cover a lease-breaking fee on your apartment and a little extra cash to help with the move."

"I'm on a month-to-month so that shouldn't be a problem." I was getting kicked out anyway. "There's one thing though." *Breathe, Cambria.*

I had to calm my enthusiasm and rationalize my thoughts. I wanted this job. I *needed* this job. There was one issue I dare only raise now that I had the job. Patrick sighed into the phone.

"Thank you so much for offering me the position. I would love to accept the job. However, I have a daughter— she's three—and the amount of smoke is a concern. I'm hoping you'll consider changing the carpet at least."

"Oh, the smoke." He sounded surprised. "We'll be doing the whole works on the apartment. Carpet, paint, counters. I've already discussed this with our new maintenance man, and he said he could get rid of the smell, and then we'll air out the lobby. That shouldn't be a problem."

"New maintenance man?" My heart sank. "What happened to Chase?"

"He is the new maintenance man."

Happy jig.

"Now," Patrick continued. "I would prefer for you to train alone. Once you move in, I'm fine with your daughter being there during office hours."

I may have peed my pants. "Thank you so much, Patrick. I promise I'll do an exceptional job." It felt like my chest had been pumped full of helium.

"Thank *you*," Patrick said with an odd fluctuation of his stern voice. I was too high on excitement and relief to be bothered by the implication. "I'm glad you're up for the challenge. Have a good night."

"You too." I hung up. *Yes!* I threw my arms up in silent victory and smacked my hand on the shower rod. Causing it to crash into the tub. Taking my shampoo, soap and Lilly's bath toys with it. Lilly screamed. Now I had to put a frightened toddler back to bed and clean up my grubby bathroom. But who cared? Life just took a major upswing toward fabtabulousness. Which isn't a word.

∽≈

"But totally should be," Amy conceded when she arrived early Monday morning. "I think it should be our new mantra."

I opened the front door wider for her. All I could see was the top of her blond and pink bun piled high on her head over the mound of clothing and shoes cradled in her arms. The girl had the figure of a ruler. Unless she had a pair of magical Spanx in there, I doubted I'd be able to squeeze into any of her doll-sized clothes.

"I love that idea. We should bedazzle it on some shirts and start a Facebook page. *The Fabtabulous Females of Los Angeles.*" I laughed at my wittiness. Amy did not. "Too far?"

"You lost me at bedazzled."

"That's the best part."

"Let's concentrate on the task at hand before we start adding rhinestones to stuff." She emptied her load onto my bed and spread out the clothes. She had on a pair of denim shorts that looked like Lilly cut them, all frayed and stringy, and a black tank top with a pink bra strap sliding off her shoulder. She was roughly eighty-percent leg, five-percent torso, and the rest was all boob. I was the Ethel to her Lucy. The Mary Ann to her Ginger. The Patrick to her SpongeBob. I was the typically scripted shorter, less cute, rollier best friend. I provided the comic relief and the logic. It was a role I was comfortable with.

"If I'd known you were planning on bringing your closet, I would have come to your place instead." I leaned against the doorway, watching her hold up a shimmery, low-cut shirt, eyeing it with a tilt of her head. Amy had always been my go-to stylist when more than a Target Mossimo shirt and jeans were required. Amy and I went back a long way. We'd bonded back in third grade over Lisa Frank pencil boxes and our mutual love of the monkey bars. Sometime during that year, while hanging upside down from the bars, the tips of her blond braids touching the sand and my Einstein hair remaining unmoved (it tends to look the same whether I'm upright or upside down), we pinky-promised to remain best friends forever. Even in high school, when she was president of the drama club, and I was on the soccer team, we remained close. Sleepovers every Friday and Saturday nights, shoving notes in each other's lockers, we even went to sophomore Homecoming together. (We weren't exactly what you would call popular. We had each other so it didn't matter—too much.)

Some years ago, while watching a *Project Runway* marathon, Amy sat up, having an epiphany of sorts, and announced we were moving to Los Angeles to pursue her acting career. She didn't ask me to come along, nor had I asked if I could. Neither of us questioned it. We did everything together. I'd long since dropped out of college, and she was working as a waitress, a job she hated. "What do we have to lose?" she had asked, and I couldn't think of anything. So off we went.

Maybe it was because we were both only children or maybe it was because we were both the same kind of crazy. Either way, we built a lasting friendship seasoned with trials, tears and an ocean's worth of Diet Coke—as well as the occasional makeover.

Amy tossed the shimmery shirt back on the bed. "I brought everything because I wasn't sure what state your hair was going to be in." She turned around and her clear blue eyes widened in exasperation.

"What?"

She grunted and dug through the pile again, pulling out a white shirt that looked as if it belonged to Lilly. "We need to pull attention away from what you have happening on top of your dome." She pointed to Einstein shoved into a knot on the top of my head. "Here, try this on."

She handed me the shirt, and I held it up to half of my chest. "This is not going to fit."

"Trust me. I'll have you looking like an apartment manager in no time."

"Do you even know what an apartment manager is supposed to look like?" I pulled my oversized green shirt over my head and shimmied my way out of a pair of black yoga pants that were stained with the remnants of every meal I'd eaten since Friday.

Amy shrugged. "Not exactly. But I have a good idea of where I'm going. Plus… yikes. Cambria, honestly." She took a step closer, shaking her head. The diamond stud in her newly carved nose caught the overhead lighting. I went crossed-eyed looking at it. "When was the last time you plucked that brow? You realize there are supposed to be two, right?" she asked rhetorically.

After an hour of tweezing, blow-drying and bobby pinning, Amy stepped back to admire her work. "Voilà!" She kissed the tips of her fingers and tossed them into the air. "Perfection. You know I'm not doing this every morning, right?"

"I know," I whispered, barely able to squeeze the words out. The Spanx Amy talked me into were not conducive to breathing. Dots danced in my peripheral vision. "I wanted to look good on my first day, that's all."

"Suuuuure you did." She leaned in and yanked one more hair off my face with her tweezers.

"Ouch!"

"OK, now you're done." She tossed the hateful instrument back into her bag. "I've gotta get going. I have an audition in—" She checked her phone. "Fifteen minutes. I'll come back and grab my stuff later. Tell the cute maintenance guy I said hi. Love ya." She kissed the air and bolted out of the bathroom. "Bye, baby," I heard her say to Lilly, who was lying on the couch in a *Mickey Mouse Clubhouse* trance.

I hoisted myself off the toilet seat and turned around to get a look in the mirror. I was wearing the *tight* white shirt, tucked into my own *tight* black pencil skirt—the one everyone said I looked good in. But I hated the skirt because it made my butt look three times bigger than it already was. Apparently, that's a good thing. Small gold hoops dangled from my ears, which complimented the gold chains drooping down my chest. Einstein was tamed into a tight bun at the nape of my neck, and my feet were crushed into a pair of Amy's red stilettos. My face was creatively painted on, which deviated from my usual mascara, lip gloss and blush routine. I didn't look like an apartment manager per se. More like a librarian who moonlights as an escort. If I wasn't almost running late, I might have changed.

As it was, I hustled out as fast as my skirt and stilettos would allow, scooting Lilly along, feeling frazzled and clumsy. Three steps out the door and I was in Mrs. Nguyen's apartment dropping Lilly off. Mrs. Nguyen worked from home as a seamstress, and Mr. Nguyen (I couldn't pronounce their first names for the life of me so we kept it formal) worked mostly as a mason and sometimes as a pedicurist at his cousin's salon. They were both in their sixties and barely spoke English. And they were the sweetest human beings I'd ever encountered. We referred to them as Lilly's So-Cal grandparents since my parents were in Fresno and Tom's were in Tahoe. They'd been helping me with Lilly since the day she was born. Having them next door would be the only thing I'd miss about living in what I'd lovingly nicknamed Crap-o-la Apartments.

"I love you." I kissed the top of Lilly's head and brushed a dark curl behind her ear. Her heart shaped face, sparkling hazel eyes and pouty lips always made it hard to say goodbye. "Be good," I warned.

"She good. Go, go." Mrs. Nguyen waved me off, drying her hands on the apron tied around her waist. "You be late. Go!"

"Tạm biệt!" Lilly yelled after me as I ran down the stairs. She'd become quite fluent in Vietnamese thanks to her So-Cal grandparents.

As soon as I reached my car, it began to drizzle. My Civic moved along at a sluggish pace behind all the drivers going at sloth speed while they marveled at the wet stuff dripping from the sky. I even saw a news van parked near an exit. A female reporter stood in front of the camera wearing a yellow poncho, gesturing to the strange phenomenon foreigners referred to as "a light mist" and we Southern Californians called "Armageddon." Any deviation from warm and sunny turned the freeways into a parking lot.

I compiled a mental list of reasons why I dared to be late

on my first day while racing toward the sad brown doors. Traffic didn't seem a suitable answer. There was always traffic.

*I was in a terrible car accident, and despite the fact there isn't a scratch on me, I almost died.*

*I stopped to help another because I am a responsible Samaritan.*

*I was looking at the surrounding apartment buildings, you know, checking out the competition.*

*Oh, that's a good one.*

I grabbed the rusty knob, using my momentum to push open the door. It was locked. I bounced off it like a rubber ball and stumbled backwards, barely missing the mud puddle.

I threw my purse back over my shoulder, searched around the stucco archway for a doorbell, and found one hidden behind a plant. It took two rings before Joyce appeared, engulfed in a fluffy pink robe and her hair still in curlers. She hadn't drawn in her brows yet, and her face was crinkly and pale. "Good morning, Joyce," I said sweetly, pretending my heart wasn't hammering in my chest.

# Chapter 4

*The Lessor will be hereinafter referred to as "Landlord," and the Lessee will be hereinafter referred to as "Tenant." The parties to this lease agree to the following:*
*Tenant agrees to not engage in disturbingly loud activities that may nauseate other tenants on the Premises.*

"Morning. You're early." I was ten minutes late, but who was I to argue? "Come on in." Joyce opened the door wider, allowing me enough room to scoot past her. "You look *nice*. A pair of jeans and a shirt will do if you want. Patrick isn't picky about wardrobe."

My face went cherry. I pulled at the hem of my skirt. "Sorry."

"Don't be sorry. Maybe letting the girls out will help you rent apartments." She was serious. I forced a chuckle, pulling at the top of my shirt. Willing it shut to no avail. "Check the machine while I finish getting ready, and then we'll start."

I searched around for a pen and pad of paper. The answering machine wasn't hard to locate given it was twice the size of my head and at least as old as Joyce.

*You have seven new messages.*

*Message received 7:45 p.m.*

*Joyce, it's Larry. Yeah, hey, my toilet stopped working, and I need Bob to come take a look at it. Soon, please, cause I gotta go. Thanks.*

*Message received 8:33 p.m.*

*It's Martha. Whoever lives in Apartment 32 is outside, uh, relieving himself. Just thought you might want to know.*

*Message received 8:35 p.m.*

*Joyce, it's Silvia. I don't normally complain, but the tenant in Apartment 32 is urinating on his highly visible upstairs balcony. It's incredibly rude and disturbing, not to mention unsanitary.*

*Message received 2:15 a.m.*

*Trent would rather spend his only weekend off with his ex. So, let me know what I need to do to get him off my lease.*

*Message received 2:19 a.m.*

*I haven't seen my kid in a few months, and Alexis is getting all volatile over nothing again. She threw a pot at my head.*

*Message received 2:20 a.m.*

*I didn't throw a pot at his head! He's such a liar.*

*Message received 2:21 a.m.*

*That's it. I'm moving.*

*End of messages*

I stared at the primordial machine, my lower jaw nearly resting on my cleavage.

"Any messages?" Joyce took a seat on the other side of the L-shaped desk. Her eyebrows were back on, her pale cheeks rouged, and her red hair was looking extra voluminous and highly flammable. Not a good combination for a woman who smokes as much as she does.

"A few," I answered.

"That's the first thing you'll do every morning. Never bring the phone into the apartment with you at night. Trust me. You get people calling at two in the morning wanting to look at vacant apartments. If someone needs to get ahold of you, they'll call the emergency line, and that is directed to your cell phone... Why aren't you writing this down?"

"Oh, sorry." I sat up straight and poised my pen. "I'm ready."

"Good," she continued. "Speaking of emergencies, don't ever call Patrick unless it's a big one. He likes his managers to handle everything. The less work he has to do here, the happier he'll be, and in your case, you want to make him really happy."

I dropped my pen. "Why is that?"

"Because the new maintenance boy put up such a stink. He went on and on about how he didn't want to work with you or something like that. Patrick offered the job to someone else, and someone else after that, but everyone turned it down, so here you are. Or was I not supposed to tell you any of that?"

*I was Patrick's third choice and Chase's last?* That was a comforting tidbit of information.

Joyce brought her hand up to her chin; the track lighting turned her skin translucent and her bulging veins a purplish blue. She thought for a moment before reaching her conclusion. "Nope, I was not supposed to say anything. Patrick specifically told me not to. Forget it."

It felt like a bus had rolled on my chest, parked and unloaded a convoy. "Joyce, I can't forget it. Why would Chase say anything? He doesn't even know me." Surely she had to be talking about someone else. Chase wouldn't do that. He was kind, loving, compassionate, hot and an amazing, toe-curling kisser... or at least he was all those things in my imagination. I'd only met him once, and he'd already been tattooed on my brain. It said *I Lust Chase* in Lucida Handwriting twelve-point font right across my striatum, and tattoos are a pain to remove. I would know. I had one laser treatment to try to remove the dolphin permanently stuck to my lower back, but the pain rivaled childbirth, and the cost nearly killed me, so I opted to live with Flipper forever.

"It's my fault, really. I thought if you met him you'd be more inclined to take the job. Now forget about it. That ship has sunk." She swiveled her chair around and yanked open the filing cabinet, removing a manila folder.

*That ship has sailed? Or sunk?* Either way, I guess the ship was gone. What a disappointment. I wanted to sail on that ship.

Joyce swiveled back around. "What did the messages say?"

*Messages?* Oh, the messages. I cleared my throat, attempting to remove the basketball-sized lump now wedged in there. "Trent is possibly cheating on Alexis, and she threw a pot at his head and would like him to move out, even though she denies throwing it. Now he's moving. Larry is pissing on his patio because his toilet is broken."

Joyce nodded along, as if this were an everyday occurrence. "Alexis and Trent have been having problems since she started snooping on his Facebook thing. Don't worry, they'll be fine, and I'll have you write out a maintenance report for Larry's toilet." She shrugged.

"That's it?" Even at Crap-o-la Apartments no one had been caught peeing on their patio. Having sex, yes. Peeing, nope. "Should we write Larry up? I mean, what are we going to do about him pissing on his patio?"

"Fix his toilet." She handed me the maintenance notebook. "Fill out an order, and give it to Bob."

"Bob? Why Bob? What about Chase?" Did he hate me so much he'd rather quit than work with me? *What could I have said to him?* Such a waste of Spanx.

"Normally, Sundays and Mondays are our days off. He won't be around much until Friday anyway. He starts full…" Joyce's voice trailed off. Her eyes were fixated on something outside the large window next to the desk.

I swiveled the chair around. A woman stormed through the breezeway. Her pink robe flapped behind her like a cape as she treaded toward the office. "Who's that?" I asked.

"It's Silvia Kravitz." Joyce sighed with a shake of head. "Please, for your own sake, make a better impression this time."

*This time?*

A chime echoed through the lobby, announcing a visitor, followed by the sharp tapping of heels across the linoleum floor. A woman with ten-too-many facelifts appeared. It was the love child of Gollum and Joan Rivers. Her silk robe hung off one shoulder revealing the thin strap of her red nightie. On the other shoulder a parrot sat so still that I questioned if it were alive or a prop.

"Hello, Silvia, this is Cambria, the new manager," Joyce greeted from her chair.

Silvia's bulging eyes met mine, and I smiled. "Hello, nice to meet you." I walked up to the counter and held out my hand. Silvia eyed it suspiciously and slowly placed her fingertips into my palm, as if waiting for me to kiss the backside of her hand.

I shook her fingers instead, eyeing the unmoving parrot. Silvia reached over to the sanitizer propped next to the brochures advertising a *spacious studio*, gave it two pumps into her palm and began slathering it on.

"Is there something I can do for you?" I asked.

Silvia groaned. The parrot repositioned him, or her, self on her shoulder. "It's happening again. Look what it's doing to Harold."

"Who's Harold?" I asked. She gave me a look, trying— and failing—to move her brow. "Oh, is… is he Harold?" I pointed to the parrot.

"You know I'm not one to complain." She looked over my shoulder at Joyce for backup, but Joyce remained silent. "It's every day. Morning, noon and night. It's…" She leaned in closer. "It's unnatural," she whispered.

"Unnatural?" I whispered back.

She nodded. "Unnatural." She reached into her pocket and pulled out a saltine cracker, took a small bite, and then handed the rest to Harold. He grabbed it with his claw and attacked it with his beak, sending crumbs down Silvia's chest and into the wrinkled cleavage peeking out from her nightie.

I looked back at Joyce who was now doing a crossword puzzle. "Can you elaborate on what is so unnatural?" I asked Silvia, keeping my eyes away from Harold, who was now picking the cracker crumbs out of her cleavage.

"No!" She closed her eyes and placed her hand over her chest, forcing Harold back to his spot on her shoulder. "Come with me right now. You can hear for yourself what we have to put up with. Because Joyce refuses to see for herself." She clapped her hands together. "Come, come."

I turned around and mouthed "What do I do?" to Joyce.

She shrugged. "I'd follow her if I were you. But be careful. Harold bites."

*Harold bites?*

Silvia's silk robe rustled behind her as she walked through the complex, her heels clacking against the wet pavement. Harold perched himself backwards to better keep a tiny eye on me.

We passed the pool and arrived in the third courtyard. It was my first time in the banned area. It mirrored the first, except for the ominous feel to the air and the black door on the second floor at the top of the back staircase. Apartment 40. Plywood covered the window. Cobwebs coated the top corners of the door, and "Forty" was sprayed in red, dripping paint. I squinted, trying to read the weathered note taped above the doorknob.

*Management never…*

Silvia snapped her fingers in front of my face. "Concentrate, new apartment manager." She flipped her bleached hair and trotted forward. I caught one more glance back. The "Forty" looked like it could be the title to a horror movie, a really gory one. The plywood wasn't as weathered as the door, indicating the window had to have recently been broken—hopefully not by a stray bullet or a dead body. Yikes. Goose bumps prickled down my arms and up my neck. "Apartment Manager!" Silvia yelled.

I shook off the concern. "Coming."

"Hurry up!"

*Note to self: Patience is a virtue you don't possess. So fake it, Cambria.*

I took the stairs up to Silvia's apartment. She stood at the door with her arms crossed, foot drumming, face frozen in shock. She pointed down to my feet. "Those have to be removed before you may enter my home, always."

"Of course," I obliged, and yanked off Amy's stilettos. My feet sprang back to life. Feeling slowly returned to my toes as they sank into the plush tan carpet. It felt heavenly. It smelled heavenly—fresh lilacs and vanilla. Cool air wafted from the air-conditioner stuck in the window. The apartment looked staged for an open house. The furniture firm and untouched, vacuum lines perfectly spaced along the carpet. A bookshelf containing framed photos of a beautiful brunette posing in a garden, posing in a swimsuit at the beach, standing with Muhammad Ali, and another of her with an actor I recognized, but I couldn't remember his name. I guessed the woman in the pictures was Silvia, with her original face on.

She placed Harold on his perch next to the couch and snapped around to face me. "Well?" she asked.

It's like she was speaking in code. "Well…"

"Listen."

I took another step in, eyeing Harold. I heard muffled voices. I followed them down the hall into the bedroom where the sound became painfully clear—and was followed by a repeated thumping against the wall.

*Oh, please, no.*

"Can you hear that?" she shouted over the husky moans coming from the other side of the wall. Two oil paintings hung above the bed and swayed with each thrust, threatening to swing off the nail holding them to the wall. "Do you see how disturbing this is?"

I saw. I heard. I agreed. I found myself nodding my head along with the rhythmic humping.

"Go talk to them. They don't listen to Joyce. Maybe they'll listen to you. It has to stop, or I'll move!"

The sexing couple was now screaming. It was awkward. "I will make a note and speak with them later when they aren't so… busy."

Boom!

One of the paintings swung off the nail and landed on the bed. "That means they're done. You can talk to them now. Go. Go." She clapped her hands together.

"Right, OK. I'll go do that." *Is this really happening?*

I grabbed my shoes on the way out and took the four-step journey to the neighboring apartment. I stared at the door—thinking of all the things I would rather do than speak to strangers about their loud, unnatural sex life.

I raised my hand and knocked twice. The door creaked open, and an old, old woman poked her head out, her short, thinning gray hair pointing in every direction.

*You have got to be kidding me.*

I forced my mouth to move. "Um… I'm the new apartment manager… and… um… *hi.*"

The woman opened the door wider, allowing me a full glimpse of the white sheet wrapped around her sagging unmentionables. "Hey, Hon, look. It's the new apartment manager," she yelled to the old man sitting in a recliner wearing nothing but boxer shorts, smoking a cigar. "Say hi," she scolded. The man raised his hand, not taking his eyes off the fishing show he was watching. "I'm Clare, and that's Bill. I was about to bake you some welcome-to-the-neighborhood cookies except I got a little distracted." She smiled—*Oh hell, where are her teeth?*

I looked at the floor. "That's actually why I'm here. Your bed backs up to your neighbor's bedroom, and if you could keep that in mind, that would be great." I hoped she understood my point, because saying sex in front of a toothless grandma required more maturity than I currently possessed.

"Hon, your snoring is bothering the neighbors again!" she yelled to Bill.

"Oh, it's not the snoring," I quickly added and leaned in closer. "Do you have a large headboard?"

Next thing I knew, I was standing at the foot of her bed—a wooden bedframe with four tall posts that nearly touched the popcorn ceiling. She readjusted her sheet. "See, it's just average size."

*That's what she said.*

"It's not the size, more so the sound when it crashes against the wall," was my roundabout explanation. Grandma stared at me. I gave the foot of the bed a hard shove with my thigh, causing the headboard to slam into the wall. I then gave it three more steady shoves to drive the point home.

Grandma made an O with her wrinkled lips. "I can fix that." She grabbed a throw pillow from the chair next to the bed and shoved it behind the headboard. I gave it another hard thrust. The pillow kept it from ramming the wall.

"That seems to work. Now if you could, you know, try to keep it... *quiet*... that would be helpful."

"I'll try my best," she said with a contrite smile, readjusting her sheet again.

# Chapter 5

*Tenant understands that the community Dumpster is used for the disposal of TRASH ONLY.*

*Resident said she'll try her best to keep her voice down while intercoursing,* I wrote later on my time card. *Tried to follow up with Silvia, but she didn't answer the door or my phone calls. Left message saying, "I took care of Clare and Bill, and will follow up as necessary."*

Patrick wanted an hourly chronicle of my training. Aside from my conversation with nearly naked Grandma Clare, I spent most of the day sitting at Joyce's kitchen table eating Doritos and watching her smoke. She told me stories of when she first met Bob, growing up in Chicago, and how she became an apartment manager to pay for her son's college tuition.

We took a short break to go over unclogging a garbage disposal with the end of a broom. A skillset put to use when Apartment 8 tossed a used condom into theirs (I didn't ask questions). Then Joyce and I assumed our positions at her table while I listened and she talked about anything and everything except the job. I wasn't sure how to write this out on my time card without sounding like I sat and ate all day, which is exactly what I did. Even though I was third choice, I had to sound productive.

*Thoroughly reviewed application process,* I wrote next, even though Joyce only casually mentioned something about rental applications in between Bob's kidney transplant and her bunion surgery. *Discussed medical benefits…*

Joyce dropped a key ring on top of my time card. "Lock up the office when you're done," she rasped.

I swiveled the chair around to face her. There were at least forty keys of all shapes, colors and sizes shoved on the small ring. None were labeled. "How do I know what key goes to what?"

She touched a gold one with her bent forefinger. "This opens every door. I don't know what the others do."

"Thanks. That's *helpful?*" I'd already forgotten which one she pointed to.

"Don't lose those," Joyce warned. "And I'll see you in the morning."

"Happy packing," I sang and flashed an exaggerated smile. She had confided in me earlier that, as a kind gesture for her years of faithful service, Patrick had hired a moving company to pack for her. According to Joyce, "three dimwits with big muscles and no shirts" arrived. She was not about to let them touch her delicate possessions and promptly shooed them away.

I begged her to invite them back, even offered to personally supervise their bubble wrapping. I wouldn't mind babysitting some dimwits with big muscles. It seemed like the perfect distraction from the cute maintenance boy who turned out to be a dimwit himself.

She rolled her eyes. "Finish the damn time card, and take the trash when you go. If you can manage," she quipped, wanting the last word before shuffling back to her apartment. The rusty hinges screeched as the door reunited with the frame, and she flipped the lock loudly for effect.

Laughing, I swiveled back around and dropped the keys into my bag. I enjoyed our easygoing banter. It made the nicotine headache I'd been rocking all day sufferable.

"Hellooo?"

The tube top brunette from the day I interviewed stood behind the counter. This time she wore a red bandana as a shirt.

She snapped her gum. "I know you, right?"

"Yes, Cambria. I fell down next door."

"Ooh, right, right, right. You, like, work here?" The Valleyspeak accent was strong in this one.

"I'm taking over for Joyce."

"So sad. I like her. My Boo will be totally bummed." She pouted her glossed bottom lip.

"What apartment does your *Boo* live in?" I asked.

"He's in Apartment Thirty-nine." She giggled, and plucked a rental application out of her knockoff Prada and slid it across the counter. "I printed this off the website." *We have a website?* "I'm moving in with him. Yay me." She clapped. "Joyce said if I wanted to live here I have to, like, have an application in or whatever."

"That's correct." I had no clue. "I'm sorry, I didn't catch your name."

"Wysteria, with a y, it's totally my work name, so you can call me Alice, cause that's, like, my real name. It's on the app." She pointed a freshly painted crimson fingernail at her name. The "i" dotted with a heart.

"Nice to meet you, Alice. I need a copy of your driver's license." I skimmed the application. All the information appeared to be in place. Previous rental history, contact information, employer... *The Palace. Occupation: striptease artist.*

Surprisingly, I knew of The Palace. I'd interviewed there, thinking it was a restaurant. And it is: a topless one.

Alice handed me a copy of a student identification card from a college I'd never heard of. Which meant nothing. There were over fifteen junior colleges and trade schools in the area. At least that's what my mother said at the end of every conversation. "I totally left my license at a club and haven't gone to the DMV yet. Please don't tell my Boo. He gets really mad when I lose stuff, and he's totally sick with a gnarly cold right now." She held up a Vons bag filled with remedies and smiled until her bra started singing. "Oops. Hold on a sec." She pulled her phone out of her cleavage and answered. "Hi Boo... no, I'm on my way right now." She pointed to my shirt and mouthed, "Super cute. I totally want."

I gave a thumbs-up.

She opened the door. "I told you, I was going to go get some stuff... I'm walking back now... don't worry..." I could hear Alice arguing with Boo until the door shut behind her.

I glanced down at my shirt; it was threatening to pop open with my next breath.

*Thanks, Amy!*

Whatever. It was quitting time.

The carports horseshoed the building with a single, narrow space marked for each apartment. A rickety gate guarded the entrance, squawking the arrival of each car as it passed through. The driveway looked to have been paved sometime during the Vietnam War and not touched since. My heels slid into the cracks veining through the asphalt, and I hurried across, trying not to get hit by one of the many cars speeding over the bumpy terrain. It was a real life game of Frogger. I managed to make it to the other side with only a scuffed toe.

The Dumpsters were pushed up against the maintenance garage. Just seeing the word *maintenance* brought my blood to a boil. I'd been wracking my brain all day trying to figure out what I could have said to make Chase not want to work with me. What would cause him to go out of his way to call Patrick and ask that I not be hired? If the other two applicants hadn't turned down the job, I would have been screwed. It didn't make any sense. *Maybe I was drooling? Maybe he didn't like that I had asked him for advice? Maybe he was just a Grade-A Douche?* I had no idea, but had every intention of finding out, soon. In the meantime, I pointed my nose to the sky and strutted past the garage even if it was closed, and even if Chase was nowhere near it. It was good practice.

I threw open the lid to the Dumpster and swung the trash over the side, with a quick glance down before I released... *What the?* I gasped. A button flew off my shirt and hit the side of the Dumpster with a "ping."

# Chapter 6

*Tenant agrees to refrain from all illegal activity while on the Premises.*
*This includes all Common Areas.*

An assortment of wallets covered the bottom of the bin along with a black backpack. I counted thirty wallets in total. All looked new and quite expensive. I wouldn't have given one or two wallets any thought, but thirty? It wasn't right. Why would someone throw away so many good wallets?

With a quick glance around to be sure no one was watching, I dropped my purse and hoisted myself up, resting my stomach on the side of the bin, teetering like a human seesaw, and reached... *oomph!* I would have face-planted at the bottom of the bin if the backpack hadn't broken my fall. It smelled like fish and gym socks, yet still better than the office.

I awkwardly moved into a catcher stance and began gathering the wallets into a leathery mountain. Each still had identification inside along with gym passes, Vons Club cards, meal cards from Café Rio, unopened condoms and business cards. No credit cards, debit cards or money. I scanned the IDs in search of a familiar face. All belonged to California drivers, and all addresses were located in the Los Angeles area. All were male, and none looked familiar.

These were stolen, I realized. Someone stole the wallets, took all the cash and credit cards, and then dumped them in here. What other explanation could there be?

The trash truck had bounced down the driveway only a few hours earlier, so these would have had to be tossed recently. The rickety gate only opened with a transmitter, and the pedestrian gate required a key. It couldn't have been someone passing by, looking for a quick place to dump his or her stolen goods.

I turned my attention to the backpack. Unlike the wallets, the backpack looked worn, the coloring faded and the stitching frayed. The pain shooting down my face told me it wasn't empty either, and being that it hadn't detonated when I landed on it, chances were it wasn't an explosive.

Realizing I was now dealing with a potential crime scene, I figured I should probably stop getting my fingerprints all over the evidence. I grabbed a Popsicle wrapper that was stuck to the inside of the bin and used it to unzip the backpack. The notion of calling the police rather than tampering with evidence hadn't dawned on me yet. Irrational decisions traveled through my mind by way of rocket, while logic voyaged by donkey. It wasn't until the backpack was open flat and I was staring down at the contents that logic finally did stroll in.

A large, white glove splattered with red, a handful of zip ties, and a black ski mask—all scandalous items on their own—were minimized by the handgun in the middle of the pile. The dark tarnished barrel sparked a fear deep in my Spanx'd gut.

A small, blue rectangle lid stuck out from behind the mask. I knew what it looked like, although I had to be wrong. *That would be absurd.* However, the entire day had been absurd what with the horny grandparents, scary doors, unmovable faces, parrots rounding second base and now a gun in the Dumpster. So, really, anything was possible.

I covered my pointer finger and thumb with the sticky side of the wrapper, and ever so lightly, grabbed the blue lid and pulled.

*What. The. Hell?*

I was right. It was exactly what it looked like.

"Hey, you down there! What do you think you're doing?"

# Chapter 7

*Tenant understands that Landlord does not provide security patrol, security system or surveillance video on the Premises or Common Areas.*

Joyce's head peeked over the side of the bin. "You're that pressed for cash, that you need to start Dumpster diving?" From my squatted position, everything south of Joyce's nose was hidden. The sunbursts of wrinkles around her squinted eyes told me she was smiling. Pleased with her wittiness. "Wait, is that yours?"

"No! No… no… no…" my voiced echoed around the tin bin. "I found it in here, look." I gestured to the open backpack and wallets.

Her little eyes went wide. "Stay right there," she instructed, as if moving was an option. My skirt was too tight, and my heels were too high. Leaving the Dumpster would require the delayering of clothing. With one missing button, I was halfway there anyhow.

*Note to self: Jeans and a T-shirt are definitely the right attire for the job.*

Metal scratched along the asphalt, followed by a deafening bang against the outside of the bin. *Ouch.* Joyce's head and upper torso appeared, holding the side with her curved, arthritic hands as she bent down to get a better look. "You found all this in here?" Her smoker's breath came right at me and filled the tiny quarters.

*Blech!*

"Well, what's the verdict?" Joyce asked.

With my nose buried into the crook of my elbow, I said, "Huh?" but it sounded more like, "Honk?"

"What is it?"

"Honk?"

"The test, positive or negative?"

Oh, that. I held the blue lid of the pregnancy test between my plastic-wrapped fingers and flipped it around. It answered Joyce's question with a tiny YES printed in the middle of the display.

"Well?" Joyce pressed, her eighty-year-old eyes not able to make out the small print from her stepstool.

"It's positive," I affirmed.

"That's good. I guess. Now you know so you can get out of there. Tenants kept calling the emergency line to tell me a prostitute was going through our trash. Now I get to tell everyone they don't have anything to worry about. It was just their new apartment manager." She laughed herself into a coughing fit.

I waited for her to start breathing again before saying, "Joyce, this is serious. We could be looking at some incriminating evidence here."

She actually rolled her eyes at me. "If you want to survive as an apartment manager, you're gonna have to start loosening up. Or take a Xanax. Benadryl helps too. It's just a pregnancy test, not worth jumping into trashcans over. Bob found one floating in the pool not that long ago."

"That's disgusting. But it's not the pregnancy test, Joyce. It's everything else. The bloody glove, the zip ties, the stolen wallets, the gun—"

"Gun?" I had her attention now.

"Yeah, gun." I used the pregnancy test as a pointer. "See? Gun."

Her jaw dropped half an inch. "In all my years…"

My legs were going numb. "Can you call the police while I put everything back… ouch!" A bag of trash landed on my head and spewed its contents down my back. I almost threw

up. Why wouldn't you look *inside* the Dumpster before tossing
your trash in?

Some people can be so inconsiderate.

"Hi, Ty!" Joyce hollered to the owner of (what I hoped
was) chocolate milk running down my shirt. "Ty and his wife
just had a baby girl last week," she told me.

"Yeah, I guessed that." I pulled the dirty diaper off my
head. "Can you go call now?"

Joyce thought for a moment. "Tenants are going to be
upset when they hear about this. 'Only one day on the job and
the complex has already gone to hell' is what they'll say when
police officers start showing up. Make my words." She clearly
struggled with idioms. "How about we pretend we didn't see
it?"

I pulled an empty soy sauce packet out of Einstein. "We
have to call the police, but we don't need to tell anyone that
lives here what we found. They'll probably never find out
anyway." The police showed up at Crap-o-la Apartments all
the time, and unless they wheeled out a body bag, I'd never
given it a second thought.

However, I wasn't paying two grand a month for a studio
apartment.

Twenty minutes later, I stood in front of a police officer
with my skirt on crooked, my shirt barely hanging on, and my
red stiletto straps draped over my fingers. "That's when you
found the gun?" the officer asked, eyes serious and lips pursed
as she scrawled my answers in her notebook. Another police
officer dropped the wallets into a bag with a latex-clad hand
before he walked back to the cluster of cruisers blocking the
driveway. The lights brightly alternated in the darkening sky.
Red then blue then red then blue then red then blue. It was
not the inconspicuous scene I had hoped for.

A group of residents gathered far enough to not be in the
way, yet close enough to hear what was going on. Silvia stood
in the middle with Harold perched on one shoulder and her
silk robe hanging off the other. "And then she said she was
going to talk to them…" I heard her telling a pudgy fellow
with a bushy gray beard and a Lakers jersey. He looked like an
off-duty Santa. "She walked into their apartment, and not five

minutes later, I heard the headboard banging against the wall again, while she was in there. Then she calls and tells me 'oh, I took care of them.' Yeah, I'm sure you did." A woman decked in expensive yoga gear gasped, bringing her hand up to her mouth, while the pudgy Lakers fan winked at me.

The police officer cleared her throat, reclaiming my attention. "That's when you found the gun?" she repeated, even louder this time.

The group of residents gasped.

"Yes, it is," I replied, in a hushed voice. I scanned the crowd for Joyce and spotted her sitting on her stepstool by the Dumpster, her eyes on the madness unfolding. "Do you think it belongs to someone who lives here?" I asked the officer.

"I don't know that right now. I have your information in case we have any questions." She flipped her book shut with a snap. "If you find anything else suspicious please leave it alone and call," she said sternly.

I gave a feeble nod and another soy sauce packet fell out of Einstein. We both watched it sail to the ground with a splat.

"Not five minutes later, the headboard was banging against the wall…" I heard Silvia retelling the story to a new observer. "I'm not saying she joined them, I'm only saying what I overheard…"

I slapped my palm to my forehead.

Joyce shuffled over. She placed a hand on my shoulder for support, waiting for her breath to return before speaking. "I was just thinking," she said between huffs. "All this stuff could be linked to an armed robbery."

The policewoman and I stared at her.

"Really, you don't say," I finally said.

"The question is, though," she continued, paying no attention to my sarcasm, "who, in the middle of an armed robbery and a possible hostage situation, thinks 'I haven't had my period for a while, I should go check on that?'"

"People are idiots," the officer chimed in matter-of-factly.

"Great. I'm glad these idiots are breeding." I sighed, looking around at the group of tenants losing interest and meandering back to their apartments one by one. "It should be fairly easy to determine who did this, right? Just see which tenant is pregnant? What size were the gloves? That could determine if it was a female or a fertile male."

The officer feigned interest. "Why don't you keep an eye out, and I'll turn it over to the detectives and let them handle the rest."

*Well then.* I'd watched enough crime shows and read enough murder mystery novels to feel my input was useful.

We exchanged polite goodbyes, and the officer stalked back to her cruiser and left with the others.

Wrapping my hand around my neck, I rolled my head from side to side. My shoulders ached, and the bus was still parked on my chest, and I smelled like, well, I smelled like a smoky Dumpster.

The sun was low in the dusky sky, casting an orangey glow over Joyce's face. She was deep in thought, staring at the bag of trash on the ground. The one I never did throw away. "You'd have to be an idiot to live here and toss that in the community bin," Joyce said to me.

"You heard the police officer. People *are* idiots."

She nodded in agreement. "That is true. That is so true…" Her words trailed off and hung in the air like a raincloud above us.

The gate shook, rattled and leisurely rolled open. A silver hatchback with illegally black windows bounced over the railing and teetered across the driveway. Joyce turned and looked at the wall while the car slowed to a crawl. I could just make out the outline of a person behind the dark window. I waved, unsure of what else to do. The car stopped.

I stared.

The person behind the dark window stared.

Joyce stared at the wall.

Then, with a pop of the exhaust pipe, the hatchback roared forward and took a sharp right turn out of sight. Leaving a cloud of smog behind.

"Who was that?" I asked Joyce.

"Oh, only a tenant," she answered with a wave of her hand and swift subject change. "I think this wall is way too high to jump."

I nodded in agreement. It was a twelve-foot high, smooth

concrete wall. Impossible to climb unless you had some kind of webbing abilities, like the Spiderman I nearly ran over.

*Hmm.*

The fact I was entertaining Spiderman as a possibility told me it was time to go home. Before I left, I had to ask, "Anything like this ever happen before?"

She shrugged her bony little shoulders, staring up at the wall. "Not on my watch."

# Chapter 8

*Tenant agrees to observe a speed limit of no more than ONE MPH while driving in the carport area.*

I lay in bed with the *Frozen* blanket pulled up to my nose. Lilly sprawled out next to me deep into REM cycle while I stared up at the stiff yellowish peaks and bumps of the popcorn ceiling. Cars zoomed down the busy road, their headlights flashing across the popcorn as they passed one after the other in a constant rhythm. Sirens wailed, feet pattered along the sidewalk, and the occasional drunken outburst followed by a scuffle commenced outside my window.

My body yearned for slumber, but my mind wasn't about to surrender. It had more important things to do, like repeating everything from being the third choice, to the gun in the Dumpster, to Chase, to the black door, to the pregnancy test, to my loud neighbors currently getting high outside my front door. Every detail, every smell, every possible theory played out in my mind like a never-ending bad movie.

Something heavy was lurking around the corner, waiting for me to get comfortable before revealing its ugly head. I could feel it. Was this feeling intuition or paranoia, though? It had always been difficult for me to differentiate the two. I had a habit of sprinting to the absolute worst possible conclusion, and then sticking to it, unable to let go even if I wanted to, hostage to an exaggerated mind and the continual "what ifs." Some would call this a fatal flaw—and those "some" would be every guy I'd ever dated.

Sometime around dawn, I convinced myself I was being overdramatic—again—and everything was going to be fine. The items in the trash were left by a random criminal looking for a good place to toss his or her evidence. The owner of the backpack likely snuck in behind a car. There wasn't a dangerous impregnator living on the property waiting to take my wallet, zip-tie my hands, kill me, and deposit my body somewhere along the Pacific where it would never be found. Leaving poor Lilly motherless... Nope. That wasn't going to happen. It was all going to be fine because I couldn't afford for it to turn out any other way. Therefore, dwelling on the possibilities was a useless endeavor.

Instead, I spent the rest of the sleeping hours watching instructional YouTube videos on how to escape a hostage situation (specifically with zip ties) and checked the news to see if any armed robberies had been covered. Nothing. Only gang shootings, stabbings and hit-and-runs had been highlighted on *The LA Times*' website. Plus a news story of a woman who released a jar of bed bugs into her apartment manager's office as revenge. That's when my mind slipped back into the pessimistic realm of thinking, so I turned off the computer and took a swig of Benadryl.

The next morning, after a few deep breaths, I rolled out of bed and dressed in the recommended jeans, along with one of my many solid-colored Mossimo V-necks. With newfound determination, I was ready to apartment manage like no woman had ever apartment managed before.

I arrived (on time) for the next three days of training, eager to learn as much as Joyce was willing to teach me (which wasn't much). Thursday afternoon, two police officers strolled in with a three-page photo lineup in hand. I always imagined these sorts of things happened "down at the station" with a room full of police officers and the witness standing behind a one-way mirrored window while a line of criminals walked across a stage, looking glum and scary. Something more official, especially when dealing with guns and hormones. This was casual and inconsequential as neither Joyce nor I recognized any of the faces. All were white males with spider web tattoos on their necks.

I still kept a vigilant eye, especially when dumping the trash, and I questioned Joyce more about the black door and what exactly I should expect from Kevin. "He's... interesting," she had said. "The best thing you can do is leave him alone. Stay far away."

"What do you mean, interesting?" I pressed.

"I mean... you'll just have to hike that bridge when you get to it."

I crossed my arms on her kitchen table, careful not to knock over the bowl of Cheetos in front of me. "Do you think the gun and pregnancy test could have belonged to him?" I asked.

She thought for a moment, ate a Cheeto and said, "He has put on a little weight."

Even if I was frustrated by the vague responses, I had to laugh at that one. "Just because there was a pregnancy test doesn't mean it was a woman."

"It doesn't?"

"You know what I mean. Do you think it could have been him?"

She smirked, as if remembering a joke, and then shook her head, handed me a bag of Spicy Doritos and continued on about the new place she and Bob had purchased in Nevada—a pre-fab house near Reno.

The moving truck rolled up late Thursday to collect all of Joyce and Bob's furniture and boxes. We were forced to move our "training session" to the lobby, where Joyce continued to share her stories while I listened and snacked (the training period was becoming troublesome for my waistline).

I suspected retirement was more difficult than she was letting on. She had devoted twenty-five years of her life to the care of the property and the residents who had lived there. Her avoiding all things pertaining to the actual job was a defense mechanism, or so I thought. She had not yet accepted the idea of someone taking over the reins. Because of this, I was sensitive and didn't press the issue. I was a fast learner and confident in my BS'ing abilities. Once she taught me about rent collection, I'd let Google cover the rest.

I imagined her emotions would surface on her last day. I imagined a lot of well wishes from the residents, maybe some thank-you cards, gift baskets, tears, hugs, maybe a dog pillow from naked Grandma Clare. In my head, I was going to have to shoo her off the property. Force her to leave.

That was not the case.

When I arrived Friday morning, Bob was at the helm of their Oldsmobile donning a driver's cap with his gloved hands resting at ten and two. Joyce sat in the passenger seat, the seatbelt strapped over her shoulder and a houseplant in her lap.

"But… but… Joyce," I stammered, shocked. The plan was for her to stay until closing. How was she going to get a proper send-off if she wasn't even there? It was rent day, and I didn't have a clue how to even do rent. "Well," I continued, finding the words to properly express my appreciation. "I first want to say thank you so much for everything, and I promise—"

"You're welcome," she interrupted, reaching for the door and pulling it closed. Bob slammed on the gas, rubber burned, and the car smoked and screeched before disappearing down the driveway.

Joyce was gone.

# Chapter 9

*Tenant acknowledges that Landlord is neither a physician nor a psychologist and is not qualified to give medical advice at any time, nor does he or she want to.*

"OK, fine, where's Joyce then? Because she'd never do this to me," the resident from Apartment 3 asked, cupping the edge of the counter, her knuckles turning white.

"I told you, Joyce left this morning. I'm the apartment manager now. According to your lease, the rent is due on the first. I'm not sure how asking you to pay the rent on the apartment you are renting is so offensive to you."

She released the counter and stood up straight, hands on hips, head cocked, angry face on. "That's fine. I'll talk to my lawyer about this."

The front door swung open, and Mickey, the resident from Apartment 19, walked through. An older, round man with dark hair and thick scars running down his dark forearms. "I'll kill you, I'll take you to hell and bury you there," he mumbled to no one in particular while Apartment 3 hammered on about her lawyer. I leaned over to see if a Bluetooth was in either of the man's ears. Both were empty. "The government is gonna take it…" he continued as he walked to the other door and swung it open. "Gonna take it…"

"Are you even listening?" Apartment 3 whined.

I cleared my throat. "Something about a lawyer who is going to sue me for asking you to pay rent?"

"This is just... no... I'm not doing this." She threw her hands up, then turned around and left.

Who knew collecting rent would be so difficult?

I'd already heard everything from "my grandma died" to "a gypsy stole my money." Larry, in Apartment 32, couldn't pay his rent because of his hemorrhoids. I didn't ask for specifics, but he shared them anyway. I was ready to pay his rent for him if he would stop talking about it!

*Blech!*

Five o'clock arrived, and I happy-jigged over to the lobby doors and flipped the locks. I'd successfully made it through my first rent day, collecting nearly half the rents. I hoped the rest would be waiting in the drop box, with the late fees attached, when I returned Sunday (a.k.a. Moving Day).

All ancient equipment powered down. Lights off. Einstein re-tamed. Two layers of lip gloss applied, and I was ready to tackle one last item of business before I scurried home to finish (and start) packing.

Chase had arrived in the morning with a crew of men recruited from the Home Depot parking lot. Within minutes, the carpet was gone, the walls were primed, and the toilets and sinks were trashed. We had not exchanged pleasantries since he was far too busy doing his job, and I was far too busy Googling how to do mine. I was ready for him though.

During my shower the night before, I prepared a cleverly scripted speech, expressing my anger in an eloquently condescending way. I held up a bottle of Pantene as Chase's proxy and told it I was an honest, hard worker and even if he attempted to sabotage this job for me and my small, defenseless, hungry child, I was not one to hold a grudge (which was mostly true sometimes). I reminded the shampoo I was now its boss, but I did it with a glower that said "watch your back" and a hair flip that said "I'm too good for you," and then I sauntered off (well, as much as I could in my tiny shower), swaying my booty in a way that said "Mmm hmm, coulda had this and blew it." Oh, it was good. I took another shower in the morning to perfect my glower.

I had seen the hired workers leave, but I knew Chase was still working because *he* had to check in with *me* before he could leave, because *I* was *his* boss.

*Mwhahahahaha.*

I stepped into my apartment. The last time I'd been there was shortly after Joyce had peeled out of the parking lot. So much had already been accomplished. The Smurf carpet was now a plush pecan color. Cream linoleum covered the dinette and kitchen floors, the walls were a shiny eggshell, and the tiled counters were now bare wood, ready for the laminate.

I strolled down the hallway, amazed at the difference. I peeked in the first bathroom. The uninstalled toilet sat near the door, and the sink was in the bathtub. It was still so surreal to think I'd get *two* full bathrooms. TWO. A luxury I hadn't had in my entire adult existence. The smell of freshly applied paint and newly installed carpets abolished my doubts and replaced them with pure, childlike excitement.

I'd been treading for so long, barely able to keep my head above water. Now it was time to swim. This was the fresh start I'd been waiting for.

I stepped across the hall into the master. With my hands clasped over my heart, like a child at Christmas, I looked around. My stomach bubbled with all the possibilities. I had a bedroom all to myself.

Only me.

Just mine.

All mine.

Mine. Mine. Mine.

All... by... my... self...

It was a notion far more depressing than I'd anticipated. A tinge of loneliness stabbed at my heart.

As promised, Joyce's massive armoire towered in the middle of the room. I ran my hand across the smooth surface, tracing the dark, natural swirls with my finger, deciding if I should paint it, stain it or trash it. I yanked open the cabinet doors, releasing a batch of hoarded nicotine. I coughed and gagged and slammed it shut.

*Trash it. Definitely trash it.*

While waving my hand in front of my face, warding off the offensive smell, the squeal of a drill pushing a screw into the wall caught my attention.

*Showtime!*

I peeked in the master bathroom and saw Chase standing on a stepstool, holding a bronzed light fixture against the wall with one hand while the other worked the power drill. Drywall dust coated his hair and stuck to the scruff on his face. He was intently focused on his job, and I was intently focused on his bicep.

I sincerely believed I'd find him repulsive after what he said to Patrick. Unfortunately, he was just as attractive as the day I met him, if not more. Suddenly, all my anger soared out the window, and I started hyperventilating. My insides flipped and fluttered and twirled like a damn acrobat. I turned into one of those annoying girls who forgot their convictions the moment a cute boy arrived. I was a total cliché, and it didn't piss me off, which totally pissed me off. I couldn't move because my legs were all watery, so I stood there staring like an idiot.

Chase stepped down and admired his work, crossing his arms over his chest. I wanted to run away, go look for my convictions and staple them to my forehead so I wouldn't lose them again, but I couldn't tear my eyes away.

Finally noticing my wobbly presence, Chase turned and delivered an infectious grin. I wanted to slap him and kiss him and fire him and… *Ahhh! Get a grip, woman!*

"Hi," he said.

"Hi," I said back.

"How's it going?" he asked.

"Fine, you?" I asked back. It was a tantalizing conversation.

"Good. I just finished," he said.

*Finished?* I glanced up at the fixture. It was upside down and crooked. The caulking around the toilet was thin in some parts, thick in others, and mostly globby and smeared all over the floor. *Is that medicine cabinet on backwards?*

I tried to open it.

*Sure is.*

Lilly could have done a better job. This was my fresh start, my chance to swim. How was I supposed to swim if I couldn't even open my medicine cabinet?

And just like that, my convictions returned, my legs re-solidified, and my glower appeared. "Are you serious?" I asked in an eloquently condescending way.

He looked around, confused, scratching the scruff on his face and causing the drywall dust to fall to the ground. My legs started to go all liquidy again. I imagined him as a bottle of Pantene. "I'll be back tomorrow to finish the first bathroom..." I wasn't sure if this was a question or a statement.

"I'll also need you to finish this one," I said, glower still in place. "I'll send you a text with the items I'd like you to address, specifically, the giant armoire in my room that I need removed, please." Hair flip. Glower. Hair flip. "Now, before I leave, I wanted to discuss our working situation."

"Situation?" he looked confused.

"Yes, situation." Hair flip. Hair flip. *Ouch.* Neck kink. "I know you didn't want to work with me, and I wanted to assure you I have a very high—"

"Who said I didn't want to work with you?" He took a step closer, placing his drill on the paint-spotted counter.

"It doesn't matter, what does is—"

"No, it does matter. Who said that?" he pressed again, mirroring my glower.

I grunted. This was supposed to be a one-sided conversation. "Joyce mentioned it. It's not important—"

"Why would she say that?"

"Would you stop interrupting me?" I snapped. I was losing momentum. "I wanted to assure you I have very high standards regarding... stuff..." *Dammit.* I forgot what came next. "Please know I plan on working here for a long, long time. You can find someone else to maintenance if you don't like me." *Did I just say someone? Crap.* "Somewhere, somewhere else to maintenance," I quickly added.

Chase stared at me. I squirmed. He asked for permission to speak with an arch of his brow. I nodded my approval. "My buddy applied for the job as well, and I wanted him to get it, that's all. It wasn't personal. I don't even know you. I like working here. I don't think there's any *situation*."

"Huh," was my response, because I couldn't think of a better one. During my rehearsal, the Pantene bottle never spoke of any friends. It never spoke at all. Joyce could have mentioned the friend. It would have lessened the blow. "OK, then, well, glad we got that out of the way. I'll text you the items I'd like you to fix tomorrow. You may leave." I turned and sauntered off as planned, swaying my booty until I whacked it on the doorknob. Ouch.

My hipbone throbbed. I pretended not to notice, and kept on swayin' until I was out of his sight.

# Chapter 10

*Tenant agrees to use the emergency line for real emergencies only—Fire, Flood, Blood.*

Despite the hundred-and-one-degree heat, a rental truck on the brink of exploding, and a cranky toddler, Tom, Amy and I still managed to get all my belongings from one apartment to the next. Interestingly, Patrick didn't offer the shirtless dimwits to help with my move. That's what happens when you're third choice I guess.

By the time we lugged the boxes and furniture from my old apartment to the truck, chased the woman who stole the items from the back of the truck, then unloaded everything into my new apartment, we were beat.

Tom, as a kind gesture, took Lilly for the night so I could organize and unpack.

And unpack I did.

I unpacked an entire box of Joe Joe's cookies like a boss. Dipping each one into a jar of Cookie Butter. The sweet, creamy, chocolatey, buttery goodness rolled around my mouth and slid down my throat, bringing so much joy to my stomach. I relaxed on the couch, propped my sore feet up on an unlabeled box and licked the cookie buttery deliciousness off each throbbing finger. One of the perks of being an apartment manager was free cable. My television was atop four boxes functioning as my entertainment center. I now had hundreds of channels of mind-numbing entertainment at my disposal. An indulgence I hadn't enjoyed in years. *This must be how the other half lives*, I thought while watching reruns of *Law and Order*.

Not wanting to be completely unproductive, I grabbed a box marked *Lilly* and dragged it to her room. I then set up Lilly's new bed. A pink plastic toddler bedframe I had purchased for five dollars on Craigslist. It was gently used, only a few scuff marks, which became invisible once I pushed it against the wall. Her old crib mattress fit perfectly inside it. I arranged her stuffed animals next to her pillow and folded her princess blanket at the foot of the bed—the Frozen sheets were all hers now. I couldn't wait for her to see it.

*That was exhausting.*

I hauled my tired body to the kitchen and set the alarm, flipped off the lights and closed the blinds. The warning beep from the alarm echoed through the apartment while I heaved my mattress down the hall and through my bedroom door, dropping it on the ground with a loud thud. That mattress and I had had our fair share of moves. When I was ten it went with me from my parents' house to my dad's condo. When my dad married that woman, it came with me to my mom's apartment. It followed me to college, then L.A., and all the random places I dwelled in between. It was with me when I lost my virginity during my first (and only) year of college. Alex Simon was the douche... *ahem...* I mean boy's name. He was my first real boyfriend. He was my first real love, or so I believed at the time. Three months later, the solid springs of my mattress held my devastated body after I discovered Alex had also visited Stacey's mattress and Courtney's and Isobel's and Leah's...

My mattress had been vomited on, strapped to the top of cars, shoved into moving vans, hung off the back of a truck. It was soaked in tears of heartache after Tom sent me to Alcatraz, tears of defeat when I lost my job, tears of joy when Lilly finally potty-trained. The floral print had faded, the stitching frayed, and the springs were visible through the thinning fabric. It's actually kind of gross, I realized.

*Note to self: With first bonus check, purchase a slightly soft, mostly firm, mostly new mattress.*

Unable to muster the energy required to shower, I unsnapped my bra and pulled it out through my sleeve, dropped my jeans to the floor and curled up in my new comforter—a housewarming gift from my mom. It had arrived Friday morning, priority mail, which had to cost a pretty penny—a penny I knew she didn't have. "Some things are worth spending money on," she had said when I called to thank her. "And you moving out of that apartment is definitely one of them. You're far too pretty, with way too much potential, to be…"

The white fabric puckered every few inches, creating the most elegant, comfy, grown-up looking texture I'd ever owned. I cocooned myself in it, laying my head on the matching pillowcase, in my very own two-bedroom apartment, an apartment I wasn't about to be evicted from. An apartment that didn't have bars on the windows, or neighbors getting high outside my door, or parole officers frequently visiting, or couches in the walkway. I even had a ceiling fan cooling the sticky air to a sleepable temperature. Installing the fan hadn't been on Chase's to-do list, but he'd taken it upon himself to do it anyway. I almost forgave him for forgetting to remove the ashtray-smelling armoire. Almost.

For the first time in a long time, I looked forward to a night of peaceful slumber, allowing my thoughts to turn to nonsense as I drifted…

Ring… ring… ring… ring… ring.
*Is that my phone?*
*What time is it?*
I rolled over and grabbed my cell off the box working as my nightstand. *The emergency line!* I bolted up and threw the phone to my ear. "Hello, this is Cambria," I answered, my hand over my chest, my breath hitched in my throat. I'd been the sole manager for three days, and the building was already on fire.

"Hello. You have a call on the after-hours emergency line. To accept, please press one," an automated woman's voice with a pleasant British accent instructed. I gulped and pressed one, anxiously placing the phone back up to my ear.

Three rings later and I was connected. "Hello, this is Cambria."

"Hi, this is Ty," the caller said. "Someone's in the pool. I wouldn't normally say anything, but I've got a baby trying to sleep."

*Phew. No fire.* "I'm so sorry, Ty. I'll go speak to them right now."

Pants on. Bra on... the floor. Phone in hand. Keys in pocket. Cold water on face and I was out the door. According to paragraph three on the fifth page of the *House Rules*, the pool closes at nine. It was nearly midnight. This, of course, was a major infraction. I strutted along the pathway, feeling quite important, ready to lay down the law. *This is my town now... or... er... community.*

My confident strut slowed to a walk... to a shuffle... to a stumble... to a complete... stop. I felt my eyes go wide as saucers. My heart skipped three beats. I was a braless statue carved of flesh, unable to move. My brain had yet to process what it was looking at.

Then, finally, my frontal lobe grasped the situation and screamed and recoiled and forced my eyes closed with a violent shiver of my body.

Penis.

A penis attached to a hairy man who was very wet, obviously cold, and much too old to be skinny-dipping. Maybe late thirties, early forties? He swayed around on the pool deck with a boogie board tight in his grasp. Then, the naked man stretched his board in front of him and slid across the pool. The hazy, underwater lights made the auburn hair covering the man (covering all the man) shimmer as he sailed to the shallow end.

The penis... *ahem*... man exited the kidney bean shaped pool and ran back to the deep end. He had a potbelly, a skinny face covered in small scars, and a black tattooed snake wrapped around his scrawny arm. I was trying to keep my eyes above the abdomen.

I pushed open the pool gate, catching the attention of the skinny-dipper before he descended across the pool again.

"What apartment are you in?" I asked, trying to sound authoritative.

He scoffed as he got out of the pool. "What apartment are *you* in?" the skinny-dipper countered while swinging his board under his arm, nearly falling over in the process.

I crossed my arms and took a wide stance. "I'm the apartment manager."

"Pfft, no you're not. Joyce is. Go away." He slid across the pool again.

I met him on the other side. "Joyce retired. I'm the new manager. And you're not allowed to be out here this late, and you're never allowed to be out here naked. Now, what apartment are you in, or who are you visiting?" *Please say you're a visitor.*

"Joyce retired?" he asked, grasping tight to the pool railing. "My prayers have been answered!" The board went flying into the pool, and before I knew it, the skinny-dipper was wrapped around me.

"Get off of me!" I yelled.

An upstairs porch light flicked on, and a woman's head poked out. "Keep it down!" she yelled. The door slammed, light turned off, and I was still in the skinny-dipper's embrace.

"Get off," I repeated, more quietly. I wouldn't want to disturb anyone again with my own problems, like being assaulted by a hairy naked man. *Honestly.*

Skinny-Dipper released me and took a step back, scanning me from head to toe with a disapproving shake of his head. My frontal lobe was still playing catch-up. "I never gave Patrick consent to hire a new manager. What's your name?" he asked, closing his eyes, like he had just fallen asleep.

"No, what's your name?"

His eyes popped open. "What?"

I reached into my back pocket to retrieve my phone. This seemed like a good time to call the police. "*Your* name?"

He looked around to see whom I could be talking to. Realizing we were alone, he placed his hand over his furry chest. "Me?" He sounded offended. "Who am I? I am the owner of this entire property, that's who I am, and if I want to swim around here naked, I can."

Crap.

"You're… you're… you're *Kevin*?" My voice rasped in my ears. It felt as if I had swallowed a bucket of sand. In my head, Kevin was a teenager with a bad attitude. Not a forty-year-old nudist.

The porch light flicked on again. The same head poked out. "Would you keep it down? I'm trying to sleep."

"Yeah." Kevin nodded. "Keep it down, apartment manager." He flashed a sardonic smirk and leaned into the pool, grabbing the strap to his board. "Try to be a little more considerate," he said before walking off, the board scratching along the cement behind him.

*I feel sick.*

ஒ௸

Ring… ring… ring…

"Hello," I moaned into the phone.

"Hello. You have a call on the after-hours emergency line. To accept, please press one," the robotic British voice answered. Again.

I pressed one and waited for the rings. "Hello, this is Cambria." I pulled the phone away from my face and squinted to see the time—two in the morning. It wasn't easy falling asleep after meeting Kevin. And Kevin *junior*.

"Hey, it's Larry." His voice was shaky on the other end.

"Hi, Larry, what's wrong?" *Please don't be about his hemorrhoids.*

"I'm really upset. Kevin came by and asked if I wanted to hang out. I said yeah, since you know I haven't been able to sleep because of the hemorrhoids. We were watching a show, and then he started spankin' the dog. Then he called me fat when I asked him to stop."

I leaned up on my elbow. "Larry, you're not allowed to have dogs here."

"I don't have a dog."

"You said Kevin was spanking your dog."

"Not my dog. *His* dog," he said.

My frontal lobe caught on quicker this time. Clearly Larry shared Joyce's trouble with idioms, not that spanking a monkey would have been any better.

"Cambria? You there?"

"I'm here." *Unfortunately.*

"I've been dieting since the doctor told me to drop some weight. He hurt my feelings. I know he's the owner's son, but he shouldn't be so nasty. I mean, Cambria, you've noticed I lost weight, right?"

As hard as I tried, I couldn't formulate a single rational thought. Larry appeared to be far more upset Kevin called him fat than the fact he... *ugh.* Does workers' comp cover hypnotherapy? I definitely needed a few sessions. "Larry, I'm so sorry about that."

"You've noticed I lost weight, right?" he pleaded.

I'd known him all of three days. "For sure. You look great."

༄✢

Ring... ring... ring...

"Whaaat," I whined into the phone, stealing a glance at the clock. *Four in the freaking morning.*

"Hello. You have a call on the after-hours emergency line. To accept, please press one," the annoying computer barked into my ear. She was a patronizing little witch.

I pressed one and waited. "What?" I answered.

"Apartment Manager, this is Silvia Kravitz. You know I don't normally complain, but some of us have to work tomorrow, and Harold is in a frenzy over here. I know he's allowed to do as he pleases, Joyce made that crystal clear, but can *you* ask him to do so more quietly?"

"Wait... what?" I pinched the bridge of my nose, steadying my thoughts. It sounded like Silvia called to complain about her bird, which would be utterly ridiculous, and also a huge relief. Anything not related to Kevin felt doable.

Silvia moaned into the phone, and Harold's wings flapped in the background. I imagined he was perched on her shoulder... or in her cleavage. "I *said* I have to work in the morning, just like a lot of people around here, and I can't if the owner's son keeps playing whatever it is he is playing over there. I get he's allowed to bend the rules, but this is getting excessive. Maybe he'll listen to *you*, because I'm going to move. I'll do it."

The phone was at my ear, but my mind was off somewhere else, like in Nevada, pounding on Joyce's door, ready to unload a string of expletives. This is why she peeled out of the parking lot. This is why she never talked about Kevin or the job. She wasn't sad about retiring. She was freaking elated. I'm a fool.

I hung up. Pants on. Bra still on floor. Keys somewhere. Phone in pocket. I kicked the armoire on the way out.

Kevin's apartment bridged over the back walkway, leading out to the carports. I charged up the stairs, wishing I hadn't forgone the bra. He was playing the saxophone or a clarinet or killing a cat. It was quite unpleasant.

I knocked. The door, obviously not fully closed, slowly opened...

My frontal lobe didn't even try this time. The scene before my eyes was too far out of the realm of rationality. Kevin had the same floor plan I did, with the spacious front living room, attached square kitchen and little dinette area. The comparison ended there. His carpet had been replaced with black, scuffed rubber flooring. The walls were covered, floor to ceiling, with newspaper clippings—a random collection of headlines and articles that looked to have dated back to the eighties. Four Barbie dolls were stuck to the wall by the knife stabbed through their plastic abdomens. Blue and pink swirls were spray-painted along the ceiling, with a disco ball mounted in the center. All the kitchen cabinet doors were missing, and the seventies-inspired yellow refrigerator was wrapped in a heavy chain with the words LIVE EXPLOSIVES written in Sharpie across it.

What would I do if a tenant were receiving an excessive amount of visitors? That's what Patrick was worried about?

How did this not make the questionnaire?

Kevin appeared from the hallway, wearing pink boxers and a pair of mismatched socks. A saxophone dangled around his neck. I could almost feel him slapping me from across the room. He lunged toward the door, stopping inches from my face. A mixture of alcohol and cigarettes laced his breath. He lifted his finger up to my nose and spat, "You don't ever come into my apartment. You never come in here. Do you understand me?" I stumbled backwards. "Get out of my house, you whore!" The door slammed in my face.

What. The. Hell.

The dying cat music returned. I knocked. He didn't answer. I knocked again. The dying cat melody grew louder. You don't call me a whore and get away with it. I was many things—many, many things—but a whore was not one of them. I banged with a closed fist, three steady beats.

The neighbor's door to the right opened. A twenty-something blond drowning in a Dodgers shirt stood in the doorway, rubbing her eyes. "Can you stop pounding on the door like that? Some of us are trying to sleep."

# Chapter 11

*In regard to visitors, Tenant agrees not to invite unruly, sociopathic or felonious individuals onto the Premises.*

*To: patrickelder@eldermgmt.com*
*From: cambriaclyne@eldermgmt.com*
*Subject: Nudist Man-child*

*Dear Patrick,*

*Good morning. Last night, I received a call from a tenant letting me know Kevin was using the pool, sans clothes, at midnight. I asked him to leave, but he was quite belligerent. At 2 a.m., Kevin entered another tenant's apartment and began masturbating on his couch, then verbally assaulted the tenant. At 4 a.m., I received a complaint that Kevin was playing a saxophone. When I asked him to stop, he called me a "whore" and slammed the door in my face.*

*I have attached the contact information for several mental health services. I'd be more than happy to make all the arrangements as soon as possible, preferably today. The center in Brazil looks nice.*

*Sincerely,*
*Cambria*

I could deal with screeching parrots and sex-crazed grandparents and stolen wallets in the Dumpster. I could even listen to Larry talk about his hemorrhoids. However, I could not, nor would I, put up with Kevin. I was desperate for the job, yes. I had an overdrawn account, yes. I didn't have the funds for another apartment, yes. I... forgot where I was going with this. I couldn't leave, therefore, Kevin had to. And honestly, he needed to. Sane people didn't skinny-dip in a community pool at midnight or masturbate in neighbors' apartments.

After clicking send, I rested my forehead against the hot surface of the desk. A migraine threatened to explode behind my tired eyes, and my stomach did a nauseating flip in anticipation. I abandoned the desk in search of the box labeled *drugs*. I was in need of two Excedrin and a Diet Coke and a tub of ice cream and a nap.

One step into the apartment, and my heart sank. Unlabeled boxes towered throughout the living room and kitchen—a daunting sight. I hadn't used any kind of packing system. Walking from room to room, I shoved whatever fit into the box I was carrying—silverware with the hangers, pictures with glass cups. I then pulled the tape gun across the top and started over. Occasionally I labeled the boxes holding important things, like the Excedrin. Except that box was not readily visible and was going to require some effort to locate. My arms felt like two anchors keeping me from drifting off toward the land of productivity.

*Why is life so hard?*

Deep breath in, slow breath out. Deep breath in, slow breath out.

Ding-dong. The front lobby door.

"Coming!" I unlocked the door. Tom stood before me, looking all rested and showered and dapper. Lilly bounced up and down at his side with her shirt on backwards, hair in a tangled mess, and remnants of breakfast stuck on her face.

Tom's restful appearance and our homeless-looking child sparked a rage deep in my weary core. I clenched my teeth so hard my jaw nearly popped. "Give me." I nodded to Lilly's go-between bag slung over his shoulder.

Tom carefully draped the strap over my outstretched arm, as if feeding a ravenous animal. "Up late celebrating the new job?" he asked, taking a big step back, his foot nearly landing in the mud puddle.

I grabbed Lilly's hand and led her inside. "Something like that. Bye." I pushed the door shut with my thigh.

Lilly and I settled on the couch, her sucked into an episode of the *Mickey Mouse Clubhouse*, me actively avoiding movement. It was clear this was a ship of fools, and I was the captain, janitor, psychologist and cruise director. *"Good morning residents, we have an exciting day planned for you. At nine-thirty we have a fun game of 'why did I shove this non-food item into my garbage disposal.' At one in the morning, we have a game called 'excuses why I can't pay my rent this month.' Both games will be held on the Lido Deck. Clothing is required although not enforced if you are an offspring of the owner. Hope to see you there!"*

"Momma?" Lilly asked, snapping me back to reality. The Mickey gang sang their farewell song in the background. "Momma, where is my Minnie?"

"I don't know, sweetie. It's in one of these boxes." I licked my finger and wiped breakfast off her cheeks.

"Can you find her? Can you find her, now? Puh-leeease." Her big hazel eyes and long lashes tugged on my momma heartstrings.

"How about we go swimming?" I asked. My head pounded in time with my heart. Submerging my achy body in a pool of cool water felt like the best idea I'd ever had.

Lilly squealed. I winced. We found our bathing suits, then I packed us a light brunch before we padded off to the pool.

Lilly tiptoed into the shallow end, her arms spread out and shoved into pink floaties. I dropped myself in. The water lapped over the side of the pool and slapped the scorching cement while I sank to the bottom, watching Lilly's little feet kicking feverishly underwater.

I floated back to the surface and became a princess mermaid with Lilly. The heat was in full force, and the cold water felt heavenly. I pushed the thought of Kevin swimming naked in the pool—less than twenty-four hours earlier—out of my mind. *That's what chlorine is for, right?*

We swam. We splashed. One of us had a near meltdown over a bee in the pool. The other cried because her floaties were too tight. After a while, we mermaided our way to the steps and exited the pool. I wrapped my towel high under my armpits to hide my too-tiny pre-baby bikini. Luckily, it was Chase's day off, and no residents were around to enjoy the view either. Not that I was ashamed of my body. I had grown to accept and love my stretch marks and new curves. I just loved it more when it wasn't bulging over the side of a two-sizes-too-small bikini.

I wrapped Lilly in a fluffy towel, and we parked ourselves on a lounge chair. Within minutes, the sun had soaked up most of the chlorine dripping off our bodies. I reapplied sunscreen, protecting our freckled figures from the ultraviolet rays. Lilly sat in my lap snacking on goldfish crackers and apple slices. I leaned back, resting my head on the plastic backing of the lounger. The fresh air dulled my headache to a more manageable throb, and I allowed my shoulders to relax while soaking in the much-needed Vitamin D.

I turned and looked out to the third courtyard. I couldn't see the black door from my seat, and all was peaceful. *Kevin must be nocturnal.*

Poor me.

All I heard was the quiet footsteps of a man walking out of Apartment 36. He had a small brown bag and tucked it carefully under his jacket. *A jacket?* He looked over his shoulder and hurried out to the carports. I propped up on my elbow and watched as yet another man exited Apartment 36, same small brown bag carefully tucked into his arm. The man, late forties/early seventies/somewhere in-between, dressed in casual attire and flip-flops, also looked around the courtyard before exiting to the carports.

It struck me as odd, most certainly suspicious. "Momma?" Lilly put her little hand on my cheek, forcing my attention. "Cracker, puh-leeease."

I dug into my bag and pulled out more goldfish crackers. Out of the corner of my eye, I caught another person, female this time, around the same age, walking through the courtyard. She stopped at each door, noting the number, until she came to Apartment 36. I leaned over and watched the woman enter the apartment.

*You notice the tenants in Apartment 6 have a constant flow of visitors. The visitors tend to arrive and leave within minutes.*

I refilled Lilly's cracker supply and threw the rest of our belongings into my bag. I swung Lilly onto my hip, bag over my arm, and pushed open the pool gate. It creaked and squeaked and moaned before slamming shut, loudly announcing our exit to the entire community. I rolled my eyes and continued to creep through the breezeway toward the third courtyard. Not exactly sure of my plan, I only hoped to get there unnoticed.

The door to Apartment 36 opened. I dropped behind the nearest bush and crouched down, trying to balance Lilly and my bag without falling face first into the thorny shrub. I peeked up and watched the woman leave with the same small brown bag; like the rest, she handled it discreetly while looking around.

Apartment 36's door shut, and it was safe to get up. I could get up. I wanted to get up. But it became clear that the best way out of my position was to fall flat on my butt and proceed from there. The dirt clung to my still damp derriere, and I took my mud-butt up the first stairwell, eyeing the vacant apartment across the way. It was the perfect lookout location.

As slyly as one can with a toddler on the hip and mud on the butt, I climbed up the stairs. "This is awkward," I mumbled.

"What's awk-wad mean?" Lilly asked.

"It's when something is uncomfortable," I whispered.

"What does uncom-for-tita-ble mean?"

"It means… not comfy."

"What does not comfy mean?"

"These are really good questions. Please keep them in your brain, and I promise I'll answer them when we get into that apartment up there, OK, sweetie?"

"Hey, Cambria!" Larry poked his head out his window and waved. His long, stringy gray hair dropped down like Rapunzel's. I waved back. Then Lilly waved. Then the resident from Apartment 7 walked by and waved.

*Good grief!*

I dashed up the remaining steps, opened the door to the vacant unit and closed it quietly behind us. Lilly slipped out of my arms and ran around, free from the confines of furniture. Her little feet thumped from the living room to the kitchen to the bedroom then back again.

*I really suck at this undercover crap.*

Positioned at the window, I slid one vertical blind over to get a look down at Apartment 36. A skeletal woman waited at the door, one bone-thin hand shoved in her back pocket and the other knocking. The door opened, and a man around my age, maybe a tad older, with a small face, slicked blond hair and round, gold glasses opened the door and motioned her in. Minutes later they reemerged, her with the bag and him with a fistful of cash.

I pulled out my phone, pointed it at the door and hit "record."

*There is not enough available storage to record video.*

"You have got to be kidding me," I said to the phone. I quickly went through my pictures and deleted as many as I could. Most pictures—OK, more than 3,400—were of Lilly's cute face.

Fifty pictures gone, I repositioned the phone on a new visitor waiting at the door and hit "record."

*There is not enough available storage to record video.*

Fine. I snapped a few pictures and composed a text to *Cambria*, noting the time of arrival, the length of stay and the description of each visitor.

"Can we go home?" Lilly asked, pulling at my towel, causing it to fall to my feet.

"I'm almost done, and then we'll go," I promised.

She slapped her forehead. It was cute. So I took a picture. Then I turned my attention back to my sting. *Is that... Chase?*

It was. He strolled along the pathway, his hips swaying deliciously with each step. His dark blond hair looked extra tousled and his face extra scruffy. I wondered if he ever shaved, and what it would feel like to rub my hands across his scruff. My knees began to buckle at the thought.

*Snap to it, Cambria.*

Since technology had failed me, a second witness would be beneficial. I looked down at Chase while the phone rang in my ear. He stopped, reached into the pocket of his jeans and pulled out his phone. He stared at the screen and hesitated. He HESITATED.

He looked around and then answered, thankfully, because that would have been uncomfortable. "Hey, Cambria. What's going on?"

"Can you come up to Apartment 21?" There was a crime in progress, no time for pleasantries. He looked up at me. "Don't look up. Look at the ground." He looked at his shoes.

"Why am I looking down?"

"Because I'm trying to be discreet here. Can you come up to the apartment, slyly?" He looked up again. "Stop looking at me."

He used his hand as a visor. "I can't see you."

"That's good. Pretend like you're going to fix something in here. See you in a sec." I hit end.

About a minute later the door opened, and Chase slipped inside. He was much better at this covert crap than I was.

He looked at me and then at the ceiling. "Where are your clothes?"

I imagined my face resembled a tomato. "Er, um, uh…" I bent down and grabbed the towel, envisioning how this could be construed. I called, asked him to meet me in a vacant apartment, and to do so discreetly. Then he finds me in a bikini. I cleared my throat. "I was swimming when I witnessed some suspicious activity back here."

"Suspicious?" He returned his eyes to my fully covered body.

"Very." I pulled the blind back, and we looked down into the empty courtyard.

Lilly tugged on Chase's shirt. "Bạn là ai?" she yelled with a wave of her hand.

Chase looked down, startled, and then smiled. He dropped slowly to one knee, holding the window ledge for support. "What's your name? Wait, let me guess… hmm, is it Anna?"

"Nooo, it's not Anna." She giggled, shoving her fingers in her mouth like she did when speaking to strangers.

"No? Is it Elsa? Or wait, no, I got it. It's not… *Lilly*, is it?"

She released a full-face smile, orange cracker stuck in the gaps between her teeth, and nodded. I melted into a big puddle of mushiness right there. It was quite frustrating. It would be easier if he would commit to being a douchebag or get ugly. Then I could stop liquefying in his presence.

Lilly offered Chase a cracker, and he popped it into his mouth. Not concerned with germs, as I would have been. The affectionate exchange was becoming too much. "OK now." I clapped my hands together. "Let's get back to work."

Chase winced and used the windowsill as a cane. I offered my free hand, the other clutched to the towel. "Would you like some assistance?"

He brushed off my help. "No, just an old injury." He rolled upright. "You teach your kid… is that… Vietnamese?"

"Yep. Doesn't everyone?" I laughed at my own wittiness, as I usually did. "Do you have kids?" Single guys weren't generally proficient in *Frozen*.

"No, nieces." He moved the blind slat over and looked down. "I'm still not seeing anything."

I glanced out the window. Alice walked through the breezeway. She wore a short-sleeved green shirt and jeans. With so many clothes on, I almost didn't recognize her. "Can you tell me what's going on?" Chase asked, growing impatient.

"It's Apartment Thirty-six. I've seen several suspects coming and going, all carrying a small bag. I'm sort of a crime show junkie. So I sort of know what I'm doing. I think he's selling black market firearms. It makes sense, because if it were drugs, then why would he put it in a bag like that? If it weren't illegal, then why would everyone look so guilty when leaving? Why check the surrounding area if you're carrying, oh, I don't know, a bagel or something. It doesn't make sense. I'm thinking out loud here… There was a handgun in the backpack I found in the Dumpster. You heard about that whole thing, right?" He nodded. "Good. I'm thinking someone tossed it in there, and the resident in Apartment Thirty-six was supposed to retrieve it that night, but I found it first. Think about it. Joyce never came back here, ever. Kevin is nuts, so anything else going on here is peanuts by comparison." Phew, it was a mouthful.

Chase nodded along with my explanation. Stifling a smile. "Have you met Spencer?"

"Who?"

"The tenant in number thirty-six."

"No, why. Have you?"

"He's really nice."

"It's a cover," I muttered.

Chase raised his unkempt brows high to his forehead. I wanted to lick my finger and smooth the hairs back in place. Though that would be awkward. Almost as awkward as having this conversation in my bathing suit. "I feel like you *may* be overthinking this. I'm not seeing anyone. Couldn't he be having a party?"

Now I was the one stifling a smile. "In the middle of the day? On a Monday? None staying for more than a few minutes? All leaving with a bag?" I was clearly more versed in criminal behavior than he was. "That reminds me, be on the lookout for a white guy with a spider web tattoo. Joyce said she never saw anyone here matching that description. Maybe he is a customer of... what was his name?"

"Spencer."

"Right, Spencer."

He ran a hand through his hair. "Why am I looking for a spider web tattoo?"

"A police officer came in with a lineup of white guys with spider web tattoos. Do you think I've seen enough to warrant a call to the police now?"

"I think the best thing you can do is keep documentation in case you need it. And instead of camping out in vacant units and spying, how about I'll keep an eye out when I'm here. I'll start watching crime shows if you think it will help." I couldn't tell if he was flirty-teasing or insult-teasing. Should I be upset or aroused? This was the question every time I was around him.

"What are you doing here anyway?" I asked in an uproused kind of way (see what I did there?).

"I stopped by to grab some tools. I've got a big job I'm helping with for a different company. Speaking of which…" He checked his watch. "I've got to head out. I'll be here tomorrow in case anyone commits any felonies you need help with."

"Ha ha," I said, not really laughing, because it wasn't funny. *Who knows what will happen tomorrow?*

"Is it OK if I sneak out of here, detective?" That was definitely a flirty-tease. *I think.*

"You're dismissed."

# Chapter 12

*Tenant parks in the carport at Tenant's own risk.*

Thirty-two-year-old Spencer Bryant had lived in Apartment 36 for two months. According to his file, he paid rent on time and hadn't made a single maintenance request. According to his application, he had excellent credit upon approval and was a local dentist. Not exactly your run-of-the-mill felon, yet definitely a good cover.

*In reality, Spencer was a gunrunner (Googled that). One of his guys, who purchases guns for him, ran into some trouble and could no longer walk into a gun shop and legally buy a Glock (Googled that too) and then sell it to Spencer, who would then sell it on the black market. So he went on a crime spree, going through locker rooms, picking the locks and stealing wallets. He carried the positive pregnancy test around as motivation to get as much money as possible because his girlfriend had recently found out she was pregnant. One day he found a gun (dun-dun-duuun), and told Spencer he would deposit it in the usual spot (Dumpster). When it came time to make the drop, he decided to toss everything along with his backpack because he wanted to make a clean, crime-free start for his new baby.*

*The End.*

I printed off my theory and placed it in Spencer's file, relishing the opportunity to put the pieces together and solve a real-life crime. The brown bag was the only hitch in my theory. Did gunrunners bag their goods like a grocery store?

*Note to self: Google that.*

I closed the rusty filing cabinet and swiveled around in my chair and found a reply from Patrick on my computer.

*To: cambriaclyne@eldermgmt.com*
*From: patrickelder@eldermgmt.com*
*Subject: RE: Nudist-Man-child*

*Cambria,*

*Thank you for the mental health information, specifically the one in Brazil you highlighted. I'll pass on the information. Don't hold your breath. Please note that Kevin's actions and opinions are his own, and do not mirror those of my company or myself. Feel free to write out an incident report for his file instead of emailing me next time.*

*-Patrick*

I read the email twice to surmise Patrick's tone, and it was not happy. Joyce warned me about bothering Patrick unless it was an emergency. If Kevin masturbating in another tenant's apartment did not qualify as an emergency, then what did?

I typed up an incident report as requested and swiveled back around to the filing cabinet. The files were in order by apartment number, one through thirty-nine. No Apartment 40. I yanked opened the cabinet below and found a file labeled "Kevin." The papers were squished tight, filling the entire length of the drawer, with not enough give to fit one more. In the next drawer was another file labeled "Kevin," not quite as full. I shoved my incident report in the back and grabbed the one before it. It was handwritten in Joyce's shaky writing and dated one month prior.

*INCIDENT REPORT*

*Early this morning (around 1 a.m. I think) I received a call from Silvia Kravitz. She was upset because Kevin was playing his music loud and scaring Harold (her bird). I explained his mental disorders to her. I had already explained this when she called the week before, but I felt it necessary to explain again. I told her it's best to leave him alone. I then received two more calls before I became fed up and called the police. Kevin was arrested. Released on bail the following day, he came into my office and was very upset. When I asked him to leave, he took my vase, the one I keep on the counter to put fresh flowers in. I asked him to return it because my son gave it to me for Mother's Day the year before he passed away. He didn't. Instead, he took it home with him. I walked to his apartment to ask for it back, and he threw it out the window, breaking both the window and the vase. I will be suing Kevin for the cost of my vase.*

*Update: I received a check for my vase and a bonus for my troubles. I gave my notice, and Patrick asked if I would be willing to stay. I said I was tired of dealing with Kevin and that we already used my bonus as a down payment for a house in Nevada.*

It was the last incident report Joyce wrote.

Joyce's son was dead, as was her vase, and Kevin had a mental disorder. So much backstory to follow. It was like a giant onion—with each layer I peeled back, the more I wanted to cry. What mental disorder was I dealing with? I wondered. "Mental disorder" had extensive implications. *What do I do with the information?* Did it change the situation? No. Did it change my perspective? Yes.

In all the times we talked, in all the stories she told, Joyce never mentioned her son had died. One afternoon she'd told me of a time when her son, Josh, was nine and decided he wanted to learn how to drive. He somehow managed to get the car out of the driveway and into the neighbor's living room. She told it with such a longing fluidity to her voice, like my own grandmother when she told stories of when she was younger. I didn't think anything of it. I asked where he lived, and she had replied, "He's in paradise." For whatever reason, I assumed "paradise" meant he lived in Tahiti, near the crystal blue waters, white sandy beaches and lush greenery. I'd only seen pictures, but it looked like paradise to me. I then said to her, "I hope you get to visit him very soon." Again, I was thinking Tahiti, not an eternal paradise in the sky. I guess paradise is a relative term, and it was hard to think on all four-cylinders while trapped in a nicotine fog.

The baritone "ding-dong" summoned me from my thoughts. I slid the incident report back in Kevin's file and closed the cabinet. Tom stood behind the lobby door. He removed his aviators and flashed his signature side-smirk. "Feeling better?" he asked.

*Feeling better?*

*No! I'd inadvertently told Joyce I hope she dies soon. Kevin has an unknown mental disability, and I can't find my drug box.*

"I'm fine," I said instead. "Come on in." I opened the door wider, allowing him entrance, and locked it behind him. "Lilly should be up soon from her nap. Are you on lunch?" I led him to the office and pulled out Joyce's old swivel chair for him.

"I had a break between clients and figured I'd come by and see the new place." He took a seat, threw his arms behind his head and stretched out his long legs, crossing his brown loafers. "I was going to ask for a tour this morning except someone slammed the door in my face."

I rolled my eyes. "I didn't slam the door. It has a door closer preventing it from slamming." I gave him a *so there* look and reached down to grab an extra gate opener from a box under the desk. "Here, take this. It'll open the gate, and you can use my apartment front door from now on." I slid it across the sleek wooden surface. He managed to snatch the opener with one hand before it fell to the floor. He delivered a full-fledged smile, impressed with his own catlike reflexes, and slipped it in his inner suit jacket pocket.

"Nice catch," I said. "Oh, and before I forget, can you take Lilly to the doctor Friday morning? They're going to squeeze her in first thing, and you're usually pretty light on Fridays, right?"

He moaned and went limp, as if suddenly stripped of all cartilage. "Why is she going to the doctor?" he asked, drawing out each word.

"When we got back from the pool this morning, she kept sneezing, and her snot had a yellowish tint to it. This could be the start of a major microbial infection." Examining Lilly's mucus had become a slight obsession.

Tom slapped his hands over his eyes with a relenting sigh. As part of our child support agreement, he's responsible for Lilly's insurance and all medical bills. An agreement he wouldn't have initially agreed upon had he known how much time I spend on WebMD.

"Fine," he surrendered. "I'll take her. She sneezed twice last night, so it's not a bad idea. I guess." He belched, blowing Taco Bell-infused stomach air into his fist (and this, ladies and gentlemen, is what it feels like to be on Alcatraz). He cleared his throat and shot up straight, nose high in the air like a beagle on a hunt. "Cam, are you *smoking*?"

"What? No! Ugh." I grabbed two cans of industrial air-freshener. "Chase promised these would work. Maybe I didn't use enough."

"Who's Chase?"

"Maintenance guy." I aimed the cans high in the air and pressed the trigger, releasing a rainfall of manufactured fragrance. The bottle promised "tropical rainforest" but smelled more like cough syrup. To be fair, I'd never been in a real rainforest.

"Take it easy, Cam." Tom coughed and waved his hand in front of his face. "It's not that bad."

"I've become desensitized." I walked backwards out to the lobby, the cans high above my head, spraying every square inch until nothing more spurted out of the nozzle.

*Wow, head rush.*

Stars began dancing in my peripheral vision. I needed fresh air. I crisscrossed over to the door and flung it open. I hesitated, my eyes adjusting. "That's it! I want a day do-over," I whined.

"What's wrong?" Tom came and stood beside me, looking out at the two police cars double parked in front of the office with their red and blue lights flashing all around screaming *Look at me! I'm here again!*

I placed my hand on Tom's shoulder for support, my head still fuzzy from the tropical rainforest. "Stay here. I'm going to find out what's going on."

"Do you have any of my business cards on you?"

I pretended not to hear.

Two police officers were standing near the gate, while two others took reports from a group of angry-looking residents in the carports. Of course, Silvia and Harold were standing close by observing the situation, Silvia with a disapproving shake of her head, Harold with his judgy little eyes.

I approached the officers at the gate. One was a muscular, older man with a bulldog face, and his partner was a tall younger guy, with a long neck and a large Adam's apple. Really large. As if an actual apple was stuck in there.

"Hello," I greeted. "I'm the apartment manager. Can you tell me what's going on?"

Bulldog spoke first. "Two cars were reported stolen."

"Stolen?" I wheezed, as if the air had been pulled out of my lungs.

"It happened sometime during the day," said Adam's Apple, his apple bobbing up and down, up and down, up and down in a distractive rhythm. "You see anything?"

*See anything?*

So happy he asked, I proceeded to tell them my Spencer theory. Bulldog scrawled in his notebook until I finished. He nodded to Adam's Apple, who nodded back, and then turned around to speak into the radio on his shoulder.

"I can take you back to Spencer now if you like," I offered. Might as well arrest him right away.

Bulldog finished speaking to his shoulder and nodded to Adam's Apple, who nodded back once again. My eyes bounced between the two men, trying to decipher their nods. "We'll turn over this information," Bulldog said, flipping his notebook shut.

"What about—hey!" A finger jabbed my arm. A short woman with more lipstick on her teeth than her lips inserted herself into my personal space, her finger pointed and ready to poke again. I took a step back. She took a step closer. "Can I help you?"

"You the new manager?" she asked with a thick accent. Her dark hair was pulled into a sleek bun, and she wore a red flamenco-inspired dress.

I rubbed my shoulder. "I am."

"We've got everything we need," Adam's Apple said as he, Bulldog, and the two other officers strolled back to their cruisers. "We have your contact information if we have any questions."

"Wait one second offi—ouch! I am not going to talk to you if you keep poking me," I warned the woman.

"Manager," she snapped, her finger ready to dig into my bicep again.

"What can I help you with?" I asked as sweetly as I could, rubbing my sure-to-be-bruised arm.

"My car is gone, and I have my salsa class!"

My stomach dropped. "I am very sorry about that." I held my hand up, ready to strike if she came at me with her finger. "You can submit the police report to your insurance company, and I'll see what I can do about upping security in the carports."

She took a step closer. I took a step back. She took another step closer and then lashed me in her native tongue, her hands flailing above her head. Even if I wasn't fluent in Spanish, I caught the gist.

"Please, calm down," I said, knowing full well it was a pointless suggestion. If someone stole my car, I'd be... Who was I kidding? No one would steal my car.

"I can't calm down," she continued in English. "I have no car! I have salsa class tonight, and I pay good money for my salsa, and we have a competition this week, and now I can't go. So I lose my money for the class, and I lose my car. We don't need more security. We need Yoyce. This never happened when she was here, and suddenly you show up, and my car is gone, and they find a gun in our Dumpster. I think it's no coincidence."

"I can assure you I didn't take your car." I rubbed my arm and looked over at the group of angry residents huddled around Silvia and Harold. The sideways glances my way were a not-so-subtle hint I was the topic of conversation. Great. "I'm sorry, I didn't catch your name?"

"Daniella." She crossed her arms and looked at me expectantly.

"Daniella, what time is your salsa class?"

"Seven."

"OK." I sighed. "I'll give you a ride."

# Chapter 13

*Landlord is not responsible for the expensive stolen property you choose to leave in your unattended car.*

## INCIDENT REPORT

*Sometime between 9 this morning and noon, Apartment 3's car was broken into. Tenant claims to have had over $1,000 in cash in the trunk along with a pair of very expensive sunglasses and her laptop. She would like to be reimbursed for her stolen items. I suggested she file a claim through her insurance and not leave expensive items in the car. She then called me several names, most of which I can't recall at this moment, some I'd never heard of, and then she left.*

# Chapter 14

*Landlord shall not be held responsible for damage caused by Tenant's own maintenance attempts.*

## INCIDENT REPORT

*At approximately 11:30 this morning, Kevin came to my door looking for money. I told him I didn't have any, so he asked for the petty cash. He said he needed the money to "beautify" his patio. I attempted a rewards approach and told him I would give him half the amount he asked for now, and if he promised to wear clothes while walking around the property, I'd give him the second half later. He agreed. I gave him $20 in petty cash. He nailed a 2x4 to his patio while wearing a Speedo.*

# Chapter 15

*Tenant agrees Landlord will not be held responsible for Tenant's own acts of stupidity.*

*INCIDENT REPORT*

*Apartment 14's car was stolen sometime early this morning. Apartments 6, 11, 22, 17 and 4's cars were all keyed. There were no witnesses, and residents will follow up with their insurance companies.*

*Update: Turns out Apartment 14's car was not stolen; it was repossessed. He promised to start making his car payments again.*

# Chapter 16

*Tenant acknowledges the toilets are not trashcans.*

## INCIDENT REPORT

*Kevin called this morning to complain his toilet wasn't working. I couldn't find Chase, so I went instead. When I arrived, I found Kevin had tried to flush an entire bag of kitty litter down his toilet. His bathroom walls were covered in mold. Kevin wouldn't allow me to fix either his toilet or his exhaust fan. He also doesn't appear to have a cat, and when asked why he threw the litter in the toilet instead of the trash, he replied, "I didn't want it any more, and I didn't want it going to waste in a landfill."*

# Chapter 17

*The Premises and Common Areas may contain chemicals known to cause cancer or birth defects or other reproductive harm.*

## INCIDENT REPORT

*Kevin took all the Proposition 65 signs off the property. He was very upset with me, asking why I would use chemicals that could cause cancer. I explained these signs are posted at every apartment building, fast food restaurant, grocery store and gas station in California. He called me a liar. It should be noted that we had this entire conversation while he was smoking a cigarette.*

# Chapter 18

*Landlord reserves the right to walk away if Tenant refers to Landlord as an animal, female or male body part or any carnal activity.*

## INCIDENT REPORT

*Apartment 33's car was stolen. She confirmed she had been making car payments. I believe it was legitimately stolen. I promised to look into hiring a security patrol company. She was very upset with me, questioning why only my car had not been bothered. I showed her which one was my car and then she understood why. Still, she called me several names and threatened to have me fired.*

*Update: Submitted bids for security company to Patrick.*

*Update: "It's under advisement."*

# Chapter 19

*Landlord shall not be liable for physical assaults or property damage caused by other Tenants or Tenants' guests.*

*Dear New Apartment Manager,*

*Accept this letter as my official thirty-day notification. Our car was broken into last night, again, and my window was broken and side panel keyed. Our GPS was stolen. We will be moving to a safer apartment complex. You can return my full deposit within twenty-four hours of our departure.*

*Sincerely,*
*Rachael M. Manfeld*

I'd been the sole apartment manager for seven days. SEVEN DAYS. And the place had gone to hell. HELL (or so I'd been told by many). It had to be some kind of world record. I was on a first name basis with the police station's dispatch operator. Penny had a three-month-old baby girl and a fiancé named Pedro. I was one call away from being a bridesmaid.

I hadn't heard from a detective regarding Spencer or the backpack, and when the police arrived, they took a report from whomever had had their car vandalized or stolen, and

only looked mildly interested when I pulled them aside to
recount my Spencer theory, again. One officer humored me
and knocked on Spencer's door. He wasn't home, and that
was the end of that.

As if the crime wasn't enough, two washing machines
broke, which "never happened when Joyce was here," and just
about everyone lost their minds. I found Kevin easier to
handle than the increasing number of irrational residents.
Kevin at least had a medical reason. What exactly the diagnosis
was remained a mystery.

For being a handyman, Chase was not particularly handy.
He took hours to complete a single task, roamed around and
left tools everywhere. Expensive tools too. I had to re-fix
everything he touched, but he wasn't the one on the chopping
block. I was.

Patrick had received several complaints about my "terrible
management style." The biggest complaints (aside from the
crime I seemingly brought with me) were that I "hated the
elderly" and I "threw away other people's hard-earned
property" and was "antireligious." There was also a rumor that
I had a threesome with Clare and Bob, which, when you think
about it, contradicts the first complaint.

Life would be easier if I carried on Joyce's tradition of
never leaving the apartment (but then I couldn't continue
being Daniella's personal taxi. The woman had salsa every
night). Joyce, I learned from Daniella, didn't even leave to
show vacant units. She would hand prospective tenants the
key and let them wander around. I couldn't manage like that. I
walked the property. I showed apartments. I enforced the
rules. If you leave a dead plant on your front porch, I will
throw it away. If you hang a giant crucifix in the laundry room,
I will remove it. If you tell me the reason you haven't paid
your rent is because your arthritis is acting up, and you are too
old, and the office is too far, I will show up at your door.

I didn't make the rules. I was simply paid to enforce them.

Patrick couldn't overlook the crime or the fact that I
hadn't collected all the rents. Despite being served three-day
notices, rents were still being withheld as reparation for stolen
belongings. It was my job to explain to the residents that that's

not how life works. This would make residents mad, and they would call and complain to Patrick, and thus the cycle continued. Evictions were expensive, according to Patrick, and collecting rents was a basic job responsibility, according to Patrick. He was nearing the end of his rope. I could hear it in his voice.

According to my employee contract: *If Employee is terminated within the first thirty days of employment, Employee agrees to vacate the Premises within twenty-four hours of the time of termination.*

I was no longer swimming.

I wasn't treading either.

I was drowning.

I placed the letter in my thirty-day-notice pile on top of the others. It felt as if a pair of imaginary hands were squeezing my lungs and using my head as a punching bag. If I lost my job, my options were limited. *Where would we go?* Amy rented a room from an older woman in Burbank, a retired set designer with velvety couches, expensive glass décor, white carpet and at least twenty rescue cats. Even if I could bunk with Amy temporarily, a white-carpeted house was no place for a child, especially mine, and I was allergic to cats in a can't breathe, puffy face, pass-the-Benadryl kind of way.

Neither of my parents was in a financial position to help, but neither would turn me away if I showed up on their doorstep. Of course, then I'd be forced to come clean about Tom. Tell them that on top of being unemployed, flat broke and a complete failure in life, I was also a liar. My pride was still too intact for that option.

Worst-case scenario: Lilly could live with Tom while I scraped enough money together for a motel. When I was nearing eviction from Crap-o-la Apartments, Tom hadn't offered to let me stay with him should we officially get the boot. He of course said Lilly could, but not one mention of me. I got it. He was a womanizer and made no secret of it. He was an attractive, young lawyer (although a broke one, which I doubt he mentioned), and, as if that wasn't enough, he was a doting daddy. Women swooned. He'd met half a dozen short-lived flings while playing with Lilly at the McDonald's play yard. My presence would prove a challenge because although a doting dad was an attractive quality, the doting dad's baby momma living with him was a glaring red flag. Even if the baby momma was on Alcatraz.

My only real option was to keep my job, and I was prepared to do whatever it took.

I closed the office door and squeezed past the boxes working as my kitchen table. It was late. Lilly had long since gone to bed, allowing me time to finish up work. I'd kissed her sweet face earlier but didn't dare check on her now for fear of waking her up. I zigzagged through my unpacked apartment toward the blue glow of the television. Amy was nestled on the couch watching *Real Housewives.* She had arrived on my doorstep late Monday night in complete ruin after giving her boyfriend of two years the "marriage ultimatum." He ultimately decided he'd rather date a model from the Valley named Jessica instead.

I did what every best friend would do: I removed all social media outlets, hid her phone, provided an ample supply of Diet Coke, trash-talked her ex, kept my problems to myself, and allowed her to watch my kid while I worked.

*Really, she's lucky to have me.*

"You're the one with a drinking problem," one blond housewife on the television yelled at another blond housewife. All the other blond housewives gasped, their diamond-encrusted fingers clutching tight to their pearls and champagne-filled flutes.

"I'm so confused. I thought she had a drug problem. Or is that the other one?" I asked Amy. She didn't answer. "You awake?" I leaned over and put my chin on her shoulder. "Amy! I said no." I plucked my phone out of her hand. "I've been looking for this. I told you, online stalking is only going to make things worse."

She sat up and tucked her skinny legs under her, pouting. "I wasn't stalking *him*." We made a pact to never say her ex-boyfriend's name again. "I was looking for you."

"Here I am."

She rolled her puffy eyes. Her pink and blue greasy hair had dreadlocked, looking as if it were trying to escape from her head. The sleeves of *his* sweater were pulled down over her hands, working as a Kleenex when needed. "I was looking *for* you. I was trying to find this Chase guy so we can get more info. I want to see what he looks like."

"Why?" I squeaked. "I don't think of him as anything but the maintenance man, and even that's a stretch." Not to mention I'd already looked him up on Facebook, Twitter, Instagram, Snapchat and every other social media site I could think of with no luck. As it turned out, Chase J. Hudson was a popular name (I may have also looked at his employment file—he lived in Long Beach, had no criminal history, good credit and excellent references. Which was odd, because he was terrible at his job).

"Sure you don't," she said with a wry twitch of her lip as she tossed a throw pillow at me. I caught it with my face. "I've never seen you so googly-eyed over a boy before, and I love it." She laughed for the first time since "Jessica from the Valley."

"Gee, thanks," I said.

"You know what I mean." She wrapped a dreadlock behind her ear. "For the longest time you were so stuck on Tom, whom we both know is never going to settle down, and when he does, it will probably be with some model named *Jessica*, like, from, like, the Valley. Tramp."

"I told you, I don't like Chase. He's a colleague... ugh." I may be able to lie to myself, and I may be able to lie to my parents, but there was no lying to Amy. She knew me too well. I buried my head in the pillow and face-planted into the couch. "Why are guys that aren't attracted to me so attractive?"

Amy wrapped her long, bony arm around my waist and dropped her head next to mine. Spooning me in *his* snot-covered sweater. "If I knew the answer I wouldn't be here," she whimpered, digging her face into my shirt and snarfing up a snot bubble. "Why do I need this stupid boy?"

I flipped to my back. "You don't *need* any boys," I said with conviction. "You were Burn Victim Number Three in a *Grey's Anatomy* episode and Dead Girl Number Four in *Zombie Time Machine*. You don't need any boys. You deserve a man."

Amy sat up. "You're totally right." She ran her hand under

her nose, leaving a streak of snot on her left cheek. "We're hot, strong, independent, confident women. We don't need boys. Boys who are going to say how much they love us and then follow their peckers to younger pastures." An evil smirk spread across her blotchy face. "Let's get revenge."

I'd underestimated my pep-talking abilities. I laughed, happy she'd finally entered the anger stage of the breakup grief cycle. Hopefully the "get off my couch and resume personal hygiene" stage came next. As it stood, I was one day away from giving my best friend of twenty years the "shower ultimatum."

"Funny you should mention revenge." I spoke slowly, drumming my fingers along my chin. "I just so happen to have recently learned how to remove door locks and disassemble a toilet."

BAM! BAM! BAM!

A pounding on the window forced me off the couch and onto the floor, wedged between two boxes, where I assumed the fetal position. It was Spencer with one of his spider web tattooed customers accompanied by his hormonal posse. They came to take our wallets, key our cars, zip-tie our hands and impregnate us.

I was sure of it.

Amy poked her head over the side of the couch. "Some lady is crying outside your window. I think she wants to speak to the manager."

"Is she pregnant?"

"Would you like me to ask?"

I thought about it. "No, it's probably the washing machines." Or so I hoped. "People take their laundry very seriously around here." I crawled out of my barricade, slipped on a pair of sandals and found the tear-stained-faced woman pacing outside my window. She wore an off-the-shoulder black shirt with *Pink* written in pink lettering across the front, showing off the stars tattooed down her neck and across her shoulder. She ran up to me and wrapped her thick arms tight around me, soaking the front of my shirt with tears.

*I'm a human Kleenex.*

I patted her back, unsure of what to say. If her car had

been stolen, she'd be the first one to cry about it. She'd also be the first one to not blame me, and then call me incompetent, and then storm off dramatically, and then call Patrick.

She took a step back. Mascara horseshoed her dark eyes while tears slithered down her cheeks. "I'm so glad you're home. I'm locked out, and I called the emergency line and had to leave a message. I tried getting in, but I can't get the window to open, and the locksmith is still an hour out. I know the lease says I'm not supposed to bother you unless it's an emergency, but I really need to get in." She drew a shaky breath. "Can you let me in? It's Apartment Thirty-eight."

*Phew. No car drama.*

"Of course." I was readily accommodating to anyone who had actually read the lease. "I'm so sorry. I didn't have my phone on me." *Damn it, Amy.* "Let me grab my keys, and I'll meet you there."

She nodded a sorrowful nod. I'd locked myself out numerous times and never cried about it. She did live next to Kevin though. He could come outside naked, and she'd have nowhere to hide. So I got it.

I grabbed my keys and hurried to the third courtyard, bypassing many a disgruntled tenant along the way. I slipped on imaginary blinders and trudged through the battleground, dodging the sideways glances, glaring eyes and under-the-breath insults hurled at me. Narrowly making it to the back staircase unscathed.

Up the stairs I went, past Kevin's door, and found the woman on her knees, her cheek pressed against the faded brown door. "I'm so sorry, lumber," she sobbed, stroking the weathered wood slowly with her fingers. "My lumber..."

*Umm.*

She was apologizing to the door.

Made sense. Kevin's neighbor would have to be crazy to still live there. I leaned over the woman's head and used the master key to unlock the door. She hurried to her feet and pushed it open, revealing a brown-eyed toddler on the other side.

"There was a kid in there?" I asked, shocked. Wouldn't that have been worth mentioning?

"Lumber!" she scolded the little boy. He was covered in marker and flour and makeup and chocolate (hopefully chocolate), like the rest of the apartment. Black lines were scribbled down the lower half of the walls and continued across the carpet. Flour mounds clumped together in doughy blobs all over the couch and the television and the kitchen table that, coincidently, looked to have received a fresh coat of pink nail polish. The mom in me felt terrible. The apartment manager in me began tallying up the charges... *paint $250, carpet $800, linoleum $450...* It would have been cheaper to break the window. "You don't ever lock the door on Mommy like that, ever... My television!" She released a high-pitched yelp. I cringed. The commotion could summon Kevin. He'd been quiet all day. It was quite nice. "My table!"

I stood in the doorway, rocking from heels to toes. Probably not the best time to let her know about the repairs she'd need to make. "Er... I'm going to head back now..." She didn't notice me. She was too busy inspecting the finger painting on the wall. "I'll just... close this door for you. Have, er, a good night."

I tiptoed to the stairwell, placing as little weight on each foot as possible to prevent the walkway from creaking. The old building made it difficult to get anywhere unnoticed. I held my breath as I passed Kevin's door and ever so carefully dropped my foot on the first step.

Still quiet.

Next step.

Golden silence.

Another step.

Nothing.

I released my withheld breath. The black door remained closed and quiet. Almost too quiet. A "calm before the storm" type of quiet. The only sounds were coming from Lumber's hysterical mother and muffled yells from below. Alice and her boo were arguing. I strained to make out what they were screaming about, because I'm nosy. Intense fluctuations, shrieks and thunderous grumbles, then the slamming of a door.

"Where were you?" Boo yelled.

*At least I think that's what he said.*

Then another voice, possibly Alice. "You're... planting... ducks."

*Hmmm, that can't be right.*

My snooping skills needed some work, but it sounded like things were working out for Alice about as well as they were for me.

Then came the loud, wet rumbling of someone about to eject a wad of phlegm. It came from below the stairwell.

Crap.

I pretended I was examining the railing, shaking it to be sure it was sturdy, and not eavesdropping on tenants, because that wouldn't be right. Especially if I were to be caught by another tenant.

Leaning over the railing as part of my "inspection," I found a shoeless, shirtless mass of white muscles with a buzzed head shooting a snotball into the flowerless flowerbed beside him.

I crouched down and shoved my face between the bars of the now-determined-to-be-sturdy railing. Semiautomatics and revolvers (been researching) were tattooed down the man's arms and across his chiseled abdomen, stopping at the waistband of his basketball shorts and continuing down the exposed skin of his hairy calves. He had surprisingly dainty feet for a man his size and well-groomed toenails. A small, intricate spider web was tattooed on the man's veiny neck; much like the tattoos in the photo lineup the police had brought in.

This spider web was smaller than the ones pictured, about two inches in diameter as opposed to the sprawling, full neck tattoos I remembered. I'm not generally one to judge a book by its cover, however, if I *were* a judging-a-book-by-its-cover type of person, I would say this book was a murder-mystery nightmare-inducing unhappy-ending thriller. This guy was scary. He was scary all the way from his "I'm gonna kill you" stance, to his "I can kill you with these" muscles, to his "I'll kill you with one of these instead" tattooed artillery. Was it a coincidence I found a gun in the Dumpster much like the one pictured on his left pectoral? Was it by happenstance that the police had questioned me about a man with a spider web tattoo, and here this guy stood in the same location where all of Spencer's clients had arrived and left, WITH a spider web tattoo?

*Methinks not.*

I gulped, trying desperately to coat my suddenly parched throat. Scary Guy brought a nearly burnt-out cigarette to his mouth, took in a long draw of nicotine, and discarded the butt in the aforementioned flowerless flowerbed. In paragraph six on the eighth page of the *House Rules*, it states I can serve anyone caught littering on the property with a twenty-five dollar fine.

He stuck his sausage finger up his nose and dug around until he found what he was looking for, and after a quick inspection, flicked it into the flowerbed as well. Next he folded a stick of gum into his mouth and tossed the silver wrapper into the flowerbed.

*That makes fifty.*

This was the smoking gun (literally) I needed. Scary Guy would be arrested. He'd be charged with grand theft auto, petty theft, destruction of property, armed robbery, littering… I would be called a hero for finding him, and the residents would all "shout my praise" as Joyce would say. Then Patrick couldn't fire me; he'd give me a raise and bonus instead. Chase would be so impressed he'd make out with me, and all would be right in my world again.

I dashed down the remaining steps. Confronting the man was the best idea since I'd left my phone in the apartment, and logic was still trotting its way to my brain.

I waltzed up to Scary Guy who turned his head, puffed his chest and flexed his guns. Two tiny pupils glared down at me. He'd been much shorter from my aerial view. I cleared the imaginary mucus from my throat to buy time. Surely, a smarter person would have thought this out prior to advancing. "What apartment are you visiting?" I asked in a shrilly voice. I was going for authoritative, but I sounded more like SpongeBob.

"Who are you?" he grunted, blinking, as if I were a side dish he hadn't ordered.

I balled my fists to keep them from shaking. "I'm the

apartment manager. Now, what apartment do you live in, or who are you visiting?"

"Mike," he said quickly, without missing a beat.

There were at least five Mikes who lived here, all in the first courtyard. "Mike? Really? Which one?"

"Mind your own damn business." Scary Guy was getting mad.

"Mind my own business?" I was getting equally mad. "You're coming from Spencer's apartment, aren't you? You been having fun in our parking lot? You enjoy taking cars? Missing a backpack by chance?"

The donkey finally trotted in with my logic. *What the hell are you doing, Cambria?*

Scary Guy locked his jaw and squared his shoulders. He stopped looking at me as the side dish he hadn't ordered and more like the main entrée he wanted to devour. Crap. I took a big step back, crashing into whoever stood behind me. A pair of arms wrapped around my chest, pinning my arms to my side. My adrenaline pumped, thrusting my heartbeat into overdrive. Half a dozen self-defense YouTube videos began playing through my memory.

Thumb into trachea.

Head to nose.

Back kick to balls.

Fingers into eye sockets.

Got it.

I went into attack mode.

My attacker pivoted, bobbed and bounced around behind me like some kind of super ninja warding off all my attacks. Hands grappled at my flailing limbs until they landed on my lower back and pushed me forward.

I fell into a wooden pillar holding the upstairs walkway up, and wrapped my arms around it, the splintery wood clawing at my forearms as my momentum swung me around to face my attacker.

Our eyes met.

I froze, stock-still and confused and scared and seconds away from peeing my pants.

Deep breath in and, "Ahh!"

# Chapter 20

*No alcohol permitted in Common Areas.*

"Why are you screaming?" Chase asked between breaths. He picked the black hat up off the ground and slapped it back on his head. "Why am *I* screaming?" I huffed, still hugging the pillar, scared to let it go and unsure if my legs were capable of holding me upright. "You were attacking me!"

"Calm down, everybody." Larry zigzagged in slow motion between us, flipping his stringy gray hair over his shoulder. "Everyone needs to calm down. Caaalm dooown. Let's figure this out diplomatical-baly... diploma... just be at peace before we start throwing punches." He wobbled to the right and to the left and then spun around. "Why were you beating on the maintenance man?" he asked me.

"Me?" I gasped and pointed to Chase. "He grabbed me from behind!"

Chase rolled the sleeves of his black hoodie up to his elbows, shaking his head. "You ran into me and started flapping around."

"It's true!" yelled a tween standing on the upstairs walkway. She had blond pigtails, and wore a green shirt doused in sparkles, and shorts the same size as my underwear. She leaned over the railing, holding out her phone, and snapped her gum. "I totally got it all on video."

"You what?" I let go of my pillar.

Larry gave me a look of warning and pointed his finger in my general direction. "Shhhtay in your corner," he said.

I went back to my pillar and looked over Larry's head at Chase. "What are you doing here?"

"Number thirty-eight is locked out, and her kid is inside. The emergency line forwarded to me because you didn't answer." He took a step closer. Larry cut him off, his arms outstretched like a drunken bird about to take flight.

"Shhhtay in your corner," he slurred.

"I already got sixty likes on Instagram!" the tween yelled. "Oh, wait! Make that seventy. They all totally think the chick is having some kind of seizure and the guy is way hot."

I rolled my eyes. "Of course they do." Larry kept bobbing his head like a chicken, blocking Chase from my view. "Honestly, Larry, I'm fine. We're fine. Feel free to go home and sleep it off."

Larry gave Chase a sideways glance. With a nod of his head, he cleared the space between us by stumbling to the side. Chase and I exchanged a "should we escort him home or continue arguing" look.

I went for the latter. "I was talking to... Crap!" I looked around the courtyard. Spider Webs of Death (my new nickname for Scary Guy) was gone, and Larry looked to have fallen asleep.

"She was talking to crap!" Sparkly Tween screeched with laughter and stretched her arms over the railing with her phone tight in her hand. "This is totally going viral."

"No more video," Chase warned in a deep, stern voice. The tween blushed and brought the phone to her chest, pouting her pink, glittery-specked bottom lip.

"Tell me you got video of the guy I was talking to before?" I asked her.

"What guy?"

"Crap!" I ran out to the carports and down the uneven driveway, looking into every stall as I sprinted past. How was he going to get arrested? How was I going to keep my job? How was I going to get my raise and bonus and all my acclaim and make-out session if he was gone! He had to be in the carports. If Sparkly Tween hadn't seen him, he must have slipped out the back. Except he was nowhere to be seen.

"Cambria, stop!" Chase grabbed my arm and spun me around. "What are you doing?"

I yanked my arm out of his grasp, panting, and plopped my hands on my thighs, catching my breath. That was a lot of running. "You let that guy get away. He's the one... who's been stealing... cars around here... He's about to get me fired!" *Ouch, side cramp.*

"Dammit, Cambria. Despite what you may think, watching crime shows does not make you a cop. That guy had prison tats all over him, and you decide to confront him? As if he's going to do what? Confess? You have no idea he's done anything. A couple of days ago you had Spencer pegged as a black market gun salesmen. Really, Cambria? Common logic told you that you should get into this guy's face who is twice your size?"

I gnashed my teeth and took a deep breath in through my nose. He made sense, and it pissed me off. I hated it. I hated every word of it. "Chase, as crazy as it may sound, I'm trying to keep my job. This place, apparently, was the safest compound in all the land until I showed up. I have six move-out notifications on my desk. Six!" I held up six fingers to drive the point home. "My single thread of hope is to peg all this craziness on a current resident, one who lived here when the almighty amazing 'Yoyce' was here. It will prove I'm not the problem. I'm doing my best to provide for my family and keep a roof over our heads, which isn't easy when you're dealing with parrots and washers and nudity and car break-ins and spider web tattoos and gunrunners. I'm so close to not only losing my job but my home. So forgive me for doing everything I can. I'm sorry that upsets you. Why don't you go somewhere and *not* fix something?" My bottom lip began to quiver. My waterworks grenade was about to detonate. *You will not cry, Cambria. You will NOT cry.* I was already coated in the snot and tears of others and was not about to add in my own, not in front of Chase.

A feeling of vulnerability crashed down on me like an

eight-foot wave about to take out a surfer. It was neither a familiar nor pleasant sensation.

With nothing left to say, I turned my snot-covered body around and walked away, leaving Chase speechless. I didn't expect, nor did I want, him to follow me. All I wanted was job security and a clean shirt.

My apartment door was wide open. Amy was propped up against the doorjamb all showered and preened and smiling. Her pink and blue tendrils lay perfectly blown-out below her shoulders. My red shirt, which she apparently decided to borrow, was tucked into her own boyfriend jeans. Her face was freshly painted with eye shadow, mascara, bronzer and pink gloss. She seemed to have hurdled the last stages of the breakup grief cycle while I was out apartment managing. "You were gone forever," she said, exasperated. "I was really worried."

"So you got dressed?" I cleared the threshold, ramming my shin into the corner of the box working as a side table. "Ouch!" I kicked the stupid box, crushing its contents, which sounded a lot like glass. "My life!" I groaned, kicking the box again.

"Well, hello there. Did you lock yourself out?" Amy purred. I turned to find Chase sheepishly waiting at the door, his hands shoved into his front pockets.

*Good grief.* "Amy, this is Chase, the maintenance man," I said, rubbing my shin.

Amy's eyes reached an abnormally wide circumference. "Chase?" she squeaked. "I didn't... I didn't even know you had a maintenance guy." She shrugged indifferently, and then turned toward me and mouthed *so hot.* "Well then, it looks like I have to be leaving. If you would be so kind as to give me back my phone, I'll be out of your hair."

Her bony behind had become one with my couch, and now, when I'd rather not be alone, she decided to detach herself from my furniture and make a miraculous recovery. It was far too fishy and very un-Amy-like. I couldn't press her too hard with Chase looking on. "What are you doing?" I asked under my breath.

"What we talked about," she said with a wink, and

unleashed a mischievous smile. "Gimme. Gimme." She wiggled her fingers.

With a sigh of surrender, I dislodged her phone from behind the cable box. "Thank you," she sang, plucking the phone out of my grip. "So nice meeting you, Chase, was it?" She flashed her three-grand veneers and sashayed past him.

I leaned out the door. "I don't have bail money," I hissed through clenched teeth.

"Text ya later," she called out and rounded the corner out of sight.

I stifled a groan and tossed my attention over to the boy hovering in my doorway. "What's wrong now?" I asked all snappily, folding my arms over my chest.

"I didn't mean to upset you," he said.

Really?

It was like saying *I'm sorry your feelings are hurt* or *I'm sorry you're upset.* It's an apology without admission of wrongdoing—thus not an apology at all. Under normal circumstances, I'd reject the lame attempt. However, his puppy dog eye accompaniment won me over.

"Chase, the situation upsets me," I said, dropping my arms. "The police showed Joyce and me a lineup of white men with spider web tattoos. I don't believe it's a coincidence I found a guy who matched the description here. I think he knows Spencer, and if I could have only kept him quarantined until I called the police, then he and Spencer could have been arrested, and this would all be over with. Now I can't call the police because if they show up and don't arrest anyone, everyone is just going to assume it's another break-in, which is only going to make me look worse."

He sucked in his lips, holding in a smile, as if I unintentionally told a dirty joke he shouldn't laugh at.

"What?" I asked.

"Cambria, you were going to keep him quarantined?"

"Hell yeah I was. Never underestimate a woman on the verge of ruin."

He gave me a *touché* look. "I get you're trying to save your job, but shouldn't you think things through more fully?"

I nodded reluctantly. *Guess I can give him that.*

He looped his thumbs into his pockets and leaned against the doorway, looking past me. "I see you've settled in."

I tucked Einstein behind my ear. "I'm taking more of an unpack-as-necessary approach. I did hang one picture in the hallway though." I exhaled and waited. If we were engaging in small talk, it would be his turn; if we were done, I was in need of a Diet Coke to help with my headache. That drug box was still hiding. Granted, I hadn't put much effort into locating it.

"Sounds efficient," he said with a smile. I appreciated the fact that he didn't try and sugarcoat the truth with some weak *I'm sure it will all work out* crap like Tom would have. I needed a little more pessimism in my life. I wanted to sulk and eat and cry, not be optimistic. "For reals though," he continued, dropping the smile. "You sure you're OK?"

"I'm fine," I lied.

He regarded me through squinted eyes, as if reading my thoughts. My stomach got all fluttery and my legs all liquidy. There was no time for gushiness, butterflies and sexual fantasies. I was nearly homeless.

"OK, guess I'll talk to you later. Night," I said, swinging the door shut. There was no time to deal with feelings either.

I weaved through the cardboard maze in my living room to the kitchen, picking up toys along the way like a human Pac-Man, with a Diet Coke and Brownie Petites from Trader Joe's as the end prize. Both were consumed immediately upon completion. The rich chocolate combined with the sweet carbonation made my tongue happy... my stomach, not so much. Ouch.

I leaned against the counter, rubbing my ailing abdomen. My mind churned through the events of the day. In hindsight, I should not have confronted Spider Webs of Death. I should have stalked him instead. Follow him around to be sure he came from Spencer's apartment. Telling him I was the apartment manager wasn't the best idea either. Let's just say, for example, he decided to brutally murder me in my sleep. He'd know exactly where to find me. Crap.

I pushed a pile of heavy boxes in front of the door and sank to the floor behind them, folding in half and pulling my knees close to my chest, while my mind took a terrifying trip down Worst Case Scenario Lane.

At eleven-thirty, Amy answered my thirty-two text messages, confirming what I suspected. She had gone to a bar that, according to Facebook, her ex had checked into. She planned to "casually" bump into him while flirting with everything on two legs to make him jealous. (This was her idea of revenge. My toilet plan was better.) The ex wasn't there, and she, according to the text messages that were getting drunker as the night went on, met a guy named "Rock." He had "broom" eyes, olive skin and was around five-foot-ten, two hundred "plounders" with a "rescuing" dark "herring" (whatever that meant). She followed him to a party and sent me the description so I'd be able to identify her abductor if she went missing. Because I wasn't stressed enough already.

My head began drooping around midnight, feeling especially heavy. It was a fight to keep conscious. Then came a tap on the door. I clambered up to the peephole.

*Chase? Again?*

I turned off the alarm. Removed the boxes. Unlocked the bottom lock. Flipped the deadbolt and opened the door. "Chase, what are you doing here?" I asked. His hoodie and hat were gone, replaced by a black collared shirt and a more styled mess of hair.

"When you said you were fine, did you really mean you were fine, and not doing that thing girls do when they say fine but mean the exact opposite?" He looked down at the butcher knife clutched in my hand. I mean, I had to have protection just in case.

"Oh, um, I was just cutting… *avocados*," I said, hiding the knife behind my back. "Like I said, I'm fine. Just wanted some guacamole."

"Do you want some company?"

"Yes."

# Chapter 21

*Landlord reserves the right to initiate eviction process or give notice to vacate if Tenant turns out to be a Grade-A Douchebag.*

Sunlight shot onto my eyelid like a laser, forcing me from a deep, dreamless slumber. I threw my arm over my face and rolled to the other side of the bed, except it wasn't there. It was in the bedroom, and I was on the couch. I landed on the floor.

I forced my lids open. Chase was asleep on the other side of the couch with his feet crossed and resting on my cardboard coffee table. His head hung to one side while his nose whistled with each heavy breath he took. The old me, the P.M.S. (Pre-Apartment Management Situations) Cambria would have been aching to nestle under his free arm. He looked so cozy. Despite his lack of handy skills and the fact he scared Spider Webs of Death away, he was a fine specimen of a man. He'd be almost pretty if he shaved and combed his hair, maybe too pretty. I enjoyed the scruffiness. It made him even sexier in an "I woke up like this" kind of way that P.M.S. Cambria would have been drooling over. Unfortunately, I wasn't P.M.S. Cambria any more; I was A.T.B.O.W. (About To Be On Welfare) Cambria, and I had bigger issues to deal with.

I scooted off to the bathroom to perform my usual pee,

weigh myself and declare diet starts tomorrow routine. My mouth tasted like morning, and goop had embedded itself into the corners of my eyes. In the mirror, under the still-crooked vanity light, my face looked sunken and my waist smaller, even if the evil scale refused to show any changes. Dark, puffy bags girdled my eyes, and I was so pale the auburn freckles scattered across my face looked like blackheads.

*What the?*

I leaned in closer.

*Is that... yes it is.*

CHOCOLATE. There was chocolate crusted to the corners of my mouth. I'd spent hours talking with Chase until we fell asleep. HOURS. We touched on my year at Fresno State. Lilly's cuteness. I learned he grew up in Long Beach, didn't have too much family, and went to a junior college for a couple of years only to drop out to be a maintenance man. He was not terribly forthcoming with information. He mostly asked me a lot of questions. We had glossed over many subjects, and never, not once, did he mention I had chocolate on my mouth. NOT ONCE.

I splashed warm water on my face, except more water went on the mirror than on my tired mug. Time to get dressed. Lilly would wake soon, so I only had time to change. Jeans off. Semi-clean jeans on. Snot-crusted shirt off. Semi-clean blue Mossimo shirt... *Oh no...* Voices came from the other side of the wall. It was a familiar grumble... *Crap!*

I bolted out to the living room where Chase, Lilly and Tom were all gathered. Lilly perched on top of a box with Minnie Mouse in her hands, Chase stood with his hands in his front pockets and face pointed to the floor. And Tom in his usual business attire—gray suit, white shirt, black skinny tie— looked quite debonair and extremely pissed.

"Mommy," Lilly giggled. "Where's your shirt?"

I looked down at the shirt in my hand and said a quick prayer of thanks my bra was still on. "What are you doing here, Tom?" I asked while pulling the shirt over my head.

"Picking up my daughter for her doctor's appointment. They squeezed her in, don't you recall this conversation?" he answered all lawyer-y.

"Of course I remember." *Totally forgot.* "Er, Chase, this is Tom, and Tom, this is Chase." I might as well make introductions in case that hadn't already happened. Chase nodded without taking his focus off the carpet.

"Chase?" Tom said slowly. I could see the wheels in his mind turning. "Chase, OK, that's right." He looked at me with a scathing grin spread across his face. "The 'maintenance man.'" He made air quotes around maintenance man, which would be correct since Chase didn't do a whole lot of maintenance. But I doubt that's why he air-quoted it.

We all stood there. "Awk-a-ward." Lilly broke the silence from her perch.

"Go put on the pink dress that's on your dresser." I manually turned her by the shoulders and pointed her toward the hallway. "Stay in there until we call you out." That should keep her busy for a while.

"I'm gonna go do some *maintenance,*" Chase said, his hands still shoved deep into his pockets, eyes trained on the floor. He walked around Tom, who refused to move and gave Chase the evil stare-down his entire journey to the door.

We watched the door close behind Chase. We watched Chase hurry past the windows. We watched Chase walk toward the carports and as soon as he disappeared...

"What the hell is wrong with you?" Tom and I said in unison.

"You're a hypocrite!" we yelled.

I gasped.

He gasped.

I stared.

He stared.

He who spoke last wins. We remained at a standstill, glaring at each other, blue on hazel until Tom caved. "OK, I'll say it. Last month, when you came and got Lilly, and I had whatever-her-name-is at my house, you lost your mind, even when I explained that Lilly was still asleep and never saw whatever-her-name-was. You went nuts!"

"I can't believe you're bringing that up," I snapped. "That's so different. You bringing some random woman home to have a sleepover in the room next to my child is totally reckless. I stand by my decision to go nuts. Chase and I fell asleep while talking because I had…" I took a gulp of air, knowing if I said Chase was there because I was scared, he wouldn't believe me. If he did, he'd want to know why. Then I'd have to tell him about Spider Webs of Death and the possible gunrunning situation and how I confronted Spider Webs of Death and told him I was the apartment manager. Then he'd want to know why I called him Spider Webs of Death, and I would tell him why. Then he'd want to know why I was putting our child in harm's way. Then I would say I wasn't. Then he would argue that hanging around alleged gunrunners was more dangerous than having a woman over while Lilly was asleep. Then I would call him immature because he was right, and I hate when he's right and I'm wrong. Then he would tell me I was overreacting. Profanity would be involved, and then he would storm out after I said something totally irrational. I finished the entire argument in my head. It was not how I wanted to spend my morning. I didn't know what else to say, so I pretended to cry.

Tom was unmoved. "That's not going to work this time. I had to jump through hoops to get you to forgive me and allow Lilly back over at my place."

"Oh, come on." I laughed a mocking laugh while wiping an imaginary tear away. "Hoops? Really? I asked you to please not have any more sleepovers while Lilly was there."

"But you can have sleepovers with your 'maintenance man.'" He air-quoted again.

"Would you stop that? He really is the maintenance man, and we fell asleep. That's it."

"Look, Cam. You can get whatever you want maintenanced on your own time, that's fine with me. Double standards are only your thing."

My mouth fell open. This reaction was not in his character. Mine, yes, but not his. "How have I ever, aside from this one time, had double standards? And I don't even have double standards now. We fell a-sleep talk-ing." This was getting ridiculous.

He pressed his mouth to a straight line and stared at me until his face began to relax. "Fine, I don't know how. I don't store everything that has ever happened in the history of us in my brain like you do. Lilly, let's go!" he hollered down the hall.

Lilly skipped out in her pink sundress, plastic Cinderella dress-up shoes, a leopard-print clutch and a purple beanie. "I'm ready," she said. "It twirls, Daddy. See?" She spun around, giggling, unfazed by our fighting.

"Looks beautiful, Lil. We have to go." He swung her up on his hip. "I'll bring her back later," he said brusquely.

He was crossing the line. "Like when later?"

"Like when I'm not so p-i-s-e-d o-f-f at you… or around four-thirty." He left, slamming the door behind him.

*Oh no you didn't.* I swung the door open. "There are two s's in pissed!" I yelled. Tom and Lilly were nowhere in sight, but I have last word issues.

*That's it!*

I called Patrick on the number reserved for emergencies. My life was falling apart; that was emergency enough for me. It rang twice before a sleepy moan answered. A quick glance at the clock told me this emergency could have perhaps waited until after seven. It was too late though. I was committed, as I suspected he had caller ID.

I gave Patrick the Cliffsnotes version. Starting with Spencer. (I had hoped to gather more evidence and another witness before explaining my Spencer theory, but time had run out.) I told him everything, even about the move-out notifications, which, as I suspected, were what really got his attention.

He loudly cleared the morning rattle from his throat. "This guy you saw last night, you're sure he didn't come from Kevin's apartment?"

"I don't believe so. I think that, when you look at everything as a whole, there's a strong possibility that if we get rid of Spencer, we'll get rid of the crime." I began fidgeting with a paperclip, unwinding it and rewinding it, unwinding and rewinding, determined to stay strong and not get all wimpy and unnecessarily chatty.

He exhaled. I imagined him rubbing his temples like he did the one—and only—time we met in person. "That's good enough for me then, I guess. He's on a month-to-month and has been there less than a year, so we can serve him a thirty-day notice and be done with it."

"What about an eviction?" Thirty days seemed like plenty of time to, oh, I don't know, plot revenge on the apartment manager. I began unwinding and rewinding the paperclip faster. Unwinding and rewinding.

"Thirty-day notice is cheaper and usually faster. You don't have to give a reason and don't need evidentiary support. We'll have Chase serve it."

"Why Chase? I don't have a problem doing so myself." I wanted to see the look on Spencer's face when he was handed the paper.

"I want the notice served without any conversation. He'll know he has thirty days to move, and he doesn't need to know why." It was a nice way of telling me I have a big mouth. Justified. *Bada-bing-bada-boom*. "Let me know when Chase gets there, and I'll have my lawyer send over the paperwork."

"He may still be here. I'll check."

"Still? That reminds me, I got a message from the emergency line, so I'm assuming you or Chase didn't answer right away. Did it get taken care of?"

*Note to self: Don't ever let your phone out of your sight. Ever.*

"I'm sorry. My friend had my phone. It was taken care of."

"Did Chase come?"

"He did." I thought back to our little mishap in the third courtyard and wondered if it was worth mentioning—or if I should wait for the video to show up on his Facebook feed.

"Cambria, Chase is hourly, and emergencies are overtime. Now he's there this early in the morning? I need you to be mindful of the bottom line."

The paperclip broke in half. "Oh, no. I took care of the emergency, and Chase is only here this early because he spent the night."

*Didn't mean to say that.*

"Spent the night?" His voice took on a curious tone.

"Yes... no... yes. It wasn't a sexual thing." I slapped my forehead.

*Dear Ground,*

*Please swallow me up next time I try to speak.*

*Sincerely,*
*Cambria*

There was no recovering from the sex comment. "Go ahead and send over the notice, and I'll have Chase serve it," I said, my voice small. "Please."

## Chapter 22

*Tenant agrees to not engage in any illegal activity while occupying the Premises, ever, like, ever, ever.*

An hour later the fax machine popped out the notification. I was rolled into the fetal position on the teal carpet, agonizing over the conversation with Patrick. *It wasn't a sexual thing?*

My big mouth was my own worst enemy.

I reached up and grabbed the paper off the machine.

*THIRTY-DAY NOTICE*

*Spencer Bryant is hereby required to vacate the premises in which he resides thirty days from this date.*

_____

*Cambria Clyne*
*Apartment Manager*

That's it? One sentence and a line for my signature? *He needed a lawyer for this? Screw criminal law; this is what Tom should be doing.*

My phone chirped, and I pulled it from my back pocket, still reading over the very short, very unofficial-looking notification.

It was a text from Amy. Finally. *Amy: Alive Rock was a bore at home just woke stop texting me hungover*

Nice. I slid the phone back into my pocket. Amy was fine. I could cross that off my *Things to Stress About Today* list. Next up, facing Chase after Tom's embarrassing performance. I could only imagine what was going through his head. Here he was, doing me a favor, and he's rewarded by what seemed like an overzealous ex-boyfriend, which was so far from the truth.

I found Chase in the maintenance garage. The room was a hodgepodge of every tool, screw, saw and light bulb imaginable. Only a single light bulb hung from the cobwebbed ceiling. It smelled like mildew, and the air was thick and clammy. Chase was using a toilet as a chair, working on an air conditioning unit. He bit his bottom lip, concentrating on his task. I cleared my throat to grab his attention.

He was too engrossed in his work to notice. "Hey, Chase," I finally said after three more throat clears. My esophagus was beginning to burn. "Fancy meeting you here," was my oh-so-clever icebreaker.

He smiled and wiped his brow with his forearm. "Because it's not like I'm the 'maintenance man.'" He hooked his fingers into quotation marks.

My face went flush. "I'm so sorry about this morning. Tom isn't normally that rude. It was a misunderstanding."

"Misunderstanding?" Chase repeated, with a nod of his head. He unwrapped a new filter for the AC unit and deposited the plastic on the floor. I instinctively picked up the trash and threw it away for him. Cleaning up after his maintenancing had become part of my undisclosed job duties. He stuck the filter in. "I'm assuming he's your ex?" he asked.

"Oh, no, no, no… not really, kind of, no. He's Lilly's dad. He was only mad because I give him a hard time about bringing girls around Lilly, and he… anyway, he wasn't jealous or anything like that."

He cocked his head my way. "Could have fooled me."

"Well, he did. I think he was trying to prove a point. Again, I'm sorry, and thank you for hanging out last night."

He shrugged. "No problem." He replaced the front panel

of the air conditioner and flipped it on. It purred to life, spurting out cold air. It felt heavenly. He smiled. "You know what? I think I might have fixed this." He sounded surprised. It was cute.

I went to pat him on the back, stopping midway. I only recently learned how to keep myself from dissolving in his presence. Physical contact was not a good idea. I opted for a thumbs-up instead. "Congratulations. Look at you being all maintenance," I said, and then held out the thirty-day notification. "Here's one more item of maintenance man business for you. Patrick would like you to serve it because I have a big mouth."

He wiped his hands on his jeans and grabbed the paper, quickly scanning the information. "You're really giving Spencer a thirty-day?"

I leaned against the workbench, folding my arms. "I know, right? I thought the same thing. Apparently a thirty-day is easier and cheaper than an eviction, and Patrick cares about his bottom line."

"You want me to do this right now?"

"I do. And, um, I'm going to watch you give it to him from a secret location." The bushes near the breezeway would provide the concealment I needed.

"You're going to hide? Where? Behind a bush?"

*Did I say that out loud?* "Maybe. I'm only thinking about… er… you. I'm thinking about your safety." I brought my hand over my heart and closed my eyes. "What if he goes crazy and pulls a knife or a gun or tries to take you hostage. I'll be watching to make sure things don't get out of hand." This would be my excuse if Patrick asked why I was not in the office while Chase served. "We could have some sort of signal."

"Signal? Because if you saw him with a gun that wouldn't be enough of a signal?" He laughed—it was a pleasing sound—and then flashed a smile. He sure had nice teeth— white, but not bleach white. They were natural white, like he flosses, mouthwashes and brushes twice-a-day-like-the-dentist-recommends-but-no-one-ever-does white. All were perfectly aligned except for his lower incisors that curved inward slightly—I wanted to suck on them.

*Wow.*

It was an odd, surprising desire, yet so strong. I couldn't recall ever wanting to suck on someone's tooth. *What is wrong with me?*

"You really do watch a lot of crime shows," he noted, flashing his incisors again.

I looked at my shoes, willing my face to remain its pale freckled self and not go red. "I do." *Concentrate, Cambria.* "I won't be able to hear what's happening. So if the service goes well, you could... scratch your chin. And if it's going south then... pull your ear?" It sounded stupid even as I was saying it. Chase could handle himself. For me, it would be sweet poetic justice to see Spencer's face when he discovered he could no longer screw with me.

As Chase headed to Spencer's apartment, I dashed to the breezeway to assume lookout. I plastered my back against the wall and took small side steps as if walking the ledge of a high-rise building. Einstein clung to the ivy twisting up the breezeway, and the bristles scraped my exposed skin, but blood and bald spots were not going to deter me. This man had made my life a living hell for the past... *Has it really only been two weeks?* Felt like a year.

As the end of the wall neared, I pried Einstein from the ivy and crouched behind a bush. Chase was at the door, hand positioned and ready.

Knock.

Knock.

Knock.

My stomach clenched tighter each time Chase's fist made contact with the door.

Knock.

Knock.

Knock.

Chase looked down at the papers and then up at the door, as if determining if it was worth another trio of knocks or not. I yawned.

Deciding to go for it, Chase raised his hand just as the door opened. Spencer stood in the doorway wearing dark blue scrubs with a messenger bag crossed over his chest, and a steaming travel mug in one hand and keys in the other. Without so much as a "hey there," Chase handed Spencer the paper and left, scratching his chin as he walked away—the signal. Spencer pushed his round glasses back up the ridge of his nose and read the notice again and again, shaking his head as his eyes ventured down the page. He turned it over to stare at the blank side for a while and then read it again, closing the gap between his face and the paper, still shaking his head as if he were utterly confused.

After a painful amount of processing time, Spencer sprinted after Chase, the contents of his mug splashing down the front of his scrubs. He didn't appear to notice or care. Chase responded to his name by throwing his hands up. I imagined he was saying something like, *"I don't know anything."* Then Spencer said something, I guessed along the lines of, *"Dude, man, what's up with this, dude?"* Because in my head, Spencer talked like one of the old surfer guys who hang around their VW Vans along the Pacific Coast Highway while smoking pot, even if he didn't look like one at all. But, hey, not supposed to judge a book by its cover.

Chase shrugged. Spencer readjusted his glasses and said one more thing eliciting another shrug from Chase, which prompted another readjustment of his glasses and a glance my way. There's no way he could see me.

*Right?*

"Cambria," a low, very un-surfery voice called.

*Wrong.*

I stood and began sidestepping away. "Apartment Manager, wait." Spencer leapt over a bush, releasing the last bit of the hot contents from his mug, and met me at the wall.

*Note to self: You suck at inconspicuous-ity.*

"I don't know anything," I said, raising my palms up as if he said "freeze!"

"But your name is on the bottom." Spencer pointed to my name and signature scrawled along the allotted line.

Chase stood in the walkway behind Spencer making a W with his arms. He then began pulling on his ear—the signal. *Got it.*

"Well?" Spencer pressed. He looked as if he might explode.

"Come on, man, just read the notice," Chase said, sounding more surfery than Spencer.

Spencer frowned, pushing his glasses up again. *Will someone buy this man some Nerdwax?*

"I *did* read it. It is one sentence," he said. "You don't have any basis to ask me to leave. You should be the one leaving. This place is on a grease pole to hell, Cambria, and you've only been here, what, a month?" *Two weeks.* "Everyone agrees," he continued. "We've all been talking about it. You're trying to micromanage and fix what wasn't broken. Joyce was an excellent manager, totally laid back and let us live without management breathing down our necks. I don't even feel safe leaving my car in the parking lot any more. Neither do a lot of people here. Now this. I'm not leaving. I just settled in. This is what happens when some money hungry right-winged nutjob..."

I wasn't sure how we landed on politics, but he was really starting to piss me off.

"It's your illegal side business," I blurted out.

Chase slapped his forehead.

Oops.

Spencer's mouth fell open, like a scrub-wearing trout. I backed farther into the wall, and Einstein reattached to the ivy, clinging for life. Then, Spencer hopped back over the bush and disappeared into his apartment, slam-dunking his notification into the common area trashcan on his way.

Chase made some sort of huffing sound, probably thinking something like, *"Cambria's detective skills are superior, she was obviously right."* Except he didn't look at me, tell me I was right, or even make any more noises. He turned around and walked away.

*Was that a chin scratch or an ear pull?*

# Chapter 23

*Tenant's guests are not permitted to use parking area without a guest parking permit.*

*INCIDENT REPORT*

*Chase handed Spencer Bryant the thirty-day notification and walked away. Spencer ~~found me~~ sought me out to ask why he was being kicked out. ~~I told him about the illegal behavior I'd witnessed, he did not deny it, therefore I was right. I remained quiet as instructed.~~ I provided minimal information.*

I placed the incident report into Spencer's thick file, not feeling as content as I'd hoped. Which didn't make sense. Based on Spencer's reaction, he was involved in the illegal activity around here. I was right. I loved being right. So why wasn't I satisfied?

I wiped the back of my hand along my dripping forehead. The ceiling fan was useless against the suffocating heat. The office was an oven. My shirt was a sopping mess. Einstein was in a hopeless state. An unpleasant smell permeated the air, and I worried I was the source of it. Using a pack of Post-its as a fan, I peeled off a single paper square to sponge up the sweat pumping out of my skin.

I swiveled to face the window and gazed through the open

blinds out to the courtyard. *It's so lovely.* Most would think it ordinary. No color, no flowers, the wood warped and rotting, the iron railing chipped (but secured).

To me it was beautiful, far from ordinary. In comparison to the places I had lived, it was practically the Four Seasons. Once the community was crime-free, it would be a delightful place to raise Lilly. A large patch of grass to kick a soccer ball around or blow bubbles, the sparkling pool perfect for hot summer days, the conveniently located laundry rooms, Spider Webs of Death...

I sat up.

Spider Webs of Death was strolling through the first courtyard. His biceps bulged under a white short-sleeved shirt. He had on the same black basketball shorts and a pair of flip-flops that flapped against the pavement with each step he took, echoing through the courtyard. One hand held a phone to his ear, while the other fidgeted with a key ring around his finger.

I twisted the blinds shut and stuck my finger through a slat for a less conspicuous view. Spider Webs stopped at the row of mailboxes near the lobby and stuck a key into a box. His massive torso blocked my view. Based on his location, he had opened a mailbox belonging to a resident in the third courtyard.

He collected the mail, the phone now sandwiched between his ear and shoulder. He wasn't a resident. At least he wasn't on any of the leases I'd pored over twice. He was obviously a very comfortable houseguest. On paragraph two on the second page of the *House Rules* it says, *Tenant may not have houseguests for more than three days without written permission from the manager.*

I took a burst of photos with my phone and released the blind slat to take a look at them—ten pictures of SWoD's back. Not exactly incriminating. I could turn them over to the police; maybe they've seen the back of his head before?

*If I could just get one picture of his face.*

I slipped my finger between the slats again. As if he'd heard my request, Spider Webs' face was pressed up against the window.

*Note to self: You suck at inconspi… Scratch that… Note to Self: Review previous notes to self.*

With a yelp, I brought my phone up for a quick snap of his face and dashed into my apartment. I slammed the door shut, twisted the lock and fell back against it. The gasps of my own breath sounded foreign in my ears. A fear-and-adrenaline cocktail pumped through my veins and intoxicated my brain.

Ding.

It was the bell on the counter. Spider Webs was now inside the office. The bell specifically says "ring for service" not "ring for victim."

*Ding.*

*Ding.*

*Ding.*

He was being rather polite with his…

*BOOM!*

I fell into the kitchen counter while the thunderous BOOMS of his massive fist beating against the door continued. He must have climbed over the counter or gone through the office door—either way, *House Rules* say only employees beyond the counter. It was clear Spider Webs of Death was no rule follower.

*BOOM!*

*BOOM!*

*BOOM!*

I ran to my bedroom in search of the office phone and found it on the back of the toilet. The key to any emergency situation was to remain calm and to call 911 from a landline. *Right?* My shaking thumbs clumsily punched in the numbers. I slammed the phone to my ear and ran out to the hall.

"Nine-one-one, what's your emergency?" a disembodied male voice asked.

Deep breath in, slow breath out. "I'm the apartment manager," I started, struggling to keep my voice from reaching a high-pitched *holy hell* octave. "I have a man—tall, white, muscular, thirties, spider web and gun tattoos—who is banging on my door because he caught me taking his picture, and I kicked out the person he's staying with today."

A crash against the door startled me, and I smashed into

the single picture I'd hung in the hallway. A 10x16 of Lilly's smiling face crashed to the ground where it exploded into hundreds of tiny pieces, spewing glass across the hallway and out to the living room.

"Ma'am? Ma'am?" the operator asked. "Hello?"

"I'm... I'm..." *Breathe.* "How long until the police are here?"

"Very soon. Ma'am, what is your name?"

"Cambria Jane Clyne." He needed my full name for the death certificate.

And then it happened.

Silence.

An unnerving silence louder than the pounding. I dropped the phone and raced through the crunchy terrain of the short hall that seemed to grow a mile with each step. Then came the squeak of the old hinges on the door. If I had unpacked all the boxes like I was supposed to, I would have had a clear escape path.

But I didn't.

Dropping to all fours, I slid behind a box and curled into a ball. My heart thumped so loudly I feared it would give away my location to Spider Webs, who was walking around in the kitchen. I scooted closer and pressed my forehead against the cardboard, looking at the upside-down scribble along the bottom—*Drugs*. DRUGS! If I weren't about to die, I may have laughed, and then taken two Excedrin and a long swig of NyQuil.

"Hello! Apartment Manager?" Spider Webs called out.

*Thumb to the eyeball. Knee to the nuts.* I ran through my attack plan.

Step... step... step...

I pulled my knees in tighter, steadying my breathing.

Step... step... step...

He was getting closer. My heart grew louder and felt as if it were about to leap out of my chest and run away screaming.

Step... step... step...

*Knee to eyeballs... thumb to nuts... wait, that's not right.*

Step... step... step...

"Freeze!" A brigade of heavy-soled shoes stomped

through the door and filled my cramped quarters.

I uncurled my shaky limbs, feeling thirsty, nauseated, cold. I was a flimsy mass of confusion as the adrenaline drained and the shock took over. Somehow, I ended up outside with a bottle of water in my hand and Officer Bulldog, who insisted his real name was Officer Stanwall, at my side. He kindly requested I stop calling him as such and then questioned me on the incident.

"You said you saw him getting mail?" Officer Bull... Stanwall asked in his burly, very bulldoggy voice.

"Yes. I took a picture. It's on my phone... somewhere." I took a swig of water.

His pen flew across his notepad, and with a lick of his finger, he flipped the page and continued. "He said he used the keys on the desk to open the door because you wouldn't answer."

Water dribbled down my chin. "Wait. What?"

"Did he say anything when he entered your apartment?" Officer Stanwall asked.

I thought for a moment. "He said... *hello*."

"Stop what you're doing! Stop! Cambria! Came-bree-aaaa!"

*Why?*

*Why?*

*Whyyy?*

"Cambria!" Kevin ran across the grass in his bare feet, wearing a pair of blue-checkered boxer shorts and a frown. "Cambria!" he yelled again as if I were a great distance away and not a foot from where he stood.

"Who are you?" Officer Stanwall asked.

Kevin's mouth fell open, revealing all his metallic molars. He placed his hand over his furry chest. "Who am I? I'm the owner of this building."

Stanwall looked to me for confirmation, and I nodded. "His parents own it," I said, which earned me a sympathetic brow raise from the officer.

"What did you do to Wick?" Kevin hissed.

"Who's Wick?"

"My friend," he said as if it were obvious. "I sent him here to get my mail and ask you for a parking pass. What did you do to him?"

Stanwall's bulldoggy face trained on Kevin. "You know the suspect?"

"Suspect?" Kevin threw his hands up as if declaring a touchdown and paced the walkway. "I don't believe this. He got here last night, and she's been harassing him since. Arrest this one." He pointed his hairy-knuckled finger at me.

The plastic water bottle crinkled in my clenched fist, and it took all the restraint I had not to throw it at his head. "Your friend broke into my apartment, and he has a spider web tattoo," I said through gritted teeth. This was beyond ridiculous. Mental disability or not, a woman could only be pushed so far.

"So you're prejudiced against spider web tattoos?" Kevin huffed, shaking his head. "I know lots of people with spider web tattoos. I was on the phone with him the entire time. When you didn't answer the bell, I told him to go in the office and knock on your door, and when you didn't answer, I told him to knock louder, and then he heard crashing so I told him to go in." He looked at Stanwall and cocked a thumb. "This one was taking his picture. She's a perv who sleeps with old people."

My water bottle went sailing over his head, only because I missed.

Officer Stanwall planted himself between Kevin and me. "We don't need any of that," he said with exaggerated patience. "His story checks."

I opened my mouth—to say what, I wasn't sure. It felt like I was starring in an M. Night Shyamalan movie about some parallel universe, except no one bothered giving me a script.

"So you're not arresting him?" I asked, too snippily for my own good.

"He's been taken in for violating his parole," he answered, still standing between us.

Kevin's face went tense. "You're fired," he furiously whispered under his breath.

"That's enough," Stanwall ordered in a deep, rough voice causing both Kevin and me to jump. I resisted the urge to salute. "I'll take you if I need to," Stanwall barked at Kevin with a cautionary glare. His eyes softened when they landed on me. "You OK?"

# Chapter 24

*Tenant must give 30-day intent to vacate in writing before vacating.*
*Yelling "I'm moving" is not sufficient notification.*

*Am I OK?*

That question echoed through my head later while sitting at my desk holding Officer Stanwall's card, staring at the silver and gold police emblem. *Am I OK?* I'd answered Stanwall with an involuntary nod of my head as Kevin tromped back to his delusion hideout, grumbling and puffing the entire journey. *Am I OK?* Spider Webs of Death, a.k.a. Wick, hadn't come from Spencer's apartment. He came from Kevin's. A question Patrick specifically asked before making the decision to give Spencer a thirty-day notice, and I said no. I had, true to form, overreacted. Then there was the fact Kevin fired me. Common sense said he didn't have the power to do so. Still, he had to have a little influence.

The day was turning into a compilation of my failures. Tom wasn't answering my texts or calls. Chase had disappeared. I was pissed off at Kevin, wanting so badly to verbally beat him over the head, except I wasn't sure what mental disability I was dealing with aside from a false sense of entitlement and an acute case of douchebaggery.

To top it all off, the printer ran out of ink—magenta. My attempts to explain to the machine that I only needed white paper with black print didn't work. The hateful piece of crap was going to hold my incident report hostage until I replaced the cartridge.

*Was I OK?*

No, I guess I wasn't. And there wasn't a thing I could do about it. Except sulk.

But before I could sink into a sulking oblivion—fun as that sounded—the lobby door chimed, and I knew it was Chase before I even saw him. He had a distinct, sexy man smell. A musky mixture of salty skin with a hint of soap. One of my favorite smells (second only to that sweet newborn baby smell). Under normal circumstances, his aroma would have me in a puddle of lust. Except I was already a puddle of petulance, and petulance and lustfulness are a deadly combination. There was an entire *20/20* episode dedicated to it once called *Women Who Murder* or something like that.

"Cambria, are you OK?"

"That *is* the question. After careful consideration, I've come to the conclusion I am not."

He opened the door to my office and walked in, the man scent growing stronger. "What happened?" he asked, placing his hands on the armrests of my swivel chair, leaning in close. I breathed from my mouth only and kept my eyes away from his sexy incisors.

"I'm out of magenta ink." This, I could tell from his expression, was not the answer he expected. "And the guy with the tattoos came into my apartment looking for a parking pass, but he was arrested, so Kevin fired me." I flapped my arm in the general direction of the printer. "If I had magenta, I'd give you the incident report to read. It's a real page-turner. Or, well, it's only one page, single-spaced."

Chase pushed off the chair, walked to the printer and yanked the cover open with ease. Something I attempted to do several times while the vile machine mocked me with its beeps and error messages. I had then given up and thrown my stapler at it. He pulled out the magenta cartridge, gave it a few hard shakes and replaced it. The machine hummed back to life and spit out my report.

I gave a half-hearted chuckle. Even the office equipment

was against me. "First the air conditioner and now the printer. You're on a roll today." He ignored me, his beautiful green eyes darting furiously down the page.

"This is ridiculous." He flicked the paper in his hand. "Give this to your ex." He tossed the report across the desk, shaking his head. "Better yet, email it to Patrick and copy Tom. I guarantee you this will be the last straw. Kevin was already close to getting kicked out after what happened with Joyce."

"What? Why would I give it to Tom? So he could use it against me if we should ever have a custody hearing?" Chase's mind was elsewhere. "Chase?"

He returned to the conversation. "You know his story, right?"

"Who? Tom?" *How long was I in the bathroom this morning?*

He shook his head. "What? No, Kevin."

"I know he has a mental disability and threw a vase through his window. I read Joyce's incident report."

Chase placed his forehead into his palm and laughed a hearty someone-told-a-hilarious-dirty-joke laugh. I was beginning to question the sanity of every person in the community.

"Mental health is not a laughing matter," I said, not amused. Not amused at all.

"Kevin doesn't have a mental disability." He leaned against the desk. "Cambria, you know he's gay, right?" I shook my head. His sexual preference had never crossed my mind. "I didn't think so," Chase continued. "Joyce called it a mental disability because that's what his parents called it. He's an only child, and when he came out of the closet, sometime during his teenage years, his parents sent him to a camp to 'fix it.' From what I've heard, it was pretty damaging. I don't know specifics. But he has scars all over his face from the therapy methods they used. It screwed with him pretty bad, and when he refused to seek further treatment for his 'mental disability,' his parents kicked him out and cut him off. Patrick found him living here in the gym and put him up in a hotel for a few days while he talked to Kevin's mother. She's the one who said Kevin could live here rent-free as long as he didn't contact the family. From what I've gathered, Kevin is extremely lonely. And that guy from last night? Turns out he was from San Bernardino, and he's not supposed to leave the county without notifying his parole officer. They met online a couple of days ago, and he came out to meet Kevin. I know some stuff went down with Joyce, and Kevin was pretty close to getting kicked out, but Patrick paid her off to not sue. Once Patrick hears about Kevin telling his friend to enter your apartment, I think he'll have to kick him out. That's why I said copy Tom. You have legal rights as an employee."

That was a lot of information to digest.

How terrible.

"Poor Kevin," I thought out loud.

Chase bent down and lifted my chin up with his finger, catching my eyes with his, holding me in place. "What happened in his past sucks. It does. Still doesn't give him any right to treat you the way he has."

"No, but it's a change of perspective," I muttered, Chase's finger still forcing my chin up. "How'd you know Tom was a lawyer—"

Chase's calloused thumb ran gently across my cheek, derailing my train of thought. His other hand went to my shoulder, his fingers spread, taking up the entire space between my shoulder and neck. The warmth of his touch beckoned every nerve ending in my body.

I felt the wisps of warm breath escaping his parted lips and feathering against mine. I felt the distance closing. I felt my eyes closing. I felt the desire so desperate to be fulfilled that it ached. I ached all over. The distance closed, and his lips brushed against mine. I could already feel our tongues dancing in sweet unison, savoring the taste of his mouth.

I parted my lips, an open invitation. His lips parted, accepting, moving in closer... nearly there. My heart beat in triple time. Almost there...

*NO!*

He pulled back like a hand on a hot stove, his back pressed against the door, his hands shoved deep into his pockets. I sat there with my mouth still hanging open, the feeling of his lips still hot on mine. Desire swimming around my head.

His chest rose and fell as if he had just sprinted a marathon. "I better get going," he announced, not making eye contact. The door opened, and he left. HE LEFT.

*What happened?*

I sat there, a sexually frustrated figurine. Confused. Mad. Aggravated.

*What the hell just happened?*

The familiar clanking against the linoleum freed my joints. "Apartment Manager," Silvia hollered over the counter. I turned slowly, weighted by the intense crappiness of the entire freaking day. "They're at it again," she moaned. Harold flapped. I stared. "Did you hear me? They're doing it again. I will move if this doesn't stop."

I continued to stare until "I'm OK with that" fell out of my mouth.

If Silvia could move her face, she would have scowled. Instead she scoffed and fluttered her eyes like she had an eyelash stuck in there. "Fine then, Apartment Manager. Consider this my thirty-day notice," she snapped. Harold bobbed his head up and down in agreement.

I shrugged an *I don't give a damn* shrug, because I didn't. Someone at the property should be getting some, and it obviously wasn't going to be me. Why not let the senior citizens enjoy each other in peace? Honestly, I was jealous. "It has to be in writing. Drop it off when you're ready." I smiled a patronizing smile. "And the name is Cambria, not Apartment Manager."

# Chapter 25

*Tenant shall only use Premises as a residence, not for a business.*

My Grandma Ruthie used to say, "We all have a backstory, and you can't judge anyone until you've read theirs." This was in reference to my cousin, Stephanie, who had blue hair (before blue hair was cool) and black nails (before black nails were cool) and purple-stained lips (not sure if that has ever been cool). Her nose ring was connected to her lip ring by a thin, silver chain. Black O's decorated each earlobe. When I was older, I learned that various other sensitive areas of Stephanie had been privy to a piercing gun as well. Her shoulders slumped forward, and her face remained shuttered. When I spoke, she would pretend not to notice, or she would call me names, roll her eyes, make fun of my hair and turn her back on me. I hated her. I hated being forced to converse with her. I hated when Grandma Ruthie would pull out her "everyone has a backstory" speech when I'd tattle on Stephanie for being cruel.

It wasn't until I was sixteen, while sitting in a cold, metal folding chair, looking at a 16x20 of Stephanie's shuttered face atop an easel with an urn next to it, that I finally understood what Grandma was saying. Stephanie had ended her life after a long, silent battle with severe social anxiety and depression. I never knew. I had filed her away in my mind, shoved in a folder labeled "arrogant" and "mean" and brushed her off. I never knew she was suffering. I never bothered to read her whole story.

And now I knew Kevin's. Leaving him alone was the opposite of how he should be treated. Knowing he'd been sent away, abandoned by his family, told he had a mental disability since adolescence—it didn't sit well with me. His behavior didn't sit well. I wasn't entirely sure it wasn't alcohol-induced either. If Kevin had a friend, someone who cared, then perhaps he'd be more inclined to keep his clothes on and not masturbate in Larry's apartment. At least I hoped he wouldn't. Didn't the saying go "the kids who need the most love ask for it in the most unusual ways"?

Or was it "the most unloving ways"?

What I knew for certain was the man-child needed a person in his corner. I was ready to take the role. Kevin was not going to end up like Stephanie. Not on my watch.

Pep-talking myself, I climbed the steps up to the black door and knocked. After ten more knocks, Kevin, still wearing only the checkered boxers from earlier, flung the door open.

"Can't you read the sign?" He pointed to a freshly posted note taped above the knob: Management Not Allowed.

I smiled, pretending not to notice. "I have a proposition."

"Does it have to do with you moving out ASAP?"

"No, it doesn't. It has to do with us."

He shook his head before I even got the words out. "Not interested," he said, swinging the door closed.

I shoved my foot into the doorjamb, and the door bounced back open off my blue Converse sneakers. "I want to propose a truce. We don't have to be enemies. I'd like to be allies." He perked up. Now I had his attention. "Come grab a bite to eat with me sometime after payday. Let's work together. I know how much this property means to you. You're valuable here, and I'm not just saying that because you tried to fire me. I genuinely want to be your friend. What do you say? Friends? How about next Saturday?" It would give me time to come up with how he could be more involved in the property without having him actually involved.

Kevin's mouth twitched upwards into a crescent. My heart

lifted. Everyone needs someone in his or her corner.

*I was right,* I thought just before the door slammed in my face. The wood stopped an inch from my nose.

*Or maybe not.*

I stared at the red, spray-painted number, debating if I should knock again or obey the sign. My shoulders sank with defeat.

*Perhaps it's time to start listening?*

I headed back down the stairs, my mood sinking with each drop of my foot, rejection swimming around my head like a shark preparing for the kill. So much rejection—first by Chase, who pulled away so fast you'd think I was contagious. Now Kevin. Of course there was also Tom, and how could I forget about Patrick, who rejected me twice before settling.

My life had crumbled into small, unrecognizable pieces. Much like the picture frame that once hung in the hall. I'd felt despair at various times in my life, but never like this. I'd always been able to reframe my mind, focus on my resources and find a thread of hope to cling to.

I was losing grasp of that thread.

Cutting through the grass, I hugged my chest, my eyes secured to the ground. Engaged in my pity-party-for-one, I hadn't noticed the footsteps approaching and nearly face-planted into Spencer's chest. He was holding his lease out as if he were about to make a public decree. Without saying a word (might as well start listening to Patrick), I sidestepped to the right, out of his way. He shuffled over. I sidestepped to the left. He shuffled over. I turned around and walked in the opposite direction, and he jumped in front of me. This whole keeping my big mouth shut thing was becoming rather difficult.

"Please listen to me?" Spencer finally said, pushing his glasses back up the ridge of his nose. He was still sporting his coffee-stained blue scrubs with *Dr. Spencer Bryant D.D.S.* embroidered above the pocket and blue Crocs with white socks. "I've been reading over the lease, and I believe I've taken care of everything. I'd like to show you. If things are up to par, would you consider not going through with the thirty-day notice? I just moved here, and I'd like to stay. I really hate moving." He flipped to the ninth page of the *House Rules* and pointed to the paragraph he'd highlighted. NO WATER-FILLED FURNITURE ALLOWED IN THE APARTMENT. "It says *in* the apartment, so I put them on the patio. And I got rid of my stingrays and won't be selling them any more. So there isn't any illegal activity going on either. I'd like to show you."

*Huh?*

Not speaking was no longer an option because I had to ask, "What the hell are you talking about? What's a stingray?" *Code for bazooka, perhaps?*

Misreading my confusion, he placed his thumbs and pointer fingers together to make a diamond. "They have a diamond head and are bottom-dwelling marine rays. They're fresh water, and I realize they're illegal here in California. I didn't think it would be that big—"

"Spencer," I cut him off, more confused than ever. "I know what a stingray is. Tell me what a *real* stingray is."

He stared at me with a blank expression until it hit me. "Holy crap!" I gasped. He wasn't selling firearms or drugs. He was selling fish... or... er... stingrays. "No, no, no. Spencer, I saw several people coming and going from your apartment carrying brown bags. You can't put water in a brown bag." He was a dangerous criminal. Dangerous criminals don't sell stingrays. They sell assault rifles. They generally don't wear crocs with socks and have D.D.S. after their name either... *dammit.*

"I put the plastic bag in the brown bag so no one sees. Look, I'm sorry. I assumed Joyce knew and didn't care. I moved my setup with my smaller, legal fish. Can I please show you?"

My tongue felt thick, and I struggled to speak. "Um... I... Fine, sure, whatever. Hold on." I surrendered, mostly out of curiosity. "Give me one second, and I'll meet you at your apartment." I turned around and slid my phone out of my back pocket and composed a text to Amy.

*Me: About to enter Apartment 36, Spencer Bryant, in case I die or go missing*

I hit send. If Spencer turned out to be the criminal I'd

made him out to be (and oddly, I hoped he was), Amy would be able to identify my killer.

Spencer's apartment smelled like chicken nuggets, Old Spice and latex. A card table with four plastic folding chairs was set up in the dinette area. No furniture aside from a circular futon in front of a too-large-for-this-room television, at least seventy inches, mounted to the wall with a waterfall of black, red and blue cords behind it.

*He'll definitely need to patch that before he moves.*

No pictures on the wall. Nothing on the kitchen counters. The scratchy tan carpet was filthy, littered with specks of dirt, crunched leaves and tiny papers. I followed him through the hall, past the linen cabinets, and into his room. A green comforter lay heaped on the floor next to the bare queen mattress. Clothes, sweat-ripened socks, scrub tops, boxers, grease-soaked napkins, pizza boxes and books were sprawled across the floor. A lone picture of Han Solo with his blaster pointed, hair feathered and face smoldering was hung on the wall.

"This way," Spencer said, sliding open the patio door.

I stepped outside. "You've got to be bleeping kidding me." FISH TANKS. Five long fish tanks lined the perimeter of his rectangle-shaped patio. Not the beautiful tanks with the colorful fish, fake treasure chests, artificial plants and aqua pebbles lining the bottom. Just tanks filled with water, a pump, and dozens upon dozens of light and dark blue fish.

*FISH!*

"These are Frontosas," Spencer said proudly.

I stared at him.

"It's a type of African cichlid," he explained. I had no idea what that was, but it didn't sound like a shotgun. "I breed them, they're absolutely legal, and I only sell them to my ichthyologist group."

*Ichthyologist group?*

I was wrong. Spencer had nothing to do with the crime. He had nothing to do with the guns and the backpack and the cars and the pregnancy test. He wasn't impregnating anyone. He was too busy making fish do it.

My phone vibrated in my back pocket. Amy. "Hello," I

answered, peering into one of the tanks holding a school of fish with humps protruding from their smug little fish heads.

"Cambria, what is wrong with you? Who is Spencer Bryant, and why are you going into his apartment if he is about to kill you?" I suspected she didn't remember texting me the exact same message last night.

"Don't worry, I was wrong."

Spencer knelt down and sprinkled red flakes into the tank holding the smallest Fronto-whatever. The fish flurried to the surface, grabbing the food and swimming back down to the bottom. I wanted to cry.

"You were wrong about what?" Amy asked. "Who is Spencer?" I could hear the hangover in her voice still.

"He's a tenant. A dentist who sells *fish*." The word left a bitter aftertaste.

"Like real fish or is this code for something?" she asked.

"Nope, like little Nemos."

"Frontosa," Spencer corrected, standing upright and dusting the fish food off his hands.

"Seriously?" Her voiced perked up into a sober range. "A dentist? Huh. Is he single?"

I rolled my eyes and looked around at the fish tanks, and then back up at Spencer, and then into his room with the Han Solo poster and sheet-less mattress. "I'm going to take a stab in the dark and say yes."

## Chapter 26

*Landlord is entitled to at least one mental breakdown during the length of the rental agreement.*

I felt like a scarecrow: hollow and made of only straw and clothing. No bones to keep me vertical, no brain to process the monumental mess I made. I lay on my bed, spread out like a strawy starfish, with my newly retrieved *drug* box open and on the floor beside me. I watched the blades of the ceiling fan spin around and around and around and around into a blur.

I flopped my straw-filled head to the right and got a sideways glance of the armoire still standing in the middle of the room. "I should have taken your lead and never left my apartment," I told it, as if speaking to Joyce. "I should have asked more questions about Kevin, about rent collection and the job. I have no idea what I'm doing, and I have a sinking suspicion it isn't even that hard of a job. I was wrong about Spencer. What was I thinking? That someone who sold guns illegally would bag them up like a grocery store? 'Would you like your assault rifle in paper or plastic?' Where is this crime coming from? Why did it start the same day I did? Why did Chase make a move and then pull back? Everything was fine when you were here. Why can't I leave well enough alone? Why can't I listen? Why do I make a mess out of everything I touch? Why am I talking to an armoire? Ugh." I flung my arm over my eyes.

*I've lost my mind.*

The office cordless phone rang. I felt around for it with my free hand, then brought it to my ear without looking. "This is Cambria."

"Patrick here."

"Hi, Patrick. How are you?" I tried to sound as cheery as one who talks to furniture could be. I knew why he was calling. He'd spoken with Kevin, and now I had to tell him I was wrong about Spencer and ask if he could stay.

"I heard the police were in the office today?" he asked curtly.

"What did Kevin tell you?" I thought it best to hear what version he'd given Patrick before I added in my own account.

"Kevin? I haven't heard from him. What did Kevin do that warranted a visit from the police?" Now he sounded irritated.

I gnawed at my thumbnail while weighing my options. "Nothing," I finally said, surrendering to my conscience. While I believed Kevin telling anyone to go into my apartment without my permission was wrong, I couldn't imagine what would happen to him if he were kicked out. I couldn't live with that. He needed to stay, especially if there was a substance abuse situation. This was even more clear to me after the swigs of Benadryl I'd taken. "It was just another car break-in."

"Did you give them the information about Spencer again?"

"Well, here's the thing about Spencer." I ran my hand along the rich fabric of my comforter, procrastinating. "The thing is he actually *was* doing something illegal. He was selling stingrays."

"Is that some kind of narcotic?"

"No, it's actually a real stingray. The ones with diamond-shaped bodies who dwell at the bottom of the ocean... I mean, this one is in fresh water, so in a lake. I don't think he had anything to do with all the crime. He stopped selling the stingrays and moved his fish tanks to the patio and would like to stay."

"What about the man with the spider web tattoo from last night?"

"Well, here's the thing about the spider web tattoo guy. Turns out he was visiting a friend for the night only. He lives in San Bernardino. It looks like he doesn't know Spencer and wasn't involved with any car thefts either. Spider web tattoos are quite popular apparently."

"OK. If the setup is fine, and you don't think Spencer is involved in any criminal activities, he can stay. I don't care. One less vacancy to add to the pile." Patrick's voice was tense. My stomach hurt. "I received a call from Silvia Kravitz saying you kicked her out because she complained? She also gave me another story I don't care to confirm about you and her neighbors. She told me the police were in your apartment?"

That woman was seriously getting on my nerves. "It was a misunderstanding."

"Misunderstanding?" he repeated. I nodded yes, forgetting he couldn't see me. "Cambria, this is getting out of hand. At what point do we step back and evaluate when this all started? I've never had so many calls from tenants in all my years of property management. You hastily made a decision about Spencer. Now we've got a crowd moving out next month putting you at a…" His fingers tapped at a calculator. "Seventy-percent occupancy rate? It's a bad situation. Now I have this application for an Alice Burns with a copy of a student ID card sitting on my desk. Where's her license? How do you know this is really Alice Burns? You have no photo identification? The picture on her student ID is small and grainy."

I continued to gnaw on my thumbnail. "She said she lost it, and she's only a roommate."

"Only a roommate?" he repeated, growing angrier. "Roommates still live there. Roommates still pay rent. Roommates are added to the lease. Were you even aware Vincent Romero had a three-month deposit? We only collect three-month deposits from applicants who have iffy credit. He's been a model tenant from what I see, but the point is, I have to trust my managers to look into these things. To look at the bigger picture, collect the rents, maintain at least a ninety-five percent occupancy rate and do a decent screening of applicants. Before I get the application you should have already verified employment, past rental history and done a Google search. I'm still missing some rents. When Joyce was there, she never had one single eviction. Not one. In twenty-five years." He exhaled into the phone. "I'll be there tomorrow morning so we can chat more about this in person."

*I'm fired.*

# Chapter 27

*Landlord agrees to fulfill all reasonable maintenance requests within a reasonable amount of time as long as the Tenant is reasonable.*

It felt as if I'd been punched in the stomach. I was fired. Why else would Patrick come down for a "chat"? It's the twenty-first century. We can chat via phone, Skype, FaceTime, text. No need to speak in person unless it was to serve termination papers. I took a bullet, figuratively, for Kevin, and where did it get me? Fired.

Tears clogged the back of my throat as I stormed over to Alice's apartment. I was not going down without a fight. Nope. Not me. I passed Mickey, who was arguing with himself, and then Alex and Trent, who were arguing with each other. Larry was on his upstairs balcony, nursing a Bloody Mary as he sat in an old school aluminum lawn chair with yellow and white webbing. The resident from Apartment 7 marched by, avoiding eye contact, with a stack of moving boxes in her arms.

I continued with determination to Apartment 39. Chase rounded the corner, coming from the carports, scrolling through his phone. I pretended not to notice him, keeping my eyes on the destination. Remaining employed was more important than dealing with whatever that was that happened.

With his focus still on his phone, he stopped in front of

Alice's door, cutting me off. "Excuse me," I said curtly, because I was livid—mostly because he kissed me and then ran away, and partly because I had texted him several times since. Once asking what happened. Another text with a maintenance request for Nearly Naked Grandma Clare's garbage disposal. Another asking if he received my text about Nearly Naked Grandma Clare. And the last text was an accident. I meant to send myself a grocery list, but it went to Chase instead. No replies to any. I had hoped it was because he didn't have his phone on him.

Chase looked up, startled, and then shoved his phone and hands in the front pockets of his jeans—his signature stance. "Oh, hi." He glanced over his shoulder at the door, then at me, and moved out of the way.

*Oh, hi?*

I scooted past him, careful not to inhale his scent or touch him in any way. "Did you get my text messages?" I muttered, mostly to the door, because somehow talking to wood had become my norm.

"I did. I'll take care of it," he said, lingering. Rocking back and forth from his heels to his toes.

I raised my hand to knock, waiting for him to leave. *Is he waiting for a formal order?* "Can you go do that now?" I asked.

"Yes, I can." Still lingering. Still rocking. Awkward.

I dropped my hand. "Is there something you'd like to say, or are you hanging around here for a particular reason?"

He thought for a moment. "Nope, nothing to say. I'll go take care of that now." He turned and reunited his face with his phone.

*Yeah, why don't you go do that.*

I knocked again and waited.

The click of the deadbolt sliding free preceded the clink of a chain being unhooked. A man about my age popped his head out. He had thick features, a shaved head, and long, crooked, yellow teeth.

"What?" the head asked in lieu of a salutation.

This must be Boo a.k.a. Vincent. I'd never met him before, never seen him walking around the property. According to the lease, no one else lived here. "Can I speak with Alice, please?"

"Who?"

I shook my head, remembering. "Sorry, Wysteria. Can I speak with Wysteria, please?" It's hard enough to keep all of the residents' names and apartment numbers straight, let alone their stripper names too. "Is she home?"

"What's wrong?" came a soft voice from behind.

I turned around as Alice emerged from the carports. She had on tight jeans and a black hooded sweater, her hair stringy and greasy and haphazardly wrapped in a knot on the top of her head. Her hazel eyes were hammocked in a bed of dark bags, and her face looked sunken and pale with blotchy spots on her cheeks and forehead. This wasn't the bubbly Alice sucking on a Tootsie Pop I'd first met.

Alice's eyes darted from me to Vincent, whose head was still sandwiched between the door and frame. "What do you need?" she asked, tugging the sleeves of her sweater over her hands, which pulled it down around her neck and revealed three large finger-like bruises.

"Alice," I whispered, covering my mouth with my hand. "Your neck."

She sunk her neck into the sweater like a turtle. "I'm fine," she muttered.

I turned to Vincent. His thick features remained unchanged. I looked back to Alice, who slipped her hands into the front pocket of her sweater and eyed the ground. "Do you need help?" I asked under my breath.

"She's fine," Vincent moaned from the doorway, sounding bored with the conversation.

"I'll help you get out of here, Alice." I was furious I'd somehow missed this. Too busy focusing on the man-child and Spencer and cars and backpacks and wallets and a cute maintenance boy who turned out to be a jerkball. This was my job as an apartment manager. *I think.* My job description needed some fine-tuning. I wasn't exactly sure what it was. It *was* my job as a human being to not ignore abuse. "Let's go, right now," I pressed.

Alice's eyes turned angry. "I'm not going anywhere. Mind your own business." She pushed past me, ignoring the ample unrestricted space around me and knocked my shoulder with hers.

I reached for her arm. She withdrew it quickly. "Don't touch me," she warned with a glare that could kill. She turned sideways and squeezed into the narrow gap Vincent allotted her.

"But, I need your driver's license," I said as the door closed. Far too many doors had been closed in my face. It was growing old. I knocked again, and again, and again. "Alice? Wysteria? Vincent?" I tried all the names I could remember. "My Boo? Hello? I need your... driver's... license," I begged through the faded lumber. "Please open. I can help." I pressed my forehead to the door and whispered, "Please?"

Nothing.

I spun around and pressed my fingers to my temples. This could be a classic case of my "jump to worst case scenario" mind at play. Those could have been hickeys on her neck. If there was one thing I'd learned in the past twenty-four hours, it was that my gut could not be trusted. *Hello Spencer and his fishy brothel.*

I was overdramatizing the situation. Alice was fine.

I, however, was not.

I tucked escaped strands of Einstein behind my ears and numbly returned to my apartment. I stood in the square kitchen and gazed at the chrome sink with the plastic still wrapped around the spray nozzle and the brand-new paper towel holder that didn't hold any towels.

I yanked open the silverware drawer, releasing a fresh-paint aroma, bringing me back one week earlier when I had walked through the apartment for the first time since it had been renovated—the feeling of excitement, the freedom, the endless possibilities, the relief. Oh, the relief. The relief was palpable, as if I could reach out and grab it, cradle it in my arms and kiss it.

Now it was gone.

I pulled out the silverware tray and deposited it into an open box on the floor. Then came the spatulas and whisks. Next the apron Grandma Ruthie had made me the Christmas before she died. The dusty cookbooks my mother insisted I take with me when I moved. The basket of Taco Bell sauce packets and the chopsticks still in their plastic casings. I tucked in the cardboard flaps, grabbed a brown crayon and labeled the box *Taco Bell Sauce,* because if I'd learned anything from this last move, it was the importance of labeling the essential items.

Out of the corner of my eye, I caught the top of Lilly's head bouncing across the bottom of the windows overlooking the courtyard. Tom followed behind, carrying a Happy Meal bag from McDonald's. I grabbed the remote control, found an episode of *Mickey Mouse Clubhouse* on the DVR and pressed "play."

*Oh how I'll miss you, cable.*

I met the duo at the door and bent down to give Lilly a kiss. "Did you have fun?" I asked.

She nodded, running her tongue over her ketchup mustache, and held out her prize from her Happy Meal, a Spiderman frozen mid-jump with his wrist poised and ready to web. It brought me back to the day I interviewed with Joyce. How stupid I had been not to ask more questions about Kevin, the property and the job. I'd glossed over everyone's warnings, so desperate for employment and so enamored by the cute coworker that I'd failed myself. I'd failed my little family. I'd failed my daughter.

"I love it," I said, tapping her nose with the tip of my finger and eliciting a carefree giggle. "Hey, I turned on a show for you. Can you go watch it while I talk to Daddy?"

"Chắc chắn." She giggled and bounced into the house, oblivious to the fact her life was about to be turned upside down. She settled on the couch, ironically hanging upside down, and sang along with the opening song. I shut the door, leaving a small gap to still keep an eye on her.

Tom hooked his aviators over the top of his shirt. He'd gone casual, khaki shorts, yellow shirt with the purple Lakers' logo painted across the front, and sandals, exposing his hairy toes.

"What's going on?" he asked casually.

I blinked. "What's going on?" How he managed to so easily forget about the world's troubles was incomprehensible.

My mind was like a damn iCloud, storing every detail of every good, insignificant, and bad thing that had ever happened in the history of my existence. It was all shoved in some mysterious file, hovering above my head, ready to be brought back up on a whim. "What's going on is this morning. What was that?"

He nodded, as if remembering. "Oh that. Yeah, I might have overreacted a little. I swear I know that guy, and I don't like him. I don't trust him. I don't want him around my kid." He shrugged an unapologetic shrug.

He was being completely unreasonable. This must be what it's like having a conversation with me when I'm upset. "Tom, you don't know him, therefore, you have no reason to not trust him or not like him. You don't have any right to storm in here and act like a jealous ex-boyfriend, because you're not." I winced, pressing my hand over my abdomen. The numbness had worn off. I felt everything—specifically the burning campfire of stress in my stomach.

"Cambria, I wasn't acting like a jealous ex. I was acting like you do."

*Ugh.* I dropped my face into my hands. I didn't have the energy to argue. "Tom, I just can't right now," I mumbled into my palms, and before I knew it, I was crying. The dam broke, and tears burst out. Snot seeped out of my nostrils. Spit pooled in my mouth. Every hole in my face was leaking fluid.

"Um, uh," Tom stammered, and I could see between my fingers his hairy-toed feet dancing around on the cement. "Is this a trick or for reals?" I didn't answer. "Cam?" I hated when he called me *Cam*, and I hated his hairy toes. Then he cupped his arm around my trembling shoulder, and that, I didn't hate so much.

"I'm losing my job," I said in between sobs. "And I might need you to take Lilly while I figure out where we're going to live." My salty tears slithered down my cheeks, landing in my mouth. "I don't have any money or credit, and I can't go back to Fresno because I said the stupid gay thing, and now I can't go without saying I'm a liar, but I am a liar. And I'm probably going to hell now, but I have to say so because I have no idea what I'm doing, and I'm talking to furniture."

Tom didn't say anything, he just kept rubbing my
shoulder. I leaned into his embrace, nestled under his armpit.
When my sobs turned to a manageable cry, he asked, "I'm not
really sure what any of that means. Why are you losing your
job?"

I ran my fingertips under my eyes, catching the smudged
makeup and tears. "My boss is coming to *talk* to me
tomorrow. There is all this crime in the parking lot, and it
started my first day on the job. It would be helpful if they
would have taken my car, then it wouldn't look so suspicious.
I almost kicked out the wrong guy, I got the owner's son's
boyfriend arrested, I don't have all the rents, and everyone
here hates me. Need I go on?"

"OK," he said slowly, as if carefully choosing his next
words. "How does this make you a liar who's going to hell?"

I looked down, chewing on my bottom lip. Was this the
right time to reveal my stupid lie? I didn't have the money for
a Motel 6, let alone a new apartment. I should receive
compensation for the time I'd worked thus far, which
wouldn't be much, but would hopefully be enough for gas to
Fresno and an oil change (my little genie bottle lamp looking
thing had been lit up on my dashboard for the last six months.
My car would probably explode somewhere on the
Grapevine). Going home was my only real option, and I was
going to have to explain myself then, so I might as well start
now. I took a deep, shaky breath. "I sort of told my family you
were gay, and if Lilly and I move there, I'll have to tell them
I've been lying."

Tom's arm fell off my shoulder and slapped back to his
side. I turned to face him, still chewing on my lip. He put on
his angry face. "You're not moving to Fresno with my kid.
You're not moving to Fresno period."

*Really?*

Not the part of the story I anticipated him getting upset
over. "Tom, it's much cheaper there, and I could stay with my
mom while I find another job. It wouldn't be forever, but
what am I supposed to do? Live on the streets?"

Tom brought his hands to his hips, giving me a *you're being
ridiculous* look. "You think I'd let you live on the streets? And

why am I gay?"

*Here we go.* "Well, it's a funny story, really. So you remember when I found out I was pregnant, and I said 'I think we should try and be a family'? And you were all 'I don't want to date you' and I was all 'Ouch my heart.' Well, when I told my parents, I kinda implied we were dating when I got pregnant, and then you sorta came out of the closet so we broke up. Then it all got so out of hand. I was heartbroken, and it sorta made us look better. I don't know why. I'm beginning to think there's something wrong with my head. You should know my parents are very supportive of you."

Tom's mouth hung open. His brows pressed down to a V, and his hazel eyes stared straight through me. He then closed his eyes and shook his head as if waking from a dream. "I don't ever remember having that conversation about dating."

He sure was sticking on the less poignant points of my stories here. I patted my cheeks dry, noticing Natalie from Apartment 2 eyeing me with a concerned frown as she walked past us to her apartment. I smiled an exaggerated smile and waved.

Now, back to Tom. "I was paraphrasing," I told him.

"Cam, we barely knew each other. It took me a while to get my head around being a dad. I thought you were trying to do the right thing. I never knew you were heartbroken over it."

For a lawyer, he was rather unobservant. "Does it matter now?"

He thought for moment. "Yeah, I think it does," he decided.

Lilly stuck her face in the gap in the door. "The show's over!" she announced.

"I'll be right there," I told her.

"But it's over nooowww," she whined.

"Lilly, I'll be right there," I repeated. She heaved herself to the floor.

"Lilly," Tom said sternly. "We're talking. Go sit on the couch and wait for us to finish."

"OK, Daddy," Lilly quickly obliged.

I rolled my eyes.

"Cam, you'll stay with me until we figure everything out. You're not going to Fresno. You're not going to be homeless. You're certainly not staying with the 'maintenance man.' Are you even sure you're losing your job? You have a tendency to jump to conclusions."

"Really?" I didn't know what else to say. "Thank you," I added, locating the thread of hope I'd lost grasp of. My stress lifted, a little, taming the campfire in my stomach. "My boss is coming tomorrow. I'm pretty sure he'll fire me. Wouldn't you? I was already his third choice. All the complaining and the crime that started the same day I did. I mean, literally, the exact day. The same day I started was the same day all that stuff was in the Dumpster... and the pregnancy test... holy mother crap of douche nuggets..." I started laughing. It was so obvious.

"Why are you laughing?" The concern lacing his words was even funnier than the fact I so blindly missed what had happened.

"I'll tell you later. Can you please stay here with Lilly? I have to talk to someone. I'll be right back."

# Chapter 28

*Tenant shall not keep any items of a dangerous, flammable or explosive nature on the Premises.*

"So obvious," I thought out loud, nearly singing it. Ty from Apartment 12 gave me a double take, repositioning the car seat draped over his forearm, protectively placing himself in front of his newborn. I caught my reflection in his dark glasses as I whizzed by in a flash, not even bothering with a polite smile. I had a job to save.

Through the ivy-laced breezeway and into the third courtyard I went. Determined. Silvia descended the stairwell in front of her apartment, her heels clanking against the worn stone steps, still wearing her silk floral robe. The same one she'd been sporting all week. Harold was in his usual spot, bobbing his head around, his claws digging into Silvia's shoulder. Her bulging eyes met mine. I didn't waver though. I pressed forward, maintaining eye contact.

She stopped at the base of the stairwell, one age-spotted hand resting on the railing, the other balled into a fist. I stared into her mucus-colored eyes as the distance closed between us. I once read if you should ever encounter a lion, you should stare directly into its eyes to prevent being attacked. I applied the same approach to Silvia.

It worked.

She broke eye contact and stepped around me. I ran up the stairs to Apartment 22 and knocked with both hands continuously, impatiently, feverishly and all other related adverbs. "Clare? Bob? It's Cambria. I need you, please!" I shouted.

I heard Silvia huff from below. "I knew it," she hissed.

I snapped around and leaned over the railing. "Yeah, and it was awesome!" I yelled. "Maybe you should get some. Then you wouldn't be so miserable when everyone else does."

She gasped, bringing her hand to her chest. Harold turned around, flashing me his backside. "What was awesome?" Clare stood in the doorway wrapped in a white terrycloth robe, holding her hand up to block the incoming rays of the setting sun from her eyes. "What's wrong?"

"Hi, Clare, I'm sorry to bother you. I'm looking for Chase. I need to speak with him right away." She stared at me, blank of any recollection. "He's the maintenance man. Is he not here fixing the garbage disposal?" I asked.

She continued to stare at me.

"Never mind, I don't really need him." I pounded back down the stairs, past Silvia who huffed and puffed as if she were about to blow my house down. No time. I was on a mission to save my hide. I'd already solved the entire mystery: the guns, the pregnancy test, the wallets in the Dumpster, the car thefts and burglaries. It was so OBVIOUS.

My determined march slowed to a yielding shuffle. *Was it obvious?* Had I jumped to conclusions again? Was I about to blow this entire situation out of proportion? I'd been so wrong lately.

Or had I?

My gut told me something was lurking behind the corner, waiting for me to get comfortable before jumping out and revealing him or herself. Isn't that exactly what happened? I was asleep, warm in my bed, tucked under my comforter, when I was summoned to meet Kevin. Spencer, technically, was selling illegal items out of his apartment just as I thought. Did I anticipate it being stingrays? No. Would any reasonable adult assume it was marine animals? No. Wick was in fact on parole, therefore he was a criminal, and therefore I was not overreacting when I approached him. OK, maybe when I had called the police and hid behind a box. But who knows what he was on parole for?

I was right all along.

I was going for it, I decided. Resolute and fast, I rounded the corner. Kevin stood under the archway below his apartment, wearing cargo shorts and a white tank. I almost didn't recognize him with so many clothes on. He looked out to the carports longingly, his arm draped over his protruding belly. He brought a cigarette to his mouth and took a long drag.

Kevin's presence was problematic. I hadn't included him in the plan I devised during the one-minute walk over. Chase would have been helpful. Kevin, not so much, especially considering he'd snapped the olive branch I extended. Though he never did call Patrick to tattle. If he were serious about firing me, wouldn't that be his first item of business? Telling Patrick what happened?

Perhaps the olive branch remained intact?

I tapped his shoulder. He jumped and spun around, dropping his cigarette in the process. I brought my finger to my lips before he could say anything. "Shh," I whispered.

His face contorted into an all-consuming anger. His jaw tight, eyes narrowed into furious slits, hands clenched into fists.

*Or perhaps he left Patrick a message?*

Then it happened. His jaw relaxed. His hands went limp and were promptly brought to his clothed hips. He lifted his brows high to the middle of his forehead and shrugged. "Well?" he whispered back.

It took me a moment to process the shift in his demeanor. He had not stormed away, taken off any clothing, called me a whore or slammed a door in my face (granted, there wasn't one around to do so with). "Well... how are you?" Might as well start with pleasantries.

"Fine, you?" It was the most normal conversation we'd ever had. He stuck his pinky into his ear and gave it a jiggle, pulling back to inspect his findings. For the first time I noticed the diamond studs glittering on each earlobe. His auburn sideburns were peppered with strands of white hair. Scars aside, his face had rather strong, masculine, well-defined features. He was, I realized for the first time, attractive. It's amazing what you notice when not actively avoiding staring at someone's exposed genitalia.

"Kevin," I said in a hushed tone, trying not to sound too amazed. "You really do look good in clothes. You should wear them more often."

He looked down, pulling at the bottom of his tank. His mouth twisted to the side as if deciding if making the effort was worth it. "Eh," he finally said, mirroring my hushed tone. "You here to see," he said, jerking his head toward Alice's apartment.

"Yeah, why? You know something?"

He looked around. "It depends on who's asking."

This was the Kevin I'd come to know and love, and by love I mean tolerate, and by tolerate, I mean I hadn't smacked him upside the head yet. Which had to be some kind of world record. "Me, Kevin. I'm asking you," I answered in an angry whisper. "I don't have time for games."

He looked taken aback. "Calm down, I was only joking."

Joking? JOKING? Was I talking to Kevin's reasonable identical twin brother? "Oh, sorry. Can you please tell me if you know anything?"

He folded his arms over his chest and looked around again. Confident we were alone, he leaned in and whispered, "I know everything about this place and everything about everyone." He winked.

"Ugh. I'm done. I've got bigger fish to cook."

"You mean fry?" Kevin corrected.

"Whatever," I said, pushing past him.

The carports wrapped around the building and backed up to the patios of first-floor Apartments 39, 22, 36 and 19 (the building was not numbered sequentially. It drove delivery people crazy. In my short time there, I'd already seen the pizza boy on several occasions standing in the middle of the courtyard with a receipt in one hand, hot pizza box in the other, turning around in circles as he noted each door's number, baffled. The original architect was experimenting with mushrooms when he planned the building, was my guess).

I would have an unrestricted view of Alice and Vincent's patio from the carport roof, and if the blinds were open, the bedroom. The crime started the day I arrived. Alice was the only one to technically move in on my watch. She said her name was Alice, yet everyone calls her Wysteria. Makes sense to use a stripper name. Or did it make sense to use a different name if you were using a different identity? She said she lost her license, yet she had a bag with medicine because her "Boo was totally, like, sick with a gnarly cold." You can't purchase cold medicine any more without swiping your driver's license. And I learned from my crime shows it's because you can make meth with cold medicine, so the stores track who's buying cold medicines in large quantities. Ha! See? Chase shouldn't have given me such a hard time about watching those shows when that knowledge is clearly coming in handy now. So Alice had lied. She never left her license at a club. Her name wasn't even Alice. It was Wysteria. She knew we would run background and credit reports, and her criminal hits would show up. She only turned in an application because Joyce had asked her to, and she didn't want any negative attention.

The clincher was her appearance. The day we met she was bouncy, colorful and thin. The new Alice (or whoever she was) was layered in clothing on an extremely hot day, her face was pale, her eyes sunken, and those dark spots looked an awful lot like pregnancy melasma (I'd suffered through it my entire pregnancy with Lilly).

Alice had left the office, and not thirty minutes later, I found the items discarded in the Dumpster. The bruises were still a mystery. Perhaps Vincent became violent when he found out Alice was breaking into cars? The rest added up so perfectly, I cursed myself for not catching it sooner.

The carport roof was much taller than I anticipated. Chase and his accompanying ladder would have been helpful. I squatted down, and with all my might, sprang upward with my arms outstretched, hoping to catch the top of the carport.

Not even close.

*Note to self: You are not Michael Jordan.*

That said, it didn't stop me from trying two more times. I

leaned against the rough stucco surface of the too-high wall, catching my breath.

"Here," Kevin said, appearing at my side. A freshly lit cigarette hung from the corner of his mouth. He stood in a braced positioned with his fingers intertwined.

"You sure?" I asked, cautiously inserting my Converse'd foot into his makeshift lift. I was heavier than I appeared. At least that's what every nurse said as I stepped onto the hateful doctor's office scale. *You're solid*, they'd say, and I'd want to punch them in the face.

Kevin wrapped his thumbs around my shoe for extra support. "I'm sure," he replied, keeping his cigarette balanced in his mouth. "They've been selling coke in there for a couple of months now. The guys are pretty cool. They don't make it here. They get it from somewhere else," he said, as if it should make me happy. "It's decent stuff, best I've ever had. Grabbed an eight ball from them this morning."

My mouth fell open. My frontal lobe worked frantically to decipher which disturbing piece of information to process first. "Kevin," I scolded, removing my foot. "Promise me you will not touch whatever you bought from them." I noticed his dilated eyes. "Too late?"

He brought his thumb and forefinger together, leaving a small half-inch gap between them. "Just a wee bit," he said, stifling a giggle.

And yet another piece to the puzzle—Kevin acted the way he acted because he was on drugs. Again, it should have been obvious. To be fair, I did have a hunch.

"Kevin," I mouthed, pointing to his hands. He returned them to their boosting position and squatted down to better bear the weight. I placed one foot into his hands and jumped up with the other. Kevin lifted me until I managed to hook my hands on the edge of the roof.

"You're heavy," Kevin quietly wheezed, his face turning apple.

"Just a little farther…" I inched my foot up the wall until I could leverage it on the ledge as well.

*What a sight this must be.*

With every ounce of strength pulsing through me, I made

it to the top of the carport roof.

*Note to self: Work out!*

I paused to look up at the gorgeous full moon while I caught my breath.

Then it was back to business. I army-crawled across the roof to get a better view of the patio.

The bedroom blinds were closed. Dark trash bags, filled to maximum capacity, were piled two deep next to the sliding glass door. The patio was littered with broken, plastic chairs, crinkled papers and food containers. Paragraph three on the third page of the *House Rules* says patios are to remain free from trash, broken furniture and wood-burning barbecues. There was also something in there about not being in possession of illegal drugs or involved in the distribution of them.

In short, I had plenty of grounds for an eviction.

From the reflection off the sliding door, I saw Vincent leaning against the wall directly below me. The patio door slid open, and I flattened myself against the roof. Footsteps approached. I held my breath. The footsteps stopped below, out of my line of sight. "Boo, are you, like, OK?" It was Alice. Her voice was small, submissive.

"Where the hell have you been?" Vincent asked, his voice angry.

"I told you, I was just, like, walking around. Getting some air."

*Or, like, breaking into cars, and like, being a total two-faced liar.*

"Don't play me," Vincent warned.

"I'm not playing you, Boo. I told you, you're the only one."

There was a long break of silence.

"I have to go," Vincent finally said. "I expect you here when I get back."

"You're meeting Malone at Alcove right now, right?" Alice asked, her voice louder.

"You on my phone?" he hissed, punching the wall. That had to hurt.

"No, no. I just... I heard Rev say something. I'll wait."

"You better." I heard them walk across the patio, so I

dared to lift my head. Vincent's hand was wrapped around Alice's waist as they disappeared into the apartment, sliding the door closed behind them.

I reached into my back pocket for my phone and quickly texted myself: *Vincent meeting Malone now at alcove. Rev. Alice has been gone walking property.*

I would wait, I decided, for Vincent to leave. I would wait for my feet to hit solid ground before I called the police.

The moments ticked by, the moon grew brighter and higher. Finally, Vincent left. The car parked directly under me in the carport roared, and…

*Ack!*

It happened in an instant. One second I was lying on the carport roof, the next second I was on the patio floor, with a pair of crazy, angry eyes glaring at me.

# Chapter 29

*Tenant will, at Tenant's cost, keep Premises in good, clean condition.*

I took a quick assessment of all limbs and organs. Everything was accounted for, and nothing throbbed. Hurt like hell, yes. Throbbed in a need-to-replace-a-kidney kind of way, no. I lay in a bed of stuffed, black trash bags with a hand wrapped tightly around my left ankle. The hand belonged to a man with a spider web tattoo across his neck, angry jaw, strong limbs, and eyebrows so blond they blended in with his face. I gulped. He made Spider Webs of Death look like Mary Poppins.

"When are you going to learn to not be so damn nosy?" the man asked through gritted teeth.

"Right now," I assured him, kicking my free leg. Without taking his eyes off my face, he grabbed my other ankle. "Help!" I screamed. "I'm being hel—" Before I knew what was happening, he was sitting on my legs, pinning me down, and his large, flat palm landed over my mouth, silencing my cries for help. I licked his hand. Blech. It tasted like fish.

"Who are you really?" the man snarled. I had a hunch this was Rev. "Who do you really work for?" he asked, clearly rhetorically, since his hand prohibited me from answering.

Keeping his hand over my mouth, he slid off me and moved around behind me, then hoisted my torso up with his free hand, holding me against him. Then he dragged me backwards through the patio door, my legs flailing the entire journey.

Frantic, my eyes dashed around, taking in the surroundings. A dark-spotted popcorn ceiling. Rectangles cut into the drywall along the bottom. The furnace was missing. A variety of colorful stains dotted the dingy carpet. As he dragged me over empty McDonald's containers and flattened In-N-Out cups, a Taco Bell wrapper stuck to the bottom of my shoe. The apartment smelled like burning plastic with a hint of the *Tropical Rainforest* I'd used in the office. Even in my current distressed state, I could see why Joyce asked for a high security deposit.

My tour continued down the short hallway. More rectangles. More stains. Into the living room we went. I could see the kitchen from there—the wall that separated the two had a hole so big a child could stand in it. All the kitchen cabinet doors were missing, leaving only the skeleton of what was once many-times-painted-over cabinetry. The apartment was void of any real furniture, only a few plastic patio chairs and a card table.

The spider-webbed assailant kicked a box blocking his route, sending it sailing across the room. We ended in the dinette area beneath a window adorned with thick, black curtains.

My fight or flight mode was alight and blazing, even though my attacker was twice my size and at least that much more crazy. I had a hunch he was just as stupid as he was high. My arm was released, but my mouth was still muzzled. His hot breath at my neck triggered a tsunami of fear.

"You a narc?" he growled. I tried to shake my head, but his hand was too tight over my mouth. He grabbed a handful of zip ties conveniently left on the ground. This must be the hostage room, I figured. "Put your hands together behind your back. If you don't listen, I'll go after the kid. Lilly, isn't it?"

*Lilly!*

Saying her name out loud didn't spark the compliant fear he'd intended; it ignited a fiery rage. With an accelerated rise and fall of my chest, to give the illusion his threats were working, I pressed my wrists together as instructed. Around went the shiny white tie, securely cuffing my wrists. He reached down and pulled out three more of the long ties when a knock came at the door.

I hoped it was the police coming to rescue me and take away Spider-Webbed Assailant before I, literally, dismembered him. Threaten my kid, and I will kill you. I will rip off your balls and choke you with them. Dead.

If not the police, I'd even settle for Kevin, or Silvia Kravitz. How she lived so close to drug dealers and only found the time to complain about two old people having loud sex was mind-boggling.

"Who is it?" hollered my assailant.

My breath hitched as we waited to see who our visitor was.

"It's maintenance," came the two most beautiful words I'd ever heard. Chase, despite our earlier kerfuffle, had come to rescue me. My hero.

"Not now, man," Spider-Webbed Assailant said, placing the end of a zip tie between his teeth, not detoured by my drill-toting knight in shining armor.

"Come on, man," Chase begged. "I've got to get to this before I leave." He was quite convincing, I'd give him that. I was ready for him to drop the act, though, and kick the door open. Or use his copy of the master key.

Spider-Webbed Assailant rolled his eyes and clenched his jaw, attaching the last zip tie to his circle. I didn't like where this was going—it looked like a noose.

Chase pounded on the door. "Open up! Or deal's off." This sent my assailant into a blind rage. He dropped the plastic lariat he was so carefully constructing to the ground and grabbed a roll of duct tape.

"Not one word," he warned, ripping a piece of tape off with his teeth before slapping it over my mouth. He walked to the door, his fists balled tight and forearms flexed.

"Deal's already off," he declared upon opening the door.

I shimmied my arms under my butt, pulled my knees together and looped them through my arms. *OK, Cambria, you can't screw this one up. Up high over your head, elbows together, good.*

*Now, bring them down quickly and chicken-wing your arms out to the side.*

It didn't work.

*Again.*

Nope.

*The guy on YouTube made this look so easy.*

"Come on, man, just give me a taste of whatever you got," Chase said in an uncharacteristically lazy drawl. He was either playing a role to trick his way into the apartment, or I'd missed a Titanic iceberg of a detail in the case I already solved.

*OK, Cambria, last time. Arms up high over your head, elbows together, bring them down quickly and chicken-wing your arms out and... SNAP!* My hands were free (thank you, Internet!). I ripped the tape, taking my lips with it, or so it felt, and scrambled to my feet. My Jell-O-y legs carried me to the living room. Chase standing with Rev, in no rush to rescue me.

"Cambria?" he asked, confused.

"Chase, what..." My eyes ventured down to the tiny white baggie in his hand.

*No.*

I felt sick. I felt betrayed. I felt the need to inflict bodily harm. The rage burned so deep I no longer had control over it.

"You bastard!" I lunged toward him, knocking him into the wall. I shoved him against the wall again and again and again. He didn't put up a fight. My assailant didn't try to stop me either. He was actually laughing.

Just then, the door flew open, and in stormed a heavily armored man with a rifle pointed at my face. "Freeze!"

*Now here's my knight in shining armor. Finally!*

A gang of police officers, dressed in black and carrying guns, barged through the door. One gun pointed at Rev, who knew the drill and was already down on his knees with his hands high in the air.

"Hands up!" yelled my not-so-friendly knight. "I said hands up."

"You don't understand!" I released Chase, turning around to explain.

"Hands up!" he repeated.

Chase fell to the ground, clasping his hands behind his head instead of putting them up—*he can't even follow the police officer's instructions.*

"I said, hands up, now!" the rifle-toting officer yelled.

*This isn't happening.*

"Look," I tried to explain again. "I promise I'm not—"

"Up!" Now there were three guns pointed at my head. Obviously, they were not in the mood to listen. I dropped to my knees, bringing my hands up as high as they would go.

A policeman pushed me to the ground. "Ouch! I didn't do anything," I pleaded with the man, whose knee was in my back. He forced my hands together, and slapped a cold, metal cuff over each wrist. "I'm the victim here. I promise I didn't do anything!" He led me through the door and out to the spectacle in the carports—dark SUVs, squad cars, a German Shepherd being escorted around by a policewoman, scores of people watching. I half expected a news crew to show up along with a helicopter.

"Cam!" I heard the familiar voice and looked over my shoulder to scan the crowd. Tom stood behind two police officers. Lilly was balanced on his hip, her face digging into her daddy's shoulder. "Don't say anything! I'll meet you there!" Tom yelled.

This was really happening, I realized. I was being arrested, real handcuffs and all. My feet felt as if they were made of cinderblocks, and I dragged them to the police car. One hand on my head and I was pushed down into the backseat.

Kevin came flying through the crowd. "No! Stop! That's my apartment manager," he screamed. Sometime, during all the fuss, his clothes had disappeared. A police officer wrapped his arm around Kevin's bare waist. "Let go of me! Do you know who I am?" Then he was on the ground, hands pulled behind his back and on went the cuffs.

I dropped my head back against the seat, listening to the world collapsing around me.

*There's no question about it now. I am so losing my job.*

# Chapter 30

*Tenant shall be liable for all legal expenses if Tenant should have
Landlord falsely jailed.*

My chauffeuring police officer had dark, creamy skin, a
dusting of black hair over his top lip, and a boyish face—like a
twelve-year-old dressed in a policeman's costume. Instead of a
badge and a gun, he should be carrying a pillowcase going
door-to-door saying "trick-or-treat."

He led me through the back door of the police station and
down a long busy hallway. We stopped at an unlabeled steel
door, and the officer, to my surprise, removed the handcuffs
and instructed me to wait in the chair. The room was small,
warm and gray. Two fluorescent tubes hummed from the
ceiling, filling the small space with bright light. I sat at a table
long enough to double as a bed, with an empty chair across
from me.

I inspected the red marks on my wrists, the raw burns
from the great zip-tie escape that turned out to be everything
*but* great. No doubt I'd be sitting at home instead of in an
interrogation room if the police had found me tied up. I
hadn't been booked, at least not yet. No fingerprints. No mug
shot—for which I was grateful. I caught a reflection of the
train wreck that was my face and bird's nest that was Einstein
in the cruiser's window. Call me vain, but I wanted at least a

decent-looking mug shot if I had to get one. Those follow you forever.

It struck me as odd that I'd been so dramatically paraded out in cuffs and shoved into the back of a police car only to be questioned. The information of my innocence must have come to the police while we were en route to the station. Now I'd be forced to give a full statement before I could go home.

Or so I thought.

The door opened. A woman in a suit that matched the walls stepped in. Her skin sagged, as did her ill-fitted suit.

She stared at me so intently my palms began to sweat, and then she paced over to the opposite chair, remaining on her feet, one hand on her hip, the other holding a manila folder. "I'm Detective Angela Spray," she said with a forced grin.

I flattened my hands on my thighs to keep my legs from shaking.

The detective cocked her head, staring at me with an unreadable expression. "Rough day, huh?"

I nodded.

She took a seat and leaned forward casually as if we were two long-time friends about to have coffee. "Some tea? Water? Soda?"

I shook my head.

"I have a few questions for you so we can clear this up. OK?"

I nodded.

"I need you to answer verbally, please."

"Yes."

"Can you state your full name?"

"Cambria Jane Clyne," I answered so softly I could barely hear myself.

Detective Spray either had excellent hearing or didn't care what my full name was. Or perhaps she already knew. "Thank you, Cambria." She paused, slowly drumming her fingers on the tabletop. Painfully slow, starting with her pinky and ending with her pointer finger only to start the rhythm over again. My stomach clenched. If she was trying to create a comfortable environment, one to make it easy for me to share the details of the traumatic event, then she was really sucking at it. "It's been a hard time for you, Cambria. Laid off, an eviction filed against you, new job isn't going so well, and money is tight. You've got to be feeling desperate. Needing to provide for your daughter, and then there's the added stress of being a single parent."

*Again, not feeling comfortable here.*

"I talked to your buddy Rev," she said.

My heart flipped. "He's not my buddy."

"No? He's not? That's interesting." She spoke slowly and then cleared her throat, much like I did when I was mentally preparing my next words. "You've had a lot of contact with the police recently. Haven't you?"

I nodded. "There's been a lot of crime in the community."

With not an ounce of sympathy, the detective placed her elbows on the table and stared into my eyes. I squirmed. "It's a good tactic." She chuckled, clasping her hands together. "Pretty genius really. Calling the police, making reports and telling them about this tenant who is engaging in criminal activity when you yourself were the one working with one of the biggest drug dealers in the city. Takes all the focus off you. I get it. You're in financial ruin and have to take care of your child."

"What?" I squeaked. "I don't have anything to do with drugs."

"Then why were you in Vincent's apartment?" She stiffened, like a dog ready to attack. "Why were you in the middle of a drug transaction?"

*What is happening?* "I was on the carport roof, and Rev pulled me down and dragged me into the apartment. If you spoke to him already, then you should know this."

"You were on the roof?"

"Yes. I climbed up there to see if I could find anything incriminating. I thought maybe Alice was breaking into cars."

The detective leaned back, staring at the ceiling as if her next question were written across it. The fluorescent lights buzzed and flickered, only adding to the intimidating ambiance. "You climbed an eight-foot-high stucco wall?"

"No, I got a lift up from Kevin."

"The one we arrested? The one so strung out he could

barely walk?"

I felt faint. "Look, I had nothing do with this. I'm just the apartment manager. Rev was holding me against my will. Since when is the victim treated like a criminal?"

"When we arrived you were engaged in a one-sided physical altercation with Chase Hudson. How was it you were being held against your will?"

"I was mad at him because he'd been lying to me."

"Lying to you about what?"

"About his involvement."

"His involvement in this case?"

"Sure, the case, the drugs, whatever. I was mad that he was buying drugs from Rev."

She nodded her head, as if answering an internal question. "Tell me this, Cambria. If you're just the apartment manager, innocently caught up in this, then how did you know Malone's exact location?"

"What?"

"Malone's location." She pulled a sheet of paper from the manila folder and read it out loud. "*Vincent meeting Malone now at alcove. Rev. Alice has been gone walking property.* His inner circle is tight-lipped. He keeps a low profile, nearly impossible to locate. And you expect me to believe you just so happened to come across this information?"

I was confused beyond comprehension. "How did you even know I…" Crap. *Did they tap my phone?* "Wait. No, no, no. I'm not supposed to be talking," I thought out loud. Tom said not to say anything. Keeping broke, innocent people out of jail was what he did for a living. I was both broke and innocent. "I want to see my lawyer. Right now."

She stared at me. "You're not involved with Malone at all but already have a lawyer?"

I clasped my hands together to keep them from shaking. "Thomas Dreyer is my attorney. He's here waiting for me." *I hope.*

# Chapter 31

*Landlord will be out of the office for personal or business reasons periodically during the term of the Lease.*

Requesting to speak to an attorney didn't make Detective Spray very happy, and she had no qualms about letting me know it either, not by verbalizing her displeasure, but by leaving me alone in the small, gray, hot room for several hours... or days... maybe weeks. There was no clock, no window to gauge the time. It felt like an eternity before Tom barged through the door. He'd ditched his Lakers shirt and sandals for a black suit, blue tie, blue shirt and loafers. He took a seat. "Are you OK?"

I was sitting in an interrogation room having just been cuffed and searched and stuffed into the back of a police car, and he had to ask *are you OK?* I was losing confidence in his lawyering abilities. "What took you so long? And where is our daughter?" I snapped.

After waiting in this horrid room for ages, my patience had worn thin. I was about to be tried and convicted for something I didn't do. I'd spend my life in prison with a crazy cellmate named Betty who never showered, stole my stuff and was doing time for a crime so heinous I'd be forced to sleep with one eye open.

Leaving someone like me with a wild imagination in a

small room should be deemed cruel and unusual punishment.

"I dropped off Lilly with Mrs. Nguyen and changed. I had these clothes in my car. Trust me, I hurried."

He placed a black leather folder on the table, flipped it open to a notepad and clicked his pen. "Right now, they're only questioning your involvement. You haven't been booked yet, but if you are booked, you're looking at possible charges of possession with intent to distribute," Tom said matter-of-factly, as if he were telling me the score of the Dodgers game or what he ate for dinner.

My heart thundered in my chest. I nearly flew over the table. "What? You have got to be kidding me." I stood and paced the room, squeaking my Converses from one corner to the next in three steps.

"I told you not to say anything," Tom said.

"I didn't know I was being questioned. I thought they were just taking a report."

"And they didn't read you your Miranda rights?"

I ignored him, still pacing. "I can't believe this is happening to me. Me! I've never touched a drug in my life. This is a complete injustice. I was being held hostage—he zip-tied my hands. Look!" I held out my wrists to show him the fresh red marks.

Tom grabbed my hands and pulled me closer to inspect, touching the wounds as if making sure they were real. "Cambria," he whispered. He rarely used my full name, so I knew I'd struck a nerve. "Sit down, and tell me everything from the beginning."

I fell down into the uncomfortable chair and launched into my story. "I was on the carport roof when I overheard Alice, or Wysteria, she could go by both or neither, and Vincent, the resident in 39. They were talking about Vincent meeting Malone at Alcove in a few minutes. I don't even know what that means. He left, and so did she, I guess. I didn't see her in the apartment unless she was hiding. I sent myself a text message with all the information."

I crossed my legs and uncrossed them, unable to get comfortable in the chair. Or in the situation. "The detective was talking about the text I sent myself. Do you think they've been watching me? That they tapped my phone?"

"I don't think so," Tom said, jotting down the information on his notepad. "They probably found your phone when they searched the apartment. Cam, it's not you they want. Malone is a *major* drug dealer in the area. They've been building a case against him for a long time. Then here you come with his location, allowing them to make the arrest, and then they find you in the apartment involved in a drug deal. Looks suspicious. Plus, they have Rev down the hall saying you're a customer and that's why you took the apartment management job."

"What?" I was up on my feet again, pacing the floor, wringing my hands. This had gotten out of control so fast. "Chase was the one buying whatever it was they were selling."

"Cocaine."

"Yes, Chase was buying cocaine. I was trying to leave, then the police officer came and I... *ugh.*" I fell back on the chair.

Tom dropped his pen. "I told you I knew him. I've seen him down at the courthouse before. I knew it."

"Fine, you were right, I was wrong. Would you like to write that down on your notepad?" He took me up on the offer and wrote it in the margin. "As I was saying, I wasn't involved. I was trying to get away, except... ugh." I buried my face in my hands. "Instead of leaving I started beating the crap out of Chase."

Tom chuckled.

"It's not funny."

He sucked in his bottom lip and clicked the end of his pen against his temple repeatedly, staring down at his illegible notes. "It would only be funny if he was hospitalized," he added under his breath. "Look, as I said, they're not after you. Their main concern was how you knew about Malone and why you were in the apartment." He stared down at his notes again, nodding his head. "They didn't read you your rights, and detaining you for this long is a direct violation of your fourth amendment rights." He reached across the table and grabbed my hand, giving it a reassuring squeeze. I wondered if he did this with all his clients. "Hang tight. I'll be right back."

# Chapter 32

*As previously mentioned, Landlord reserves the right to at least one mental breakdown during the Lease term.*

Any size room turns into a miniature, suffocating box when you're awaiting vindicating news—let alone an actual miniature, suffocating box. The internal battle to remain upright and sane was becoming harder to win. I was ready to confess to just about any crime if they'd let me out. In an effort to stay lucid, I concentrated on the flood of questions spinning through my head at hyper speed—*Where did Alice go? Did Vincent get away? Was he arrested? If Kevin had called the police, wouldn't they have known I was being held against my will? Would they have sent a SWAT team? Who was Rev, and where did he come from? Why would he say I was buying drugs from him? I'd never met him, had I? Did they really believe him? Was Vincent the father of Alice's baby? Or Rev? Or this Malone person? Did Joyce know about Vincent?*

Most of all, I thought about the cute maintenance guy who had betrayed Patrick. He betrayed the property. He betrayed all the residents.

He betrayed me.

It was no wonder he was terrible at his job; he was too high to fix anything.

I felt used. Sick. Confused. How could I have gotten everything so backward? He knew how I felt about him. I'm not that good of an actor, and I'm obviously terrible at hiding. He used my gag-worthy girly emotions to his advantage. It was humiliating.

Still, call me stupid, but I held on to a thread of fraying hope that Chase would not mention my name in his confession. I'd been doing his job for him for the last week. Fixing everything he had "fixed." He never did remove Joyce's smoky armoire from my room. Seemed the least he could do was confirm I was nothing more than a nosy apartment manager who was desperate to keep her job. Unless…

*Oh no, was Chase the father?*

This could have a very soap opera-y ending.

The door opened, and Detective Spray walked in. My throat tightened. My lips went numb. My stomach knotted. Her expression remained unreadable, but the door was open. Was this an invitation to leave? Was I free to go?

Then Tom appeared at the door. His face was drawn and worried, but his familiar scent was calming—woody, citrusy with a hint of fabric softener. He dragged a chair next to mine and took a seat, opening his leather folder on the table. *Sent text to Chase* was scrawled across the top.

"What's that?" I asked Tom.

"You said you sent yourself a text message," Detective Spray answered for Tom, entering the room and standing across the table from us. "Why send the information to Mr. Hudson as well?"

I was so confused, I didn't know what she was talking about, so I said, "I'm so confused, I don't know what you're talking about."

"You sent a text about Malone's location at six-thirteen yesterday evening to Chase Hudson's cell phone. Why specifically did you send the information to him?"

*Yesterday?*

Detective Spray slid a paper across the table. "These are the last dozen or so texts retrieved from Mr. Hudson's phone. Look familiar?"

I took the paper and scanned the texts.

*Hudson: 32 is fixed*

*Clyne: She just called to say her toilet is still backing up. Can you*

*re-fix, plz*
     Hudson: *Will after lunch*
     Clyne: *Nvm. Took care of it.*
     Clyne: *Not sure what happened just now? Why did you leave?*
*Thanks for fixing the printer. But can you look at 22 g/ d?*
     Clyne: *Excedrin. Soap. Bread. Peanut butter.*
     Clyne: *Sorry! Disregard.*
     Clyne: *Did you look at 22 garbage disposal? Plz*
     Clyne: *Hello?*
     Clyne: *Vincent meeting Malone now at alcove. Rev. Alice has been*
*gone walking property.*

I read the report several times over, shaking my head. "I must have texted Chase on accident. I meant to text myself. I've done this before, texting him on accident, see." I pointed to the grocery list. I remembered I was *this* close to adding tampons to the list. "I promise you, I thought I sent this to myself and was planning on calling the police once I got off the roof. I didn't know who Malone was. I only knew something bad was happening in that apartment." I slid the paper back to Spray. "Rev pulled me off the carport roof and into his apartment, zip-tied my hands, and I was only able to escape because Chase knocked on the door and distracted him." Tears pooled in my eyes. I blinked hard to keep them from spilling down my cheeks.

Spray was unmoved. "Was Wysteria in the apartment?"

I shook my head.

"Do you know where she might be?"

Tom snapped his folder shut and tapped his watch. "She said she doesn't know. You've got nothing else. I think we've been here long enough. Done?"

Spray gave him a disconcerted look. "For now."

# Chapter 33

*Tenant agrees that Landlord will seek revenge if Tenant makes Landlord's life a living hell.*

With his hand pressed firmly on my lower back, Tom led me through the station to the lobby.

It smelled like BO, onions and cologne. In that order.

We passed a man in an Ironman costume who was recounting his tale to a police officer behind a pane of bulletproof glass. It was obvious the sun had long since set, and the full moon had taken center stage.

*How long have I been here?*

We neared an old woman seated near the exit. Her mouth was void of teeth, and a gray version of Einstein sprung from her head. Several grocery bags were piled in her lap. She looked exactly as I pictured Betty, my soon-to-be cellmate.

*I don't want to go to jail.*

"Can you tell me what you know?" I asked Tom.

He loosened his tie and smiled, but it was without conviction. "We'll talk about it in the car."

"No, now. Am I going to end up back here? Maybe I need to give a more detailed report of what happened. I was so flustered, I don't think I got my point across."

"There's nothing you can do right now." He placed his hand on my shoulder and looked me in the eyes. "OK?"

I shook my head. Nothing was *OK*. Frankly, I was tired of that word. "I'm not *OK*. I was arrested today. One of my residents was dealing drugs out of his apartment. My maintenance man was buying them. So was... holy crap. Kevin. We forgot about Kevin."

"We forgot about Kevin," the old woman who looked like Betty repeated.

"Kevin?" Tom asked, ignoring Betty.

"He's the son of the owner of the building," I explained. "He was arrested too. The naked guy." Tom nodded, understanding whom I was referencing. How could you not? "I doubt his family would send a lawyer. Trust me, if you knew his story you'd be all over this."

"All over this," Betty parroted, letting out a Wicked Witch-inspired cackle. "Naked. Naked. Naked. Naked."

Tom placed a hand on my lower back again, urging me away from the cackling stranger. I didn't move. "Tom, help him," I pleaded.

He grunted. "He's the owner's son?" I nodded. "What's his last name?"

"Kevin... I actually don't remember his last name. It starts with a Mc." I bit my lip, flipping through my memory bank. Kevin's file only said "Kevin" as if he were Prince or Cher. I'd read the family trust name on paperwork before...

Betty began spitting out last name options. "McFarlin. McDonald. McDermott..."

"I love Dylan McDermott," a woman chimed in. She had a teased pouf of red hair and bright orange lipstick. She was wearing a pleather tube top and a leopard-print short, short skirt. "He was in that show *The Practice*. You look like him you know. Like a young Dylan McDermott." She pointed a crimson fingernail at Tom and winked. He blushed.

I studied Tom's profile with a musing tilt of my head. I'd never made the connection before. "You know what? I can see it now. A little... if you squint your eyes," I said to the woman. "Oh, hold on. I got it. It's McMills. Kevin McMills."

Betty applauded and then threw a starlight mint at us. It bounced off Tom's face.

"Let's go," he barked.

"But my mint," I pouted.

Tom's eyes were ablaze and jaw tight. It was the angriest I'd seen him since...well... since that morning.

"What's wrong with you, Cambria? None of this is funny. Do you realize how bad this could have been? You could have been killed. You could have been raped and then killed. You could have been tortured, raped and then killed. Why aren't you taking this more seriously?" His eyes glistened. *Is he going to cry?* "Do you realize the only reason I was able to get you out of here was because of some technicalities? What would possess you to put yourself in this situation? You just got yourself involved in a major drug operation."

I didn't answer. I didn't know how to. He was clearly upset with me, maybe because he'd spent all night at the police station, or because he knew he'd never get paid for his time, or because he was as tired and hungry as I was. Or maybe he truly was pissed at me for putting myself in this situation. Regardless, if anyone had the right to be mad it was me, but I wasn't. I was too tired and emotionally bruised to be angry—at least not yet. And I didn't want to fight with Tom, especially after all he had done.

"Thank you for everything. I'm sorry if I put you out," I said, my voice small.

"You didn't put me out, Cam." He exhaled and ran his hands down his face. "I'll go find out what happened with Kevin. You..." He looked around the room. "Just... sit here." He pointed to an empty chair next to a man with a bloody tissue up his nose. "And don't talk or leave with anyone."

*Seriously?*

Tom stalked off to speak to a policewoman behind the glass, glancing over his shoulder to be sure I was following instructions, as if I were an unruly child. His mood was out of character. He was the even-tempered "everything is gonna be totally fine" one. I was the pessimistic over-reactor. If we were switching roles, he should have discussed it with me first.

# Chapter 34

*Tenant forfeits security deposit if Tenant turns out to be a complete psychopath.*

Tom sat behind the wheel of his 4Runner, one hand draped over the steering wheel and the other clutching the armrest. His eyes darted to Kevin's reflection in the rearview mirror, then to me, then to the road, only to repeat the rotation again. Kevin was squished in the backseat between Lilly's car seat and the window. He was swimming in Tom's Laker shirt and khakis, with his feet slipped into Tom's three-sizes-too-big sandals. He stared out the window, his face etched in sadness. Tom said people can be depressed when they come down from a cocaine binge, and Kevin was no exception. Especially when you added in the possession of cocaine, resisting arrest, and public nudity charges—he had plenty to be unhappy about.

"Hey, Kevin," I said, turning around in the passenger seat to face him. "Did you happen to see Chase when you were in there?" He continued to stare out the window, not answering. "You ever see him visiting Apartment Thirty-nine?"

"He was there all the time," he said, monotone, to the window.

My heart sank. Regardless of the fact that Chase had been arrested, and that the police had his phone records, I still hung on to the hope he'd mistakenly been caught up in all this. Like I was.

"I wish you would have told me," I said. "I was completely broadsided."

Kevin exhaled, fogging the window enough to write his name in it. "I didn't say anything because you were screwing each other and I figured you must have known."

I was shaking my head before he even finished his sentence. "Nope, that's not true. Nothing happened at all."

"You wanted it to then." True. Not something I wanted revealed in front of Tom, especially after his outburst over Chase spending the night.

I flipped back into the passenger seat, fidgeting with my seatbelt. "He must still be high," I told Tom. He returned a half-hearted smile and pulled into the parking lot of the apartments. The SUV bounced over the uneven pavement until we arrived at the entryway, near Kevin's apartment.

The place was quiet, nearly four in the morning, and only a few windows showed signs of life—the blue glow from a television or the dull light of a lamp. If I hadn't spent the entire day in hell, I'd be tucked into my own bed sound asleep as well.

"Remember, Kevin, Sunday at ten," Tom said to the rearview mirror. "Keep the clothes, and wear a suit and tie if you have one."

Kevin slipped out the door without answering, slamming it shut behind him. He looked like a child in adult clothing shuffling along the pathway to his apartment.

Poor Kevin.

I leaned back against the headrest. *What a long, terrible, terrible day.* Tom looked about as exhausted as I felt, his face pale, the top button of his shirt undone and tie pulled loose.

He began mindlessly playing with the keys dangling from the ignition. I noticed the bronze circular keychain hiding in the mass of keys, the one with "I Love Daddy" stamped in the middle. A gift I had bought him for his first Father's Day. I had wrapped it in blue wrapping paper (his favorite color) and attached a homemade card with Lilly's handprint on the cover. I said it was from Lilly, but of course there was no way she crawled down to Hollywood Boulevard to purchase it for him, nor did she wrap it, tie a bow or even know it was Father's Day. Tom never said anything. ANYTHING. He barely acknowledged the gift. Not even a blasé "thanks." I was pissed. PISSED. And still bitter over it. At least, I had been until I noticed the keychain hanging from his ignition, weathered from years of use. I'd never noticed it on his key ring before. Probably because this was the most time we had ever spent together since... well... since the night we made Lilly.

"What time do I need to get Lilly from Mrs. Nguyen?" I asked.

"I told her I'd call first thing in the morning to let her know when I'd be able to pick Lilly up. I checked in with her before I knew what was happening with you." Tom let out an exhausted sigh.

"Do you think I'm going to jail?"

He shook his head. "They aren't after you, Cam. This is a huge case for them, one they've been working on for some time now. You were proving problematic at first because you kept calling the police and staking out apartments, but still, they figured you were harmless. Chase and Kevin both corroborated your story. Detective Spray was really stuck on why you sent that text message. She could have a few more questions, but you had been detained for far too..." He paused for so long I thought he had fallen asleep until he said, "I wouldn't be surprised if they contacted you for some more of that stuff."

"That stuff?" I snorted. "Did you just fall asleep?"

"A little," he confessed, flashing his signature side-smirk.

I laughed much harder than the situation called for. "Go get some sleep."

"That's the best idea you've had today." He chuckled a tired chuckle and shifted the car into reverse.

"Wait." I placed my hand on his arm. He tensed under my touch. "Let me get out first."

"I thought you were staying with me."

"Why would I do that?"

"I figured you wouldn't want to be alone, plus you said

you were losing your job, your apartment… your parents think I'm gay… ring a bell?"

Oh. That. You know it's been a bad day when losing your job slips your mind. Life had been hell since becoming an apartment manager. After Patrick found out I was not the one to move drug dealers onto the property, would he let me keep my job? Would I still want it?

I didn't know.

All I knew for certain was that Tom was right—I didn't want to be alone.

"Before we go," I said, "can I go to Vincent's carport? I want my phone back." I felt naked without it, as if I were missing an appendage.

"Not a good idea."

"Why not? I have to answer the emergency line."

He gave me a "you've got to be kidding me" look.

"What am I supposed to do then?" I asked.

"You're going to have to wait until we're sure the police have finished examining the area."

Now it was my turn to give him a "you've got to be kidding me" look.

Finally, Tom sighed, clicked his seatbelt free and reached for the door. "I can't believe I'm doing this," he groaned. "I doubt it's even up there, but I'll go check."

"Really?" I was surprised, and thankful. He was going above and beyond his lawyering and baby daddy duties. *I'll have to buy him lunch or dinner for his help.* I still had those free burrito coupons. "I promise I'll stay here and not move, ever," I teased.

Tom allowed himself a small smile. "I think I'd like that," he said, more to himself than me, looking surprised at his own words as he opened the door and slid off the seat.

*I think I'd like that?*

*What does that mean?*

I propped my elbow on the windowsill and watched Tom stroll toward 39's patio fence. Was he throwing me a life raft? A means of escaping the Alcatraz Island I'd been trapped on since I uttered the words "I'm pregnant" nearly four years ago?

No.

He couldn't be.

Or could he?

I hadn't been down the "maybe" road with him in years. Not wanting to get my hopes up only to have them squashed by his playboy ways. It was the family life I'd longed for since my parents' divorce eighteen years ago. A real family—a mom, dad, kid all under one roof kind of family. It was easy to picture Tom, Lilly and me all gathered around the kitchen table eating the mac and cheese I made from the dusty cookbook my mom had given me. Tom would make Lilly laugh, distracting her from her food. I'd playfully scold him but secretly love every second of it. Family vacations to the snow, all three of us clothed in mittens and scarfs and puffy jackets, building a snowman, or sledding down a hill. Then there'd be soccer games, me as the coach, him as the team parent, Lilly as the star player. Family pictures at the beach in jeans and coordinating shirts. Eventually, a little brother or sister would be added to the mix…

It was a warm thought. Everything I'd ever wanted.

Then my mind took a swift left turn, and the green-eyed maintenance boy entered the picture. Chase and his ridiculously perfect hips, the way they swayed when he walked. The way his jeans hung off them in the right way. In my daydreams he didn't have to be a criminal. In my daydreams he could be an upright citizen, an excellent maintenance man, and an even better boyfriend, eventual fiancé, husband, stepfather and then father. He'd be wonderful with Lilly, taking on the stepfather role with ease…

*What's wrong with me?*

Why couldn't I get Chase out of my head? Why would I ever entertain a thought with him in it? Ugh, I was developing Bonnie and Clyde Syndrome.

*Hold on.*

I'd never daydreamed or fantasized about Tom. I'd never pined over him. I'd never imagined what it would be like to be with *him*. To make love sober. To sleep in his arms. To kiss. Sure, I'd spent many nights in tears over this man I loved who didn't love me back. But was I ever in love with *him* or was I simply in love with the idea of him? In love with the family aspect he brought to the table? Of course Tom was nice, and he was also attractive—very attractive. Apparently he looked like a young Dylan McDermott. Was I attracted to him though? If I hadn't gotten pregnant, would I have bothered calling him again, ever?

*I don't know.*

It could have been post-traumatic stress, the fact I hadn't eaten since noon, or the exhaustion screwing with my mind, but I honestly couldn't answer the question.

Maybe the fact that I couldn't answer was the answer?

*My head hurts.*

This was all too much thinking for four in the morning.

*Wait.*

*Where's Tom?*

Too busy philosophizing, I'd forgotten what was happening. Tom was nowhere in sight. I pulled the keys out of the ignition and jumped out of the car, locking it over my shoulder with the remote. I headed to the wall, the one I had so ungracefully climbed hours earlier. Cupping my hands around my mouth, I loudly whispered, "Let's go, Tom."

Nothing.

"Psst, Tom. Don't worry about my phone." A sudden chill ran down my spine. I glanced over my shoulder expecting to find someone, but no one was there.

I walked slowly into the carports. It was dark. Only one of the four lights worked.

*Note to self: Fill out maintenance request for back carport lights.*

*Crap.*

*Note to self: Find maintenance man.*

*Crap.*

*Note to self: Make sure I don't find him attractive.*

All the parking stalls were filled with cars except for Vincent's assigned space, which was empty. The cement was stained with oil, and the wall looked to have been hit by a bumper on more than one occasion.

"Tom?" I called out. The air took on an eerie vibe, causing every hair on my arms to stand up. "Hello? Tom? Hello?"

"Hello," came a familiar voice from behind.

My heart leapt so far out of my chest, it was sailing over San Francisco about to cross the Oregon border by the time I realized what was happening.

Without a heart to keep me vertical, I collapsed to the ground and... died.

# Chapter 35

*R.I.P.*

Or so it felt.

Clutching my chest, I gasped for air, beckoning my heart to return. Tom wrapped his long arms around my trembling frame. "I didn't mean to scare you," he apologized, holding me tighter.

I clutched his arm, digging my nails into his triceps.

"Shh," Tom whispered, stroking the back of my head as if petting a dog. "It's OK, it's just me. You're fine."

Slowly, my heart returned to my chest cavity and began beating at a normal rhythm. The feeling returned to my legs and the air to my lungs.

"You OK?" asked Tom.

"No," I snapped. "Stop asking me that." I inhaled a long breath through my nose and released it through my mouth. In through my nose, out through my mouth. In, out, in, out...

*Calm down, Cambria. Calm down.*

Stabilized, I turned and gave Tom a fierce stare down.

"I've got your phone," he said, holding it up.

"Forgiven." I snatched it out of his hand and unlocked the screen. Eighteen missed calls, a full voicemail box, and seven text messages (one from Amy, five from Tom, and one from AT&T letting me know I was nearing the end of my data usage). All but one of the missed calls were from the emergency line. Residents calling to complain about their apartment manager being arrested, or so I figured. One was from Patrick.

"Cambria, let's go back now," Tom said. But I was too absorbed in my phone.

"Cambria!" Tom sounded annoyed.

"What are you mad about now..." I looked up, and that's when I caught the shadowed figure coming toward us. Crap.

Tom saw it too. "Let's *go*." He didn't have to tell me twice! Er, well, actually he did.

We'd nearly made it out of the parking stall when the shadow revealed its familiar face.

Alice.

My skin prickled in goose bumps. "Hey there," I said, trying to sound casual. "What's up?"

Alice was wringing her hands. She had on the same outfit as earlier, sweatshirt and jeans. Under the glow of the one working light, the bruises on her neck and melasma on her face were faint, but still there.

"I totally just came back, and everyone is gone, and there's a huge mess in the apartment." Her voice cracked.

I eyed Tom. He wasn't buying it. Neither was I.

"Sorry about that," Tom said to her. Then he turned to me. "I think I left the car running. Why don't you check on that for me?" His eyes screamed *get out now!*

"No!" Alice yelped. "I'm glad you're here, Cambria. You were right all along. Vincent trapped me. He was abusive and mixed up in the wrong crowd. You could see it. You know I had nothing to do with this. I'm desperate." She dropped her head into her hands and unleashed a tearless cry. It was a performance worthy of a 1990s made-for-television movie.

She could be crazy, and according to my theory, she could also be a hormonal criminal. So I humored her. "You're right, Alice. I know you didn't have anything to do with all of this. We're not here to get you in trouble. I only wanted my phone."

She smiled. "I knew you'd understand. I just don't have anywhere to go. I'm, like, totally broke. If only I had some way to get away from Vincent before he makes bail and comes after me."

She was beginning to tug on my heartstrings. Could I have had this wrong all along? Could she have been trapped? Was she just an innocent bystander? After all, she wasn't in jail.

"Cambria," Tom quickly jumped in. "Cambria, go back to the office and see if there's any deposit left for Alice." His voice was steady, his arms casually at his side. If it weren't for the use of my full name, I'd believe he was being serious.

He knew something. Something bad.

"Go, Cambria," he pressed again. I wasn't about to leave him alone. He had no idea she was pregnant. He'd end up dead. Heaven knows I nearly killed him a few times when I was pregnant with Lilly.

"I need you to come with me to help," I said.

"Cambria, please don't go. I need to explain to you what happened. Like, I had nothing to do with any of the problems around here."

She was nervous. I could tell. She knew we weren't buying it. Yet, standing there in front of Alice, near the apartment I'd been dragged through only hours earlier, I lost all grasp on rationality. I'd been taken hostage by rage. Blinding rage. This woman had made my life a living hell, and she had the audacity to stand here and sweetly pretend she was innocent? To ask, in a roundabout way, for money? I lost control. "I'm not going to pretend I don't know you're the reason this community has gone to hell."

Tom wrapped me in a protective embrace. "We're done here."

Click.

"No you're not!" Alice sneered, holding up a black revolver. Much like the one I found in the Dumpster.

*Why do I have such a big mouth?* I asked in my head, or so I thought, until Tom nodded in agreement.

"Put your hands up, both of you," Alice ordered, now holding the gun with both hands. Her feet were spread wide, her eyes focused. Tom held up his palms, and I followed suit.

"You're looking at two to four years right now, and if you pull that trigger, it's life," Tom stated, as if this were a helpful tidbit of information to give to a woman pointing a gun at your face. *Men.*

"Think of your baby," I said, attempting to tug on *her* heartstrings (assuming she had any). "You don't want to do this. You don't want to have your baby in prison. Put the gun down, and we'll forget about it."

Alice looked at me as if I were wearing a unicorn costume. "Like you're going to forget about it. I mean, like, you climbed into our patio. Who does that? You're such an idiot. You, like, think I didn't see you? You think, like, you didn't set this whole thing in motion yourself? Seriously? How do you think Vincent got arrested? Huh? You think, like, what, I didn't know you were eavesdropping? You think I didn't give you Malone's location? I needed to get rid of Vincent and get the hell out of here, and I knew I could count on you." She laughed a vile laugh. "You think I'm gonna let you go, like you'd actually forget about this? I *am* thinking of my baby. That's the reason I'm here. That's the reason I've done everything I can to get a better ma…" She cleared her throat. "To get out of here. To get us away from Vincent." She smiled, raised the gun and pointed it at my chest. "And I wouldn't want to have my baby in jail. You're right on that one."

In a slow-moving blur of motion, Tom leaped from my side and knocked Alice to the ground. A shot fired. Then another. A horrifying scream echoed around us. It took me a minute to realize the shrieks were coming from my own mouth. Involuntarily rocketing from my core—screams of pure horror. I fell to my knees and stared down at the blood. My hands shaking uncontrollably. So much blood. So much…

# Chapter 36

*In the event of a life-threatening medical emergency, Tenant is encouraged to call 9-1-1 immediately, not the after-hours emergency line.*

The ill-fitted gray suit detective was back, except on my turf now. "I know this is difficult for you right now," she said, forced compassion lacing her words. "Did she mention how long she'd been involved with Malone?" I was sitting in the back of an ambulance, my feet propped up on the bumper. I pulled the blanket the paramedic had draped over my shoulders tighter. My body shook as if I were sitting on an ice cap, not in seventy-five degree October temperatures. The paramedic told me I was coming down from the shock and encouraged me to lie down on the gurney, but I refused. They didn't need to spend time on me. The blood soaking my shirt was not my own.

Silvia stepped in front of the detective and handed me a glass of water. "Here, drink this." I took it appreciatively, trying not to spill as I brought it to my chapped lips. Silvia readjusted her robe, pulling it around her tiny waist. It was the first time I'd seen her without Harold. "It helps with shock," she explained, sounding as if she spoke from experience. If she could move her face, I think she would have a sympathetic expression.

She was the first of the residents to pour out of their

apartments after the gun went off, the one to call 9-1-1 and the one who wiped away the blood splattered on me.

"Cambria," the detective said. "Did she mention anything else about Malone?"

I shook my head.

"Did she say where she was planning on going?" She pressed, desperate to coax whatever information she could out of me. Unlike the other police officers that had frequented the property, Detective Spray wasn't taking down copious notes on a small pad of paper. Rather she intently studied my face with her hands settled on her hips. This was hard for her, I thought, trying to drag information out of an emotional witness. She struck me as a no-nonsense "crying is for pansies" kind of gal. A large drip coffee—black. No time for sugar and cream.

I brought the water to my lips and took another sip. The cool liquid slid down my scratchy throat, settling my stomach. "Do you know if Chase was released?" I asked her. I told myself I only wanted to know for safety reasons. Not because I cared what happened to him.

Nope. Not at all.

"She gave you nothing else on Malone?" Spray asked again. It was clear the detective only cared about Malone. How many times was she going to ask?

"No more mentions of Malone?"

*At least once more apparently.*

I shook my head again.

"OK, that's enough for now I guess. I may need to ask you more questions later."

A lump formed at the base of my throat. "I'll have to check with my attorney first," I said, turning around. Tom was strewn across the gurney inside the ambulance. When the gun had fired, I fell to the ground with a bloodcurdling scream. Then I'd gone to Tom.

He had rolled off Alice, clutching his arm. Blood spread across his shirt and all over Alice, who lay in an unnatural position, comatose. I grabbed the gun and swooshed it across the cement, under the row of cars.

"Tom," I sobbed, carefully placing his head in my lap.

"You're such an idiot. What is wrong with you?" I ripped his shirt open to find the source of the bleeding. "Where does it hurt?" I asked, not seeing any blood.

"My arm," he groaned.

"Arm?" I pulled his sleeve over his shoulder and found the half-inch opening where a bullet had grazed. "Oh, it's just a graze. What is wrong with you? You could have died." I was so mad and so relieved.

Concerned voices began gathering around us. I paid no attention. Instead, I looked at Alice. Pools of blood formed underneath her, spreading across the cement. Her lower abdomen was drenched in crimson. Tom rolled to his side and sat up with my assistance. "What can we do?" I asked.

He winced as he rose to his knees. "Take this off me," he ordered, nodding toward his shirt. I immediately did as told (for once) and yanked the shirt off, forgetting about the wound on his arm.

"Dammit, Cam. Careful."

"I'm so sorry. You OK?" He gave me a look. "I mean, aside from the gun wound thing?"

He shook his head and used his uninjured hand to point to the shirt. "Apply that to her abdomen."

I did as instructed and applied pressure to the wound on her stomach, soaking Tom's shirt. He scooted closer, cradling his arm, and leaned down. "Can you hear us?" he asked Alice.

Her eyes fluttered open, and she gasped for air, looking panicked. "Don't move," I told her. She coughed and lurched around, moaning. "Stay still."

A man in flannel pajamas came to her side, claiming to be a podiatrist and a friend of a resident—which one, I'd forgotten the moment he told me. I only kept screaming that her feet were fine.

The firemen and the police arrived shortly after, along with several EMTs, who replaced my bloody hand with their gloved ones. "We've got it," one of the EMTs reassured me.

"Wait," Alice moaned. "I didn't touch any cars, that was Rev," she told me in a barely audible whisper.

I didn't know what to say to that, so I said nothing. Scooting backwards on my butt, I leaned against the wall. My legs and arms and hands and feet were shaking uncontrollably as I watched the scene unfold, feeling as if I were looking through someone else's eyes. The men and woman working on Alice, one holding her head still, talking to her in a calm yet firm voice. The other two were inspecting the wound, pulling instruments out of their medic bag. Around the corner came another man in uniform with the gurney. The wheels rolled over the blood. A police officer was trying to talk to me, but his words weren't making sense. Then the ill-fitted gray suit detective walked up, and she too was trying to talk to me. One of the fireman was tending to Tom, whose blood-soaked shirt was at my feet.

It could have been worse. It could have been so much worse.

The sun rose, bathing the dark sky in blue and yellow hues, and the ground in glistening dew. The police cars pulled out of the parking lot, one by one. The ambulance had long since left with Alice. I turned to Tom, who was lying in the back of the ambulance. He had a butterfly bandage over his brow while the paramedic wrapped his arm in gauze. "She wants to ask more questions later," I told him.

He gave a thumbs up.

"I guess that'll be fine," I turned and told the detective. "Only, one more thing I forgot to mention." She looked at me, hopeful. "Alice didn't touch any cars in the parking lot. It was Rev. She told me before they rushed her to the hospital."

The corners of her mouth turned downward. "I know. I'll be in touch." It sounded more like a warning than a farewell.

She strolled off to her unmarked black sedan, removing the flashing red and blue light from the dashboard.

*I know?*

The blanket slipped off my shoulder as the chills subsided. The boyish-faced officer who had escorted me through the police station was standing near the entrance to Apartment 39, talking to Larry and Silvia. Larry had his arms folded over his Van Halen shirt, wide stance, and rocked slightly from side to side. Silvia had her hand spread over her chest.

"Excuse me!" I called. The boyish officer held a finger up to Silvia and Larry before dashing to my side.

"What's wrong?" he asked. I swore he wasn't a day over twelve, fifteen at most. He did look rather agile and eager though, which was exactly what I needed.

"It's my phone," I said. It was still on my mind. Pathetic, yes. "It's somewhere in the carports, and I need to call my babysitter to let her know why we are so late picking up our daughter. Could you find it for me?"

He quickly obliged. A few minutes later, I was reunited with my phone. The screen had a few cracks on the bottom but still worked. I unlocked the home screen and sent a quick text to Mrs. Nguyen.

Next, it was time to call Patrick.

# Chapter 37

*Upon move-out, Landlord or Landlord's Agent will inspect Premises to determine the amount of deposit applied in order to return Premises to a re-rentable state.*

"What's this for?" Patrick asked, nudging the plastic thimble looking thingy with the end of his pen. There were several scattered across the bathroom counter. I shrugged, not having a clue, and continued to snap pictures with my phone.

Patrick stalked down the hall, his yellow notepad tucked under his arm, already filled with three pages of notes. He tapped a box with his toe, shaking his head and making another note.

When I called Patrick the morning of The Incident, as Tom and I called it, he answered with the voice of a man who had reached his very last straw. He nearly fired me on the spot before I greeted him with a pleasant salutation of, "I'm sitting in an ambulance and was just held at gunpoint and as a hostage for the second time tonight."

His response? Nothing. He said nothing. I would have thought he had hung up if it weren't for the female voice in the background repeatedly asking, "What happened? What's wrong? Tell me, Patrick."

Once he recouped enough to form words, we agreed to meet as planned. After I explained what had happened, I suspected he wouldn't be firing me any more.

I was right. Instead of handing me a notice of termination (which I saw when I peeked into his bag, already signed and dated), he handed me a bonus for all my "troubles." I opened the envelope, readjusting my sore body on the ugly chair across from the even uglier couch in the lobby, and stared down at the three thousand dollar check with my name scrawled on it. It was enough to bring my bank account to positive and put a deposit down on a new apartment, should I choose to leave. "I'll understand if you want to look for a new job," Patrick said earnestly. He looked tired.

Biting my lip, I stared down at the money that would only go so far. "I think," I replied, "I'd like to stay. I would like to be trained though." I realized over the course of the last week how little I had learned from Joyce and how little Google knew about property management. Patrick readily agreed, and it was back to business as usual (with a negotiated extra week of vacation time and free laundry, you know, for my troubles).

Back in Apartment 39, Patrick stared through the hole in the wall between the kitchen and the living room. "This never should have happened. Inspections should be done at least twice a year. We got lazy," he said, making note of such on his pad. It took nearly a week to get the eviction processed for the apartment before we could enter. Warranting two visits in one week from Patrick. The most he'd visited the community over the last five years he said to me, before promising to start making monthly inspections. For which I was glad. I found his company quite pleasant. "You heard from Kevin lately?" he asked.

I nodded. "He says the plan is to get him into rehab instead of doing jail time." I'd prodded Tom for more information at breakfast. He kept silent on the subject, scooping a forkful of pancakes into his mouth instead. I'd spent the night at his apartment. I had spent every night since The Incident there. Cuddled up in Lilly's bed, wrapped in her Frozen comforter, nearly hitting REM before my head hit the pillow.

The day after The Incident, we were both too physically exhausted to make food, so we opted for IHOP. Lilly sat next to Tom on the booth, enjoying her pancake covered in syrup and whipped cream and chocolate chips with a cherry on top. Her eyes grew about six inches when the waitress slid the plate in front of her, and she gasped and giggled and clapped as if she'd just won the lottery. I pushed my Southwest-style omelet around the plate with my fork. My stomach had not quite settled. Tom nudged my knee under the table with his, making sure I was all right. He'd, of course, offered to help me with workers' comp and to file a lawsuit against Elder Management for negligence or whatever. But I wasn't interested. I was ready to start a career and get out of the limbo I'd been in for far too long.

It wasn't until the waitress dropped the check on the table that I realized I was living out one of my Tom fantasies. We were sitting at breakfast as a real family—mom, dad and child all enjoying a meal. It was picturesque (aside from the bandage around Tom's arm, the cut on his eye, and the dark bruise on my cheek I'd discovered when I woke). I caught Tom staring at me over the table, and I couldn't help but blush. The awful truth though, was he didn't throw me into a nearly combustible state like the green-eyed maintenance boy. The guy I still couldn't get out of my head.

Was physical attraction really that important? I nearly came unhinged in Chase's presence, and where did that get me? It got me here, in an IHOP with a bruise on my cheek and a campfire in my stomach and a life raft from my baby daddy. Maybe someday I'd leave Alcatraz, jump in the raft and paddle to shore.

Maybe…

Patrick groaned, kicking part of a broken plastic chair out of the way. "What really gets me is Chase," he said, running a hand over his bare head. "I've always had a good read on people, and he struck me as a real standup guy. He had good references, excellent credit, no criminal hits, and he was inexpensive. You know how hard it is to find anyone to work for minimum wage? It was too good to be true I guess. Maybe he wasn't that great at his job, but for that price, I could live with it." He jotted down a thought on his notepad.

"Aren't you glad you didn't hire his friend?" Part of me

was still bitter about being third choice, especially now. Would either of his first two choices have basically solved an entire crime on their own?

*Methinks not.*

"What friend?"

"His friend who applied for my job."

He scrunched his bushy brows together. "No, I don't recall anyone mentioning they knew him. I was going to offer you the position the day after you interviewed, then Chase called and told me you cheated on your application and he didn't think you'd be a good manager. At the time, I believed him to be a straight shooter. So I offered the job to two other seasoned managers who both turned it down, mainly because of the horror stories they'd heard about Kevin."

"Are you serious?" My heart swelled. I was the first choice? It was the confidence booster I needed to confirm my decision to stay and pursue a career in property management. And yet another mark on the *reasons you should stop thinking about Chase* list. Any sane person with a heartbeat and a brain would scream FORGET ABOUT IT. Especially when looking at all the evidence—the way he'd made an advance only to pull away (douche), the drugs (liar), the arrest (criminal), the job sabotage (even bigger douche).

# Chapter 38

*Newly remodeled one-bedroom apartment. Gorgeous downstairs unit, easy access to the carports, large patio, wonderful location. Luxurious pool, spacious laundry rooms, stunning courtyards. $2,900 a month. Must provide two forms of identification, paycheck stubs, references...*

"The entire apartment is brand new from the carpet to the walls to the kitchen cabinets," I said in my best sales-pitchy voice, running my hand along the newly installed countertop. Patrick and I had gone back and forth on color options over the last month while Apartment 39 was being restored. I pushed for color, wanting to add yellow, green and blue hues to liven up the space. Patrick wanted grays and whites and browns—blah. We "compromised" and went with silver countertops, beige cabinets and tan carpet. Baby steps, I told myself.

A short, curvy woman with a thin black side braid stood in the kitchen, bouncing the drooling baby boy wrapped around her chest in one of those mile-long cloth-wrap things I never was able to figure out how to use with Lilly. Speaking of Lilly, she came skipping around the corner, nearly knocking into the young mom. "Sorry about that," I said, shooting Lilly a *cut it out* look, which she completely ignored.

She waved off my apology. "No worries. I love the family atmosphere of this place." She opened the brand new dishwasher, noting the instruction manual still inside. "Why is everything so new?"

"Fire." It was only a slight exaggeration. "It just came on the market, and I'm sure at this price point, it'll go fast. I have applications in the office if you'd like to fill one out?"

She kissed the top of her baby's head. "What are the neighbors like? Are they nice, like good family people?"

I chose my words carefully. "The neighbors are *quiet*." It was only a slight exaggeration. Kevin had been gone for a couple of weeks now and wouldn't be returning for some time. "There's a family with a little boy upstairs."

She smiled. I had her.

I locked the apartment behind us, and we traveled back to the lobby for an application. Larry cut across the lawn with a box labeled *Harold's Things* in his arms, Silvia walked behind him with Harold, supervising the move of her belongings. I'd arranged a transfer from her apartment to the vacant unit across the courtyard. It only shared a wall with Larry, and he was more than happy to have a new neighbor. They both enjoyed complaining—her about everyone, and him about all his physical ailments. Perhaps they could complain to each other and keep me out of it.

Or so I hoped.

Silvia's apartment was already rented out to a wonderful couple who I was thrilled to have—Mr. and Mrs. Nguyen. Mr. Nguyen had started as our new, and much improved, maintenance man (he actually fixed the things he touched and wasn't a drug-addicted douche nugget). I'd introduced him to Patrick shortly after Chase was arrested (and never heard from again), and the two hit it off. Of course, Patrick ran a thorough background check prior to approval, and Mr. Nguyen passed all checkpoints with flying colors. I didn't have to micromanage his hours either as his apartment counted as part of his compensation along with a salary.

Lilly was thrilled with the thought of having her So-Cal grandparents back, and Mrs. Nguyen promised she'd teach Lilly how to sew. And the fact that Mr. and Mrs. Nguyen were hard of hearing paired perfectly with the loud lovemaking of their neighbors, Clare and Bob. Another win for Cambria.

Back in the lobby, I opened the door for the young mom, who was beaming at the prospect of occupying "the best apartment in the complex." She filled out the application. I took her driver's license. Checked it twice. Then one more time for good measure. Faxed it over to Patrick, and we were done. I politely shooed her out of the lobby and locked the door. I knew I was late. I knew I'd be late when I stopped to show the apartment. If I could rent it, the risk would be worth it. At least I thought so. I wasn't sure anyone else would see it that way, aside from Patrick maybe.

Lilly bounced up and down on my hip as I sped through the community. Residents either waved or scowled as we passed. Most had forgiven or forgotten about the crime sprees, my arrest and the gunshot. The threesome rumor had lost momentum (hallelujah). Only a few apartments remained vacant, although a steady flow of traffic and a motivated apartment manager (me) had already filled most of them. Patrick was impressed.

By the time I made it to Apartment 36, I could barely breathe. (I still hadn't exercised. It was on the list.) I pounded on the door, checking my watch. My phone was vibrating in my back pocket. I knew who it was, and I knew why he was calling. Not answering would give the illusion I was driving to the location I should be at.

Amy opened the door. Her blond and purple-streaked hair blown out to perfection, framing her face. "There's my girl," she sing-songed and reached out for Lilly. "You ready for a fun day with Auntie Amy?"

Lilly squealed.

"Make sure you're super careful," I said, handing over Lilly's bag. "Don't let her out of your sight, and she can't have anything with soy because she has this rough patch of skin below her ear, and I think it could be an…"

Amy put her hand on my shoulder. "Breathe." She took in a deep breath and exhaled slowly, inviting me to join her. I took heed and inhaled and exhaled to make her happy. "You sure you don't want me to go with you?" she asked.

My stomach was all butterflies, and my throat felt about two sizes too small. Still, childcare was more of a concern than my nerves. "I'll be fine. Where's Spencer?"

"Right here," he hollered, emerging from the hallway in jeans and a white polo shirt. He'd made significant improvements in the wardrobe and décor department since he began dating Amy. His apartment now had a white couch and a blue love seat, decorative rug, art on the wall, and a real kitchen table. It smelled of fabric softener and cinnamon. It was only a matter of time before Amy would be submitting her own rental application to join Spencer's lease. I was thrilled.

"Where are you guys going? The park?" I asked, my phone vibrating again in my pocket.

"The Aquarium of the Pacific," Spencer said, grinning. He placed a hand on Amy's shoulder and said hello to Lilly. He had waited until their third date before springing the fishy brothel on her. Turns out he's a decent guy who treats her like a queen. She decided she could live with the whole fish thing, as long as it remained on the patio.

I fidgeted with the bottom of my shirt. "That's in Long Beach, right? I mean, that's kind of far to drive, and it's super busy... What about going to McDonald's instead?"

Amy cocked her head and gave me a look. "She'll be fine. We'll be fine. You will not be fine if you don't get out of here right now. Go."

She had a point. I kissed Lilly's head. Made one more plea for McDonald's. Was told to leave.

Thirty minutes later, I pulled into a parking space at the courthouse. As usual, I crawled over the center console and passenger seat to exit the car, and raced inside. I found Tom pacing the hall, his phone at his ear. My phone vibrated in my back pocket.

I wore a pair of black slacks and a blue-collared shirt, the most professional outfit I could find at Target. Amy and I had our hair blown out the day before. Einstein was so silky and long, I couldn't stop running my fingers through it. I'd spent the night before watching makeup tutorials, practicing the smoky eye. I was going for a sexy business casual look, and based on Tom's gaping expression, mission accomplished.

I had to look my best, especially today.

Tom lowered his phone and stared. "You look... *good.*" He blinked, hard. "Why are you so late?"

"This girl showed up and really wanted to see an apartment." I smiled a *sorry not sorry* smile. "I'm here now."

He ran his hand down his face and grunted. "You have any idea how serious this is?"

I scoffed. Of course I knew how serious this was. I was the one who had to take the stand. I was the one who had to sit through hours of questions from multiple detectives. "Tom, I'm ready. I can do this."

"Here's the thing. You probably don't have to now."

"What?" I'd been stressing for days, and rushing all afternoon, and now I might not even have to testify? "Why not?"

Tom looked around the busy hallway and led me to a quiet corner near the drinking fountains. His hand lingered on my arm—a life raft. He'd thrown me several not-so-subtle life rafts over the last month, and I'd pretended not to notice. I hadn't made my mind up yet. I hoped today, this trial, would give me the closure I needed to move forward in my love life. My feigned ignorance was only going to last so long. Plus, a big part of me enjoyed watching him try. If he really wanted this, if he really wanted me, then he'd have to come right out and say it.

"It looks like one of the detectives on the case blew his or her cover and came forward to testify. The D.A. said there's enough incriminating evidence to put Rev away for a long time without your testimony now."

"Really? Do you know who it was that came forward?"

He shook his head. "You don't need to find out either. Let's go, and you can have some peace of mind knowing you won't have to face Rev." I wasn't sure how much peace I could have knowing Alice's trial had not been set yet. She survived the gunshot, but her baby wasn't so lucky. She would still be forced to stand trial, and I was concerned she would blame Tom or me—or both of us—for the death of her unborn child. She would plot revenge, stalk us, take us hostage—or worse, our daughter—and finish us off as she intended to do that night. My "worst case scenario" mind was clearly still alive and well.

"I want to watch," I announced, charging down the hall. "Which door?"

Tom shook his head and pointed the way. The last courtroom I'd entered was for Kevin. After a guilty plea, the judge sentenced Kevin to court-ordered rehab after a three-month stint in prison. Tom had wanted rehab only, without any jail time, but Kevin arrived without shoes or a shirt on, so he had to work with what he had.

I had high hopes the rehab and jail time would serve him well. Patrick promised Kevin would have a home to return to. I remove the cobwebs over his door and placed a "welcome" mat in front. I was still in his corner, maybe because of my cousin Stephanie, or maybe because he'd had a crappy childhood, or maybe because I saw Kevin as the underdog, and I loved a good underdog story—it was the most relatable.

Only two days before, I received my first letter from Kevin.

*Dear Kamebria,*

*Hi! I hope you and your child are doing well. I am doing alright. Jail sucks but my new cellmate is cool. I wrote Patrick and said I think you should get a raise. So you should be seeing that in your paycheck soon.*

*Being here has made me realize I really need to get my act together. I promise once I get out of prison I will be a model tenant. I promise I won't play my music loudly or let sexual offenders hide out in my house. I won't piss on the mailboxes, and I will wear clothes when I use the exercise equipment. I'm going to be really quiet and helpful. Like you said before, I can help you manage the place! I'm looking forward to it.*

*I also wanted to ask you a few favors. Can you please water the plants on my patio? I also need you to go into my apartment but don't look in the* <u>*kitchen or bathroom!!!!*</u> *I have a pet snake named Viper in my closet, and he needs to eat one mouse a week. I keep the mice in a brown box on my dresser. In my hallway closet, I have a few plants, and I need you to water those on Mondays and Thursdays. I have a heat lamp on a timer, and I need you to make sure that is coming on. Can you please get my mail and set it on the floor by my bedroom door? I also need you to evict Larry. Make sure he is gone before I get home.*

*If I think of anything else, I will write you again. Thanks for the letter. You can visit again if you want.*

*Sincerely,*
*Kevin P. McMills*

*P.S. My first cellmate, Doug, will be calling you. He just got out last week and is looking for a new apartment. I gave him your name and number so you can hook him up. I told him all about the place, and he said it sounds real nice. I told him to put me down as a reference.*

I read the letter twice before folding it back up and shoving it into the envelope.

*Note to self: Don't show anyone named Doug an apartment alone, ever.*

This courtroom was much bigger than Kevin's. Men and women of all ages and races made up the jury. The judge, an older African-American woman with red half-moon glasses resting at the end of her nose, presided. The gallery was near empty. I chose a seat in the third row behind the defendant and sat down, placing my bag on my lap. Tom sank into the chair next to me.

A hot flash hit me like lightning when I caught sight of the back of Rev's head. His hair had grown out a little since I'd last seen him and he was now sporting a suit. He looked like a creepy Chia Pet, which is kind of redundant. My hands shook, and sweat sprinkled my forehead.

"That's it, we're leaving," Tom whispered, starting to stand.

"I'm fine," I said, slowing my breathing and trying to calm down. "Fine," I repeated to myself.

*Breathe.*

Then it happened. The air shifted. A scruffy-faced man took the stand, swore in and sat. Chase. He wore a fitted dark blue suit, white shirt and a solid yellow tie. His normally shaggy hair was slicked back and wrapped behind his ears.

The District Attorney stood behind a wooden podium, a pudgy fellow with a comb-over of silver hair. He asked Chase to state his name for the court. Chase rattled off a series of numbers instead. Tom's jaw dropped about a foot.

Chase wasn't the bad guy. He wasn't a bad guy at all. He was the exact opposite. He was the good guy. A guy who had been protecting me all along. He'd tried to stop Patrick from hiring me to keep me off the property he knew was overrun with drug dealers. He'd been so shocked when Spencer admitted he was participating in illegal activity because he had likely done a sweep of all the residents and determined him harmless (which he was). He was terrible at his job because he was too busy doing his *real* job. He was disappearing, and reappearing when I needed him, and after everything that had happened, my gut was right. Chase was no druggie. Chase was no maintenance man either.

Chase was an undercover cop.

"My role was originally a doper," Chase began, his hands folded in his lap. "I had approached the defendant about purchasing half an ounce of cocaine in exchange for two hundred oxycodone placebo pills and some cash. The defendant immediately shut me down. We had reason to believe the defendant had connections to a bigger case I'd been involved with. He then took up residence with Vincent Romero. The defendant introduced Vincent and his girlfriend to Malone, and Vincent began dealing out of his apartment. We were having a hard time keeping track of them and going unseen because of the location of the apartment, so I took on the role as the maintenance man at the property, having assumed the identity of Chase Hudson. I was then able to build a good rapport with Vincent and later the defendant, who is the brother of Vincent's girlfriend. We witnessed the defendant break into several cars and orchestrate the theft of several others. We had to keep watching because we knew he'd lead us to Malone eventually. Rev and Vincent asked that I keep the apartment manager out of their way. I did so in order to keep up a good relationship. On one occasion, the defendant sold me an eight ball, and on two separate occasions he sold me a gram. The point of my cover was to gain access to his boss, and on the seventh of October, I received an anonymous tip with the exact location of Malone, who had been running a major, deadly drug operation. We verified and made the arrest. We also arrested Vincent Romero on scene. Once the lead detective on the case confirmed the arrests, I went to the defendant's apartment. He was agitated and didn't want to answer the door. Once he did, I found the apartment manager inside. It was later confirmed during a confession by the defendant that he had taken the apartment manager hostage with plans to get her out of the way." He paused.

*Breathe.*

I breathed in slowly, exhaled slowly. Chase continued. "Once he agreed to sell me a gram, we were able to make the arrest. I'd planned on staying undercover, so I was arrested too, as was the apartment manager because at the time we weren't sure of her involvement. But she turned out to be in the clear."

For a few glorious seconds our eyes met, and that spark exploded around us. He'd blown his cover so I wouldn't have to testify. Chase, or whatever his real name was, returned his attention to the District Attorney and casually lifted his hand and scratched his scruffy chin—the signal.

Everything was fine.

# Chapter 39

*I and/or We have read and agree to abide by the terms of this lease. In witness thereof, the Parties have executed this Lease on this day.*

*From: joyceplummer@eldermgmt.com*
*To: cambriaclyne@eldermgmt.com*
*Subject: FW: FW: FW: FW: FW: FW: URGENT*

ONCE YOU'VE STARTED READING THIS YOU CANNOT STOP OTHERWISE YOU WILL DIE>:<<# *The...re was a boy named Ro..y>> who was hated by everyone. Ever..yone made>> fun of Roy and no one lis...tened so he killedhimself. Noone not..iced >> until people started disappearing. He haunted them down..andkilled them>, one by one. Brutally torturing each. If you don't forward this to 22 people in the next 1.23 seconds then Ro..y will haunt you for the>,> next twelve months >,< and then kill you...with...a plunger. < You've been warned. Roy has already brutally murdered over<...// a thousand..people</ who deleted this email.*

I laughed.

*What a lovely note.*

At least I knew Joyce was still alive, considering she had sent at least three "you will DIE if you don't forward" emails a day for the last month. Some tales were so old I remembered reading them in high school. Patrick was also on Joyce's daily chainmail list. Neither of us had heard how she was doing otherwise and decided the time to become concerned about her wellbeing was when the emails stopped... or Roy showed up. Luckily, neither had happened.

*Delete.*

I scrunched my knees up to my chest and shoved my sweater over them. The office was a freezer—sixty-degrees outside and five degrees cooler inside. My teeth chattered, my lips were chapped, and my skin was dehydrated. I'd never survive a *real* snowy, blizzardy, mittens-and-earmuffs kind of December like the rest of the country was experiencing, and I was fine with it. I'd take crisp, smoggy air, bare trees and the occasional rainstorm over frozen pipes, shoveled walkways and slippery sidewalks. It sounded like a lot more work. Being a So-Cal apartment manager had its benefits.

The lobby door opened, and Mr. Nguyen backed in, tugging the six-foot noble fir Lilly and I picked out from the Christmas tree lot down the street. It was only after we said hello to Santa, drank our weight in eggnog and paid for the tree, that I realized I had no way of getting it home. In came Mr. Nguyen to save the day, just as he had when Apartment 6's ceiling began dripping muck-colored water at three in the morning, and when the pool's heater broke, and when Larry got his ponytail stuck in the garbage disposal. He was a lifesaver. Patrick called us "the dream team" because we were. One hundred percent occupancy and a friendly maintenance man who could fix everything you asked him to, plus the things you didn't even know needed fixin', and he could give you a pedicure while he was at it. Christmas bonuses were on their way.

Still, I'd be lying if I said a ping didn't stab at my heart when I caught a glimpse of the embroidered "maintenance" above Mr. Nguyen's shirt pocket. I had a small sliver of hope that Chase, or whatever his real name was, would contact me after Rev's trial. Show up at my apartment and profess his love. Or send a letter. Or an email. Maybe a friend request on Facebook?

Nothing.

Not one word.

He'd been whisked away after his testimony, never to be heard from again. It was possible he was already on a new job, having done his judicial duty by ensuring Rev got the twenty-five years in state prison he deserved. According to Tom, Chase didn't show up at Vincent's trial, where he was sentenced to five years. As for the mystical drug lord Malone (whom I'd only seen pictures of—he looked like Mr. Clean), his trial had recently ended with a life sentence. I was able to keep tabs via various news outlets covering the story. If Chase had shown up at Malone's trial, it wasn't significant enough to be covered.

Alice's trial had been postponed again, and again and again. It was bordering on ridiculous. Not only because she deserved to rot in prison, but because there was a chance Chase would show up to testify, a very small chance. "Less than a one percent chance," Tom had said when I asked, not hiding his frustration with the question. He was cute when he was jealous.

Regardless of the missing ex-maintenance man, it made for a happy holiday knowing all who had inflicted harm were safely tucked behind bars. For now.

"You want this in apartment or out here?" Mr. Nguyen yelled. He was as kind as he was loud.

He stood the tree upright, fluffing out the branches and sending a rainfall of needles to the ground. I inhaled the memory-inducing pine scent. Mmm. My third favorite smell.

I went to the lobby and shoved my face into the tree, fully emerged in the aroma of Christmas. Nostalgic joy bubbled in my stomach as I ran my hands along the branches. Happy childhood memories flashed through my mind. "Would you hate me if I asked you to get another one for the office?" I asked directly into his ear. Patrick said he'd personally see to it that Mr. Nguyen get fitted for hearing aids in the New Year. Mostly because talking to him on the phone was grueling.

He shook his head. "No problem! I go now!" He was out the door before I could thank him.

I propped the tree up near the counter and stood back to admire the view. Piling presents underneath would be far less stressful this year than Christmases of the past. *Everything* would be far less stressful.

I was finally swimming.

Tom, Lilly and I would be spending Christmas Eve and Christmas morning together, as a family. Not that Tom and I were *together*—yet. After a month of deflected advances, he came right out and asked, "What would you think about you and me... trying?"

At the time, I didn't know what to say. It was late, nearly midnight, and I had been binge watching *The Walking Dead*. Not the best time to be tapping on someone's door wanting to talk about feelings. "Trying what?" I asked, still wanting to make him work for it.

He delivered his signature side smirk. "Trying to see if there's something between us."

He was going to have to do better. "I don't really understand what you're getting at, Tom."

"Sure you do." He reached across the threshold and wrapped his arm around my waist. My insides leapt at the touch of his hand across my back, my stomach butterflied when he pulled me closer and cupped my cheek. I gulped. I was nervous, excited, apprehensive. He leaned down, slowly dropping his lids. I followed suit and soon our lips met. At first, I felt nothing. Like kissing the back of my hand. My thoughts wandered back to *The Walking Dead*. It can't be a good sign if you're thinking about zombies when your lips are pressed against another person's lips.

He tilted my head to the side, pulled me in tighter, pressing his body against mine and *really* kissed me. Kissed me hard. The hearts and flowers and fireworks reappeared. My knees went weak. My adrenaline thundered. The world spun. All else forgotten... for a moment.

The relationship hadn't moved past the flirty/occasional make-out stage. Not yet at least. Maybe it was because we had a child together and the relationship deserved respect. Slow and methodical consideration. It was too important to screw up. Or maybe it was because I hadn't fully recovered from Chase. Either way, I wasn't quite there, but a life raft was ready for when I was. Assuming nothing or no one interrupted the path we were on, I suspected I'd be using the life raft soon. It was a warming thought.

Mr. Nguyen arrived with another beautiful tree. It was in a stand and leveled within minutes. He then dashed off to handle a new maintenance request. It was nice having a maintenance man who enjoyed maintenancing.

I dragged the tree in front of the window facing the street and began untangling hundreds of strands of colorful bulbs. I'd found a dusty box of Christmas decorations in the maintenance garage filled with lights, wreaths, plastic Santas and a menorah, which went on the countertop.

While untangling, Mickey from Apartment 19 walked through, arguing with himself. "Hi, Mickey," I said automatically, my attention on the web of primary colored bulbs. He flung open the door. "Bye, Mickey... Ugh, this is a mess."

"Need some help with that?"

My heart skipped two beats. I dropped the box, afraid to look up. My mind was playing tricks. It had to be. Things were going good. No, things were going great. I was falling for the father of my child. I was gainfully employed. I was happy. I was swimming. I had no time for liquidy limbs.

Maybe it wasn't Chase. Maybe it was Roy distorting his voice to screw with me because I deleted his email.

"Cambria?" It was Chase. It was his voice. It was his smell. It was his sensual energy. The sexy man scent overpowered the Christmas tree, and my legs turned to goo— an all-too-familiar feeling. Roy couldn't have that kind of power.

I rolled my sleeves up to my elbows. *It sure is hot in here.* Deep breath in, slow breath out. I turned to face him.

It was Roy.

He beat me with a plunger.

I died.

That would be an easier scenario than the one standing in front me.

Chase. His hair was shorter, styled and darker—light brown. Only the faintest appearance of a five o'clock shadow brushed his jawline. The scruffy "I woke up like this" Chase had nothing on the groomed "I could be an underwear model" Chase. He had on jeans and a red hooded sweatshirt with USC printed on the front in bold yellow lettering. I didn't know what to say, so I made a squeaky noise that could be interpreted as "Hello."

He twisted his mouth to the side. "Maybe I shouldn't have come," he said more to himself than to me.

"No..." I didn't know his name. It could be Bartholomew or Dan or Peter. It was hard imagining him going by any other name than Chase.

"My name is Xavier," he said, as if reading my mind. *Holy crap!* He's an undercover cop. He could read minds. Not literally. Part of his job was to get a read on people. I'd seen it on the hundreds of crime shows I'd watched. He had to know I was pining over him the entire time he was here. That's embarrassing.

*I feel sick.*

"You OK?" he asked.

My insides were hyperventilating. "I'm fine. A little surprised, that's all." I was determined to have a normal *hey, haven't seen you in a while* conversation with Ch... I mean, Xavier. "What brings you by?" I asked casually. "We don't have any more drug dealers I need to know about, do we?"

He took a step closer, close enough to touch. *Control yourself, Cambria.*

"I wouldn't know. I'm not undercover any more. I went to uniform with a different agency."

"What?" I suspected that meant he was a regular police officer now. "Why?"

"It was time."

"Oh." I paused to regroup. "By the way, sorry for, you know, hitting you that night. I don't think I've ever hit anyone before."

He laughed. It had a charming, musical sound. "I thought it was awesome. Here you were, face-to-face with two druggies, and instead of cowering, you went all Tyson. You can definitely hold your own. I like that."

"Thanks." I blushed, biting my lip.

"Hey, how about I help you with these lights?" He grabbed the box and pulled out a wad of white lights, colorful lights, big lights and small lights all mangled together in a ball.

I laughed. I couldn't help myself. "No offense, but from what I remember, you aren't particularly handy. Or was that part of the cover?"

"Hey, I fixed the air conditioner," he said with pride.

"It broke the following week."

His shoulders drooped. He looked genuinely sad, as if I just told him Santa wasn't real. "You know, it was a lot harder than I thought it would be. Doing this job and mine. I bet if I gave it my full attention, I'd be a good maintenance man."

"Without a doubt," I humored him.

"Fine, no lights." He dropped the box on the coffee table. "Let's do dinner."

"Dinner?" I chuckled. We went from drugs to Christmas lights to dinner. No matter how hot he was (and he was), I couldn't run off with him like some schoolgirl. "Chase, I don't even know who you are. I mean... Xavier." That was going to take some practice.

"What do you want to know?"

"I don't know... Do you have a wife and kids at home?" It had crossed my mind, numerous times.

"Do you think I'd be here asking you out if I did?"

I shrugged. People are idiots. You never know.

"No," he finally answered.

*Phew.*

"I've never been married. Never been close to anyone. Not a good idea when you're doing what I was doing for a living. I *did* grow up in Long Beach as I said. I *do* have nieces—four of them—and three brothers and a sister. I'm the second oldest. I *did* go to Long Beach City College, except I didn't drop out to do maintenance, obviously. I transferred to USC. I'm fluent in Spanish, Cantonese, and I can get by in Japanese. Still working on it. I root for the Angels. I run for fun. I could watch *Seinfeld* all day. I went undercover six years ago, and this is the first time I've worked in uniform. Anything else you want to know?"

"How old are you?"

"Thirty-three."

"Chicken or beef?"

"Vegetarian."

"Morning or night person?"

"Night."

"Do you have a cat?"

"No. Goldfish named Fish."

"Was that really an old injury you had the day we were spying on Spencer, or did you hurt yourself chasing bad guys?"

"Neither. I fell off a ladder getting a wasp's nest."

"Did you... wait, you fell off a ladder?" I laughed. I laughed until tears blurred my vision. "I'm sorry, it's not funny... except it is."

"I am actually a pretty agile guy. I thought the nest was already dead." He laughed along with me.

*A man who can laugh at his own expense is a keeper,* Grandma Ruthie used to say.

I wiped my eyes. "Seriously, I have one more question. Did you really tell Patrick not to hire me because you were trying to protect us or was another undercover cop trying for my job?"

"To protect you."

That's what I thought.

"I was pissed when I heard you got the job," he continued. "You also made my job difficult by being so..."

"Nosy?"

"I was trying to think of a different word. But, yes, nosy. Squad cars were here all the time, from a different agency. You staking out apartments. Hiding on top of carport roofs." He narrowed his eyes. "I still can't believe you did that."

"You *can't* believe I did, or you *can* and wish I hadn't?"

He smiled. "I *bleeping* wish you hadn't." He leaned over and placed his hands on my shoulders. His touch was warm. "Dinner?"

I bit my lip. "Lilly should be home any minute..."

"We'll order pizza. Look, you and I both know I'm not here just to take you out to dinner and catch up. It's more." He leaned in closer. I inhaled his sexy man smell.

*Curse you, timing.*

# Epilogue

"You're, like, way too sweet," I said, batting my un-mascara'd lashes. I slid my finger up and down the thick metal telephone cord… up and down… up and down, smiling innocently. He liked it, I could tell. His cheeks flushed, and he leaned in closer to the glass separating us, running his tongue over his lips. Guys were so predictable. So easy. If the D.A. wasn't a chick, I would totally be free right now. "You really think I look cute in this?" Another bat of my lashes followed by a lip pout. He told me I looked hot, whatever. The jumpsuit was gross. It felt like I was wearing a box. It hid all my assets. Plus, like, it was blue. Gag.

Blue is bad luck.

My mother only wore blue. She would strut around in her tight blue miniskirt and bang whoever was willing to give us a place to crash and enough heroin to keep her going. That was before she shoved 100 mg of dope into her arm and left me to the state—damn whore. I was dragged around from home to home, getting felt up by horny pricks pretending to care about me so they could collect a check every month…

*Yuck, don't think about it, Wysteria.*

I drew in a breath, moving around on the hard metal stool, trying to shake the memories. Jail had a way of doing that to you. Too much time to think. It totally sucked, like, being trapped in a mental jail was worse than any sentence the judge could give. I'd been awake since, like, midnight, just lying on the piece of crap cement block they call a mattress. My mind swept through memories I'd long since shoved into a closet, wrapped in heavy chains, and thrown away the key to. Memories like the cold, leathery feel of my mother's skin when I found her on the floor. The smell of vinegar and urine coming off her gross dead body. The wheels of the gurney carrying her away, the sound of them going over the carpet— swish, swoosh, swish, swoosh, swish, swoosh. It played through my mind on repeat like a Justin Bieber song —swish, swoosh, swish, swoosh.

Vincent liked blue. That should have been my first clue. He wore a blue shirt with dark blue jeans the first day we met. I was leaning against the bar, studying my nails, bored. It was a slow day, and then in came Vincent. At first I wasn't really feeling it, but a girl's gotta do what a girl's gotta do. Plus I was totally indebted to Cash, my low-life boss, who had lent me some money earlier in the month for rent. The thing about loans from Cash was they came with heavy interest—his sexual interests. I was desperate to pay him back so he'd get off my back, literally.

Vincent wasn't grabby and rough like most guys who came in. He bought a few dances, tipped me decent and offered to buy me a few drinks. He seemed like one of those, like, real gentlemen type of guys I'd only ever heard about, but doubted their existence. He had a job in construction and a really nice apartment, and wasn't on parole, didn't beat me, or cheat. Heaven knows I fell hard and fast. *My Boo…*

Then came Rev.

*Damn Rev.*

He wasn't even, like, my real blood brother. We were in the same home for a while growing up, and we just sorta clicked in a nonsexual way, which was different. I wasn't used to having a guy around who wasn't trying to get laid.

Come to think of it, Rev was wearing blue the day I introduced him to Vincent.

Like if someone invented a time machine, I would totally

go back and not introduce Vincent and Rev. Like not at all. Then Vincent wouldn't have become involved with Malone, and things would have been different. I wouldn't be sitting here in a gross, blue frumpy suit.

I mean, I got it. It wasn't totally all Vincent's fault. I mean, you like, can't make that kind of money working nine-to-five. It was too tempting for Vincent, and he totally ignored me when I asked him not to start dealing for Malone. But, like, it happened so fast. Rev moved in, and, just like *that*, the apartment became a crack house.

I went from way totally happy to total misery in, like, minutes.

That's when we started fighting, bad. I wanted out, bad. I was done. Vincent wasn't going to, like, let me walk away, not without a fight. He had changed. I would have to leave town. Sneak out without leaving a trail. Sneaking away isn't cheap, and I didn't have the money, and I didn't want to hit up Cash for it.

I grabbed Rev's old backpack, figuring it had some crack in there I could sell to get some extra money. Cause, like, Vincent would seriously kill me if I touched his stuff he had to sell. Like, hunt me down and murder me dead.

The backpack was filled with a bunch of crap I didn't need. Like I'm actually going to wear a mask over my face? Honestly. The only item that proved useful was the too-big-for-my-small-hand gloves. I found a wallet in the trashcan at Taco Bell, covered in hot sauce, and strapped on the gloves to get it. No matter the desperate circumstance, there was no need to ruin a decent manicure.

I didn't even need the guns. The biggest weapon I had was the double-Ds right in front of me, and I used to them to get the funds I needed to bail. Finding targets was easy, distracting them even easier. All were men. All were mid-lifers with minivans and a wife and kids and dogs and boring-as-hell lives. I could recognize these guys from, like, a mile away— they were the type who would come to the club in the middle of the day in the middle of the week. Anyway, I flirted. I flashed. I did a little more if I needed to, then took the bastards' wallets and got the hell out of there, fast. I made an easy five hundred as well as some stuff purchased on the cards before they were declined. Including a pregnancy test...

I was so happy when I saw the positive sign on the pregnancy test. It was a boy. Not that I'd had one of those sonogram thingies. I had a feeling. I already had a name too. There was an adorable little boy who lived above Vincent named Lumber. He was just about the cutest kid I'd, like, ever seen. A totally adorable name.

*Lumber...*

Wanting to do right for Lumber, I tossed everything, aside from one of the guns in the backpack—a girl can never be too careful when shacking up with drug dealers. I totally made a promise to clean up. I wanted to be a better mom than that whore. I knew I could be.

I didn't tell Vincent, not yet. I wanted to show him how committed I was, because that was totally his biggest complaint. That I was not super into him any more. He was so naggy. You'd think we'd been together for, like, years, and not weeks the way he was all whiny about it.

Ugh, and then there was Joyce. Vincent said she never noticed anything. So I was totally upset when she kept badgering me to turn in an application if I was going to live there. Vincent told me to take care of it. Whatever. I used the ID of one of my friend's cousins, Alice Burns. I mean, like, what's the harm?

Vincent was happy to get Joyce off our backs, but then totally pissed when he heard she was quitting. That made him all crabby again. Rev was breaking into cars, and I was all like, "You guys are gonna get caught," and they were all like, "shut the hell up." I was not going down with them. It was time to find another man. Making those bruises on my neck was a totally awesome idea. Guys like girls in distress.

I tried to get the maintenance man, Chase, cause he was super-hot, and even though he was one of Vincent's clients, he wasn't strung out like the naked guy upstairs. But he was a total dud. Then I met *him*. A lucky find, really. Just happened to be walking around in the carports, and I caught him checking me out and, like, sealed the deal. A few times. Lucky for me, I was with him when Rev was arrested.

Even luckier for me is that he came to visit and thinks I look hot in a frumpy blue jumpsuit. I mean, he wasn't much to look at, but seemed like a real gentleman, so of course I went for it. I mean, it would be problematic that he, like, lives in the same building as Vincent, but since Vincent's been put away for a while, I don't see too much of a problem—aside from *her.*

"Hey, Wysteria," he said, tapping the window.

I jumped and shook my head. *Too much time to think.* I batted my lashes in his direction. "Yes, my boo." I began stroking the metal phone cord again.

He readjusted on the stool. "Can you tell me what exactly happened? I was so worried, and this is the first time they've let me see you."

*Ugh, what a wuss.* But a girl's got to do who she's got to do to get by. It took way too much energy not to gag. "You're too sweet. They, like, had me at the hospital for a long time because of that whore, Cambria. She put me there and killed…" I closed my eyes. I didn't really like to think about it. It kinda sucked.

"Who did she kill?" he asked all concerned-like. He was a serious wimp.

I bit my bottom lip and placed my hand up on the glass again. "Our baby. She killed our baby. I was totally pregnant and didn't even know it. After Vincent and Rev got arrested I knew we could you know, be together. Cause, like, I told you how horrible Vincent was to me. You saw the bruises. But then I went back to the apartment to pack my stuff, and that's when that guy Tom, he's, like, her boyfriend or something, showed up."

Plus they were both wearing blue. They knew what blue did to me.

"He was acting all shady, and then she came and started acting all shady, and I knew they were going to try and turn me in. I sorta lost it. I mean, I had one of Rev's guns for protection from Vincent, but I wasn't going to actually, like, pull the trigger. I just wanted to scare them. Wipe the smugness off their mugs. Then he attacked me, that guy Tom, he jumped on me and that's when I lost our baby." I wiped my eyes with the back of my hand. They were totally dry, but he was falling for it. Sap. Like it could actually be our baby. Whatever. "The damn apartment manager was wearing blue. It's a bad color, which is why I can't wait to get out of here and out of this damn jumpsuit." I tugged on the hideous apparel again. It was seriously the ugliest, but I had to be more upset if I wanted to land this guy. "I basically did everything I had to in order to get away from Vincent and be with you. I already told the District Attorney everything. But it could be another year before I'm out. You sure you can wait that long?"

He nodded, his face all pouty like. He was a total pansy, in bed and life too, but there was something different in his eyes now. Like a fire, something scorching inside of him, and it was way hot. "Don't worry about it, baby," he said. "I'll take care of it."

Now he was talking my love-language. "You know, if your apartment manager and her guy never showed up, I would still be pregnant, and we could be together with our baby. Just the three of us." I threw some fuel on the fire, wanting him to rage. It was way hot, and the thought of Tom and Cambria getting theirs was even hotter. "We'd be together forever. I know it, Boo."

"Don't worry, I'll take care of it."

# A Note from Erin Huss

Hello!

I want to personally thank you. Yes, YOU, the one with the book/phone/Kindle/tablet in your hand. You're awesome, and don't let anyone tell you otherwise. It took six years of on-site property management and three years of writing to get here, and I appreciate you taking the time out of your busy life to read *For Rent*.

If you enjoyed the book, it would make my day if you left a review on Amazon. The more reviews I get, the more books I can sell, the more sales I have, the more See's Candy I can buy, the more See's I eat, the more energy I have to write. And don't you want to know what happens next?

I'd also like to invite you to join my mailing list to stay up to date on my latest news and special sales, and get a free ebook of *Can't Pay My Rent* (normally $2.99)! You can sign up here: http://bit.ly/erinhussnews

My sincerest thanks,
Erin

P.S. Read on for a sneak peek of *For Hire*, a humorous novella about Cambria's journey to becoming an apartment manager.

# Acknowledgements

Writing a book is hard. Writing a book when you have five small children is *really* hard, and it took a village of remarkable individuals to turn this idea into a novel. I first want to thank my husband, Jed. Your unwavering support and love mean everything. To my children, Natalie, Noah, Ryder, Emma and Fisher, you are my motivation in all things. Thank you for letting me be your mom.

A HUGE thank you to Adria Cimino and Vicki Lesage for not only taking a chance, but for your superb editing skills, patience and knowledge. I'm honored to be a part of Velvet Morning Press.

Thank you to my mother, Barbara Stotko, for continually telling me I could do anything; my dad, Tim Hogan, for your endless support; Tyler Hogan for being the best brother an annoying big sister could ask for; my step-dad, Mark Stotko, who met me as a teenager and still wanted to marry my mother, and for loving my family as your own blood since; my best pal, Katie Ledesma, for losing sleep while going over plot twists with me; Cody Christiansen for being my go-to lawyer; Christina Christiansen for being the sister I always wanted/needed; my in-laws, Janean Huss, Rod Huss and Julie Huss, for taking me in and allowing me to use the Huss name. I wear it proudly.

I want to thank my beta readers, all those who read the first few (terrible) drafts and the final one—Jordan Elliot, Brittney Zeedik, Katie Ledesma, Barbara Stotko, Tia Howard and Lucy Woodhull. Thank you to Sam Young for taking a young, relatively inexperienced apartment manager and allowing her to manage your flagship property. Thank you to Ashley Stock for the author picture and early-on beta reading. Iris Handy Peugh, thank you for *Crap-o-la*. To all my Santa Maria and Westlake peeps—love you ALL!

I want to thank all the readers of The Apartment Manager's Blog, some who have been with me since 2009.

Your support means so much. THANK YOU!

I feel like I wouldn't have the confidence to write if it weren't for my grandma, Melba Raynaud. She told me from a very early age I should be a writer. Look Abuela, I finally listened!

# About the Author

Erin Huss is a former on-site apartment manager and current blogger at The Apartment Manager's Blog—a chronicle of the comical (and often bizarre) accounts of property managers. Erin lives in Southern California with her husband, five children, two dogs, and lots and lots of fish.

Keep up with Erin online:

Newsletter: http://bit.ly/erinhussnews (and get *Can't Pay My Rent* for free—normally $2.99)
Website: TheApartmentManagersBlog.com
Facebook: TheApartmentManagersBlog
Twitter: @ErinHoganHuss
Instagram: ErinHuss
Email: ErinHuss@gmail.

# Other Titles by Erin Huss

Check out the rest of the Apartment Manager series:

*For Hire*, a novella where Cambria just needs a job—any job—no matter how nightmarish.

*Can't Pay My Rent*, the original book of 31 real-life reasons why tenants claimed they couldn't pay their rent, free when you sign up for Erin's mailing list: http://bit.ly/erinhussnews (normally $2.99).

*Still Can't Pay My Rent*, the hilarious sequel to *Can't Pay My Rent* with 31 more real-life excuses for not paying the rent.

*Move-In Special*, a sequel to *For Rent* (Coming 2017!)


Read on for a sneak peek of *For Hire*...

Excuses come in 31 flavors...
*Can't Pay My Rent*

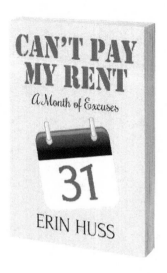

*Why can't you pay the rent?*

The monthly question most apartment managers find themselves asking at least a handful of tenants. In this hilarious piece, Cambria Clyne, the sassy heroine of *For Rent*, is presented with 31 real-life excuses for not paying the rent. Everything from "my identity was stolen" to "I needed drinking money for the weekend" is offered as a so-called reasonable attempt to get out of forking over the cash (or unsigned money order or check that will surely bounce).

Now the question is: How will Cambria get them all to pay up?

Get it for free! Sign up for Erin's newsletter, and she'll send you a free ebook of *Can't Pay My Rent*: http://bit.ly/erinhussnews

# FOR HIRE

## The Apartment Manager Series

ERIN HUSS

velvet morning
press

# Chapter 1

## Cambria

"You what?" I yelled over the whistling of the espresso machine. "I don't think I heard you right." Bart, my boss, was of a certain age (that age being eighty-five). He had a low, grumbly voice that had grown grumblier over the years.

"I said, I decided to sell," he repeated, raising his voice half an octave.

I used the back of my hand to push Einstein (my nickname for the dark, unruly hair springing from my head) out of my face and placed his vanilla latte on the counter. "Sell what?"

Waiting behind him, Ms. Low-Fat Cap began tapping her Prada on the tiled floor, with lips pursed and a "shut the hell up and let her make my drink!" glare locked and loaded and pointed at the back of Bart's sparsely haired head, as if about to fire laser beams from her eyeballs. If there's one thing I had learned in my six years of managing a café, it was that people took their coffee seriously. Very seriously. Life or death seriously. I will literally kill you and your entire family if you don't steam my milk to 102 degrees seriously. It was much like dealing with Lilly on the brink of an epic toddler meltdown, except I could put her in timeout. Here, I had to smile and nod and duck as the "I said extra whip" mocha came flying at my head.

"Your drink is coming right up," I told her.

She stood up straighter and feigned obliviousness, placing her manicured hand over her chest as if saying *Oh me? I'm just patiently waiting.*

Sure you are.

"Cambria, listen," Bart pressed, with his business face on.

"Yes, sorry. What are you selling?"

"It's time to close this place up," he said with an unapologetic shrug. He arched his gray, bushy brows, making it difficult to tell if he was being serious or attempting an *I'm old so I can get away with it* bad joke. I found no humor when it came to my livelihood. Not when I was on my own with a toddler to feed and bills to pay and one of the many freckles dotting my face was a shade darker than the rest and needed to be looked at. Because if there's one thing more expensive than toddlers and bills, it's healthcare.

"You're telling me you're actually considering selling the café? No way. This is a joke," I decided, shaking my head. He'd opened Bart's Café in the sixties, never married, no kids, and he'd told me he planned on dying behind the bar doing what he loved. How could he die here if he didn't own it? He'd be hard-pressed to find a buyer willing to agree to those terms.

"I'm not selling the café. I'm selling the building. This is a large lot, and a strip mall would be really good for the community."

*This is absurd.* "Bart, it's Los Angeles. There's a strip mall next door. Someone is trying to bully you into selling again. The last thing we need is another nail salon and smoke shop. I told you, I'm in one hundred percent."

He groaned, placing an elbow on the counter, looking tired. "I signed the papers this morning."

"What?" I shrieked, dropping the pitcher of hot milk I was frothing. It hit the counter, knocking over the row of paper cups waiting to be filled, and splashed its contents down the front of my apron. The boiling two percent seeped through the thin fabric, turning the metal button and zipper of my jeans into an iron, branding "Mossimo" onto my pelvic region.

Certain situations are beyond profanity.

This was one of them.

Squealing and hopping around in agony, I managed to make it to the stock room before yanking my pants down to my ankles. The first aid kit was located in the office, a good seven-foot journey. *Too far.* Frantic, I hobbled to the fridge, grabbed a carton of soy milk and pressed it on my burning unmentionables.

The cool paperboard calmed the sting. I fell back against the wall and slid down to my butt, sighing the entire way. Mike, one of many part-time baristas, darted around the corner, saw me lying on the floor with my pants down, holding soy milk to my crotch, and quickly twirled around to face the opposite direction.

"Um... you OK, boss?" he asked, staring at the required safety signs covering the wall. I imagined his face was as red as the hair on his head.

Not a good day to sport my granny panties.

"Yeah, I should be fine," I answered through gritted teeth, lifting the tight elastic of my grannies to take a look at the damage. A shiny red line ran down my lower abdomen. Not too bad. No blisters, no blood. There would definitely be a scar—a small one that would blend in with the stretch marks.

*First degree*, I thought.

"OK, um," Mike stuttered, still staring at the Safety Guidelines as if his life depended on it. "Err... Bart is on the patio, and he said for you to come out and talk to him when you're finished."

Oh, that.

A scalding milk bath had a way of erasing all other troubles. If only for a moment. "Tell him I'll be out in a bit," I said, wincing as I readjusted the soy. I needed time to overthink the situation before I talked to Bart again.

Mike was all too eager to play messenger, dashing out into the morning crowd before the sentence had completely left my mouth.

Poor kid.

I rested my head on the wall and took a deep breath, allowing the new information to settle in like a bad infection. I felt furious and sad. Betrayed. Bart carelessly delivering the news wasn't a surprise. He avoided emotions like the stomach flu. Him selling the café though, that was a shock so big it felt as if a semi had just rolled over my chest.

Mad, I took it out on the fridge door, kicking it closed with my black Converse. This backfired when I caught a glimpse of my reflection in the mirror-like stainless steel.

Einstein was pointing in every direction but south. My blue eyes were cushioned in red, puffy bags, and then there was the whole granny situation. I looked every bit the sixty-five years I felt, except I was twenty-eight.

I closed my eyes, wishing my life had a Refresh button. If it did, I would have selected pants *without* a zipper. I could have refreshed the day that Bart pulled me aside and told me he'd like to leave the café to me. He said he wanted Bart's to live on well after he was gone, and there was no one he trusted more than me. He provided information on deeds and bank accounts and tax forms. Doing it over, I still would have graciously accepted, but I wouldn't have banked my future on it. Or maybe got it in writing? Signed something? Not mentally designed business cards with "Owner" written below my name? Not have spent my own money on trinkets and artwork to spruce up the place?

*Crap.*

Determined to get answers, I charged out to the patio (after a quick, albeit awkward, aloe vera lather). Bart was in his usual spot, slouched in a plastic chair next to the parking lot. The patio was full with the regulars: Bob and his laptop, Chris and this week's girlfriend, Rachel and her Chihuahua. A group of women decked out in expensive tennis clothes chatting over lattes and taking pictures of the scones they were nibbling on.

I took the seat across from Bart, crossing my arms on the table, and studied the old man in front of me. The collar of his plaid shirt poked out from under his navy fleece, the one with the Dodger's emblem embroidered on the upper left breast. His ears looked longer and his face more creased. He had one hand resting atop a thick, unmarked, manila envelope.

I couldn't speak. I could only stare and wait. Then I remembered whom I was sitting with. Bart's viewpoint on communication was "why use words when a shrug will do?" Which is why I handled all personnel problems.

Not knowing what to say, I started with the obvious. "I'm here."

He took a sip of his latte. His face was momentarily masked in steam, leaving his brows and nose hairs glistening.

"It's good foam," he finally said, staring at the cup, running his thumb over the Bart's Café logo printed on the sleeve.

I wasn't here to talk about foam, especially not after it burned my lady bits. "Why did you sell?" We needed to stop beating around the bush.

"I was made an offer I couldn't refuse."

"By who? The Godfather? You've had a lot of offers over the years you've managed to refuse. Why now? Why not give me a heads-up? Why after everything you said about how you wanted Bart's to live on forever? And if you were going to sell, why not give me the opportunity to at least make a bid? I've poured my soul into this place."

He let out a little moan and waved his hand, as if flicking away a tiny insect trying to fly up his nose. "It's too damn expensive to keep a business alive around here. You can buy a decent cup of coffee at the 76 Station. It's not worth throwing all your eggs into this basket. Assuming you have any saved up." If eggs were money, then no, I didn't have any reserved eggs. But I had good credit. That had to be worth loaner eggs. "It would go down eventually. I'd rather it go down on my watch."

*Does he think he's doing me a favor?*

"I want to retire and have some *big* adventures."

*Guess not.*

"Here." He slid the envelope across the table. "Last paychecks for everyone and a little something extra for yourself."

I stared at the envelope as if it were contagious, unable to conjure up the right words. Perhaps there weren't any. The papers had been signed. The situation had to be accepted. The café was closing. Bart was off to a big adventure. And I was a single mother with no college education, no job and burnt unmentionables.

"I'll let everyone know," I said, fidgeting with the string-tie on my employment coffin. "What do we do with… everything?" I waved my hand around, gesturing to the tables and the chairs and the umbrellas and all the other makeup of the company that had been serving the public since 1960.

He replied with a shrug.

"I'll let you handle it then," I said, my voice small as I choked back a sob.

Bart squirmed—too many feelings happening. "Leave the keys on the desk. I'll take care of it. And... *thanks*." He stood with more spring than I'd seen from him in years and nearly galloped to his...

*What. The. Hell?*

Parked in Bart's spot was a muscular yellow Mustang with chrome rims. RIMS. He'd been driving a brown Buick with missing hubcaps for decades. The baristas and I called it the Political Time Machine because he had a bumper sticker for every Republican presidential candidate since Nixon stuck on the trunk. Now he had a Mustang. A YELLOW Mustang.

This was bananas.

Bart revved the engine, causing Rachel's Chihuahua to take cover under the chair. He drove the muscle car just as he drove the Political Time Machine. Idling out of the space, rolling through the parking lot and out to oncoming traffic, cutting off a driver or two.

He was gone, and all I got was a measly "thanks" and his empty latte cup left on the table.

I grabbed the manila envelope and unwrapped the string keeping it closed. Inside were more envelopes, each with a barista's name and then, at the very back of the stack, were two for me. My name was spelled wrong and scribed in flowery, unfamiliar handwriting. I'd been handling payroll for the last year. It was hard to believe he managed to do all this without my knowing. The first was my last paycheck, paying me through the end of the month. Good. The next check would have to cover my rent and bills until I found another job. I ran my finger under the sealed flap, careful not to add a paper cut to my list of current maladies, pulled out the check and held it up, blinking hard at the numbers staring back at me.

Bart wasn't being figurative when he said a *little* something for me.

Find out what happens next... pick up your copy of *For Hire* today!

Got a vacancy on your bookshelf?
Check out the hilarious

*Apartment Manager Series*

For new releases, deals and a free ebook of
*Can't Pay My Rent* (normally $2.99), sign up here:
http://bit.ly/erinhussnews

Made in the USA
Lexington, KY
07 November 2016